Lofty
Ambitions

Dianne L. Christner

A sequel to *Proper Intentions*

Heartsong Presents

*With love to my mother,
Annabelle.*

A note from the Author:
*I love to hear from my readers! You may write to me at the
following address:*

> **Dianne L. Christner**
> **Author Relations**
> **P.O. Box 719**
> **Uhrichsville, OH 44683**

ISBN 1-55748-634-4

LOFTY AMBITIONS

PRINTED IN THE U.S.A.

"You'd be a bad fit for city life," Korbin said. "You wouldn't have time for all your interests."

Savanna shook he

But he sensed sh  "Do you ever plar

"I'm too much of a ... ... t a kid person."

He could see that about her. "Me, either."

Seeing the same in him, her eyes batted and lowered.

Korbin stepped closer. Something deep in him warned to resist this, but desire overruled. When he pulled her to him, she put her hands on his chest and looked up, startled.

He didn't give her time to react. Didn't give himself time to think. Just kissed her. Soft at first. Gentle. Warm.

Then the fevered kiss compelled him to wrap both his arms around her. This wasn't supposed to happen.

Slowly, with unease building, he pulled back. She'd felt exactly the way he'd imagined...and more. So much more that foreboding crept into his unease. This couldn't be right.

***

Be sure to check out the rest of the Ivy Avengers miniseries!

***

If you're on Twitter, tell us what you think of Harlequin Romantic Suspense! #HarlequinRomSuspense

Dear Reader,

Welcome to the fourth addition to the Ivy Avengers miniseries. This is Savanna Ivy's story. I'm really enjoying writing about this family. Savanna is the most reclusive of them all, living near Colorado's stunning and beautiful Wolf Creek Pass, but trouble finds its way to her door anyway!

I've been watching a lot of crime shows on TV. My favorites are the reality shows, the true stories of how people try to get away with murder. We only see the stories about the murders that are solved. Just think about how many killers get away with their crimes. It inspired me to write about a man who is set up for murder. He's my hero, so naturally we get a happy ending!

Thanks for reading my miniseries. May you enjoy many more.

Jennifer Morey

THE ELIGIBLE SUSPECT

Jennifer Morey

H HARLEQUIN® ROMANTIC SUSPENSE

Recycling programs
for this product may
not exist in your area.

ISBN-13: 978-0-373-27904-3

The Eligible Suspect

Printed in U.S.A.

A two-time 2009 RITA® Award nominee and a Golden Quill winner for Best First Book for *The Secret Soldier*, **Jennifer Morey** writes contemporary romance and romantic suspense. Project manager *par jour*, she works for the space systems segment of a satellite imagery and information company. She lives in sunny Denver, Colorado. She can be reached through her website, www.jennifermorey.com, and on Facebook.

Books by Jennifer Morey

Harlequin Romantic Suspense

Ivy Avengers
Front Page Affair
Armed and Famous
One Secret Night
The Eligible Suspect

The Adair Legacy
Executive Protection

All McQueen's Men
The Secret Soldier
Heiress Under Fire
Unmasking the Mercenary
Special Ops Affair
Seducing the Accomplice
Seducing the Colonel's Daughter

Visit the Author Profile page at Harlequin.com for more titles

Mom is overdue for another dedication.
For you, Mom! Wish you were here.

Chapter 1

Each step closer to the Laughing Grass Pizzeria hammered a dark sense of foreboding in deeper. Korbin Maguire took the stairs down to the basement of the old redbrick building, certain his life was about to take a big turn. A man who took charge of his own destiny, he'd steer it in a direction he chose, but there was something else at play, and it would begin to reveal itself here, today, at this restaurant.

Under a high, ornately carved white ceiling, people filled worn wood tables, and conversation echoed in the cavernous room. It smelled like pizza, not marijuana. The latter was reserved for a fee in a private room, since it wasn't legal to smoke in public. Korbin didn't smoke the stuff but most of the people he knew did, and this was their favorite hangout.

Spotting Collette Hamilton, he headed over to her.

A bleach-blonde with heavy makeup and surgically enhanced breasts, she was borderline trashy but a nice girl nonetheless. It wasn't her fault she had parents who weren't around for her and didn't teach her how to survive anywhere but on the street. She was a woman on the brink of spending her life in and out of the judicial system. And, he'd realized recently, so was he if he didn't make some drastic changes.

Collette didn't even smile when he sat across from her. She'd sounded frantic on the phone when she'd asked him to meet her here, which was why he'd come. He had an idea what this was about.

"Where's Damen?" he asked.

"Not here." She sounded glad.

Was Damen the reason she'd asked to meet? He wouldn't be surprised. Damen's behavior as of late had raised his brow more than once. But why call him?

She'd never shown any indication of interest in him, and he wasn't interested in any other man's woman. They'd developed a friendship over the last year. She'd helped him through a rough spot and she talked to him about Damen sometimes. On the hardened side for a woman, a little easy and not very smart, she wasn't his type. But she had a good heart and he wouldn't let anyone hurt her, least of all Damen.

"You two having trouble?" he asked.

"He told me that you turned him down on the offer to work a new job," she said.

She hadn't answered his question, but that must have something to do with why she was here. Korbin was always careful about how, when and if he broke the law. He also had a tough reputation to back up his freedom of choice. No one forced him to do anything. No one messed with him. If he took a job, he took it on his own terms.

A waitress came to the table and Korbin declined to order anything. Collette had ordered a soda.

"Damen told you I turned him down?"

She nodded, almost in awe. "He wasn't happy about that at all."

"No, he wasn't." He'd yelled and threatened. Korbin had warned him about the threats. He'd only partially listened, which had been the first wake-up call. That meeting had alerted him to what might lie ahead. Trouble. And it was beginning now. With Collette.

"Korbin, you should watch your back."

"I'm not afraid of Damen." There was nothing he could do to hurt him. He had no evidence to prove his past cyber crimes. Korbin was always meticulous about covering his tracks.

Collette smiled. "No, you aren't, are you? But he's been unpredictable lately. The fact that you turned him down made him furious. I couldn't even talk to him about it. He started throwing things."

Damen's unpredictability was what bothered Korbin, but he was becoming violent? That caused him more concern. Not for himself, but for Collette. "I'm done with that type of work and nothing Damen does will change that. I'm going to find something else to do. Maybe get a real job. Maybe go see my parents." He'd been a handful to them and they no longer spoke to him. By his sixteenth birthday, he'd hacked into all of their friends' computers. By the time he graduated from high school, he'd added teachers and employers to the list. In adulthood, his expertise had attracted Damen Ricchetti's attention. No more. Damen was out of his life now. He couldn't be a part of his new direction, wherever that led.

"That's why I wanted to talk to you," Collette said. She pulled back her hair, tucking the strands that had hung over the side of her face. Korbin saw the fresh cut high on her cheek. Then she let her hair fall back down over her face.

Anger boiled to life inside him. "Did he do that to you?"

She nodded, her eyes pooling with tears. "It isn't the first time. I've had black eyes that forced me to stay home until I healed."

Korbin started to stand. "Where is he?"

"Wait." Collette grabbed his wrist to stop him. "I just want to get away from him. And I asked you to meet me here today to see if you'd help me."

He sat back down. She needed help to get away from Damen? "Why can't you tell him to get lost?" Was she that afraid of him?

"Because he won't stay lost. He's threatened me many times that if I break up with him he'll kill me. He wants me to move in with him, and I can't do that. I need to get away from here."

Korbin hadn't thought in great detail about what he was going to do or where he'd go, if anywhere. He figured he'd start with a trip to see his parents. If they'd see him.

Damen's saying he'd kill his girlfriend if she broke up with him changed the game. That made him far more dangerous than he'd anticipated and confirmed some suspicions he'd had. But first he'd step in and teach Damen a lesson.

"Of course I'll help you." He didn't have it in him

not to. He would never leave her, or anyone, helpless against violence. Damen had abused her. He was going to pay for that.

He should have become a cop.

Collette reached over and put her hand over his. "I know why you're getting out, Korbin."

Everyone associated with Damen knew that. But it was too raw to talk about.

"It's a good decision," she said in his silence.

Smothering the tide of unwelcome emotion, he asked, "What do you need me to do?"

She half smiled, a pity smile, empathizing but not saying any more on the matter. Slipping her hand from his, she said, "Help me find a place to go. Somewhere Damen won't find me."

That wouldn't be a problem. "All right. I'll need today to prepare."

"Okay. Thank you. I can't tell you how much I appreciate this. I'd do it myself but I don't have the resources you do. Damen would probably catch me before I left town."

He didn't like the sound of that. "Do you need money? A place to stay?"

"No, I should be okay. I'll just be happy to have a life free of Damen."

He'd give her enough to get by for a few months. His parents may not be speaking to him but they hadn't taken away his trust fund yet. "Be ready to leave in the morning. Meet me back here at eight." He put some cash down on the table and stood with her, putting his hand on her lower back to guide her toward the stairs. Out on the street, he looked around for any sign of Damen. Not seeing any, he walked with Collette to her car. There, he looked around again and then reached under his shirt for the gun he'd put in the back of his jeans. Foreboding had compelled him to do that. Otherwise he never carried.

"Take this."

Her mouth dropped open. "Wha—"

"Don't let him in your house. If he gets violent again, use it to get away from him."

"But…I can't kill him!"

"Then aim for his knee. Just get away from him. You only have to make it to tomorrow morning. The goal is to act normal so he doesn't figure it out. I'm hoping you won't have to use it. But just in case…"

Collette put the gun into her purse. "Okay. Tomorrow morning." She seemed worried.

"It will be okay," he said. Leaning forward, he gave her a hug, one that elicited a comforted sigh from her.

"You're a good man, Korbin Maguire." She stepped back with a smile and got into her car.

He closed her door and waved back when she did. She thought he was a good man. He wasn't, but he was going to be.

Early the next morning, Korbin woke to his ringing doorbell and pounding on the front door of his home in Lone Tree, Colorado. More pounding suggested urgency. He got up and went to the window of his second-story bedroom, which had a view of the driveway and part of the front entrance. A sedan was in the driveway and two men stood at the door. They wore jackets. Professional. Who were they?

He put on a pair of jeans and a white T-shirt and went down to the door. More pounding and ringing grew louder.

"Denver police. Open up!" one of them shouted.

Police? What were they doing here?

Korbin opened the door, leaving the security bar in place.

"Korbin Maguire?" One of the men opened a wallet to show him a badge. He was older than the dark-haired man.

Had something happened to Collette? Real worry for her swelled within him. "Yes." He released the security bar and opened the door.

"Do you drive a Mercedes AMG Black Series?" the older officer asked.

Why were they asking him about his car? "Rarely. I mostly drive my truck." He began to wish he hadn't opened the door so soon. If this was some sort of ruse…

"But you own a Mercedes AMG, correct?"

He hesitated, wondering why they were asking him about his car. "Yes. What's this all about?"

"Would you step outside, please?"

The two men moved back to give him room. Korbin didn't see any way out of this. If they were real cops—and they seemed to be—he couldn't refuse. He stepped outside onto the front porch.

"You're under arrest for a hit-and-run that resulted in death."

The younger officer produced a pair of cuffs. "Turn around and put your hands behind your back."

Did he say death?

Numbly, Korbin turned around as the younger officer handcuffed him. In the street, more police cars appeared, lights flashing.

"I don't understand," Korbin said. "I didn't drive anywhere last night. My car is in the garage."

The older officer nodded to the one who'd cuffed him. Uniformed policemen gathered in the yard.

All three garage doors opened and Korbin saw the stall where he parked his Mercedes-Benz coupe was empty. His car was gone. Only his dark blue pickup truck was in the next stall over, closest to the inner door.

"Someone stole my car," Korbin said.

"Come with us. We'll take your statement at the station." The younger officer guided him to the backseat of the sedan, reciting his rights as they went.

Had a stranger stolen his car and then run when he'd hit someone? His Mercedes-Benz coupe would be a prize for any car thief. Someone could have broken in and taken it. But how had his security system been breached? Whoever had broken in had experience. Professional experience. That's where the stranger theory fell apart. Someone had deliberately stolen his car. Someone who knew him.

This had the stink of Damen. Their last conversation filtered into his mind. Damen had accused him of thinking he was better than him and said he'd regret not partnering with him. Collette had reinforced his emotional reaction. It had led to him beating her. And then she'd come to him for help. Had Damen found out? Had she told him? Or had he made her? Korbin hadn't seen Damen anywhere near the Laughing Grass, but had he followed Collette?

It was possible. And Damen had plenty of experience breaking into buildings. And even more damning, he'd suggested the security system Korbin had installed in his house.

But if Damen had stolen his car, why leave the car at a hit-and-run scene?

All the way to the police station, questions pummeled him. By the time he was led into the interrogation room, he was convinced Damen had set him up. He'd deliberately run someone over and left the car there. His behavior was violent enough to support that assumption.

Korbin stewed with anger as he sat at a gray table in an interrogation room. The entire room was gray. Gray walls. Gray door. He'd have a gray life if he didn't find a way out of this.

The older officer—the detective who'd been at his door—entered the room.

"What happened?" Korbin asked. "Why am I here?"

He sat across from him. "I was hoping you'd tell me."

"Why was I arrested? You said it was for a hit-and-run." *That resulted in death*. "I didn't run anyone over."

"Tell me about your day yesterday, Mr. Maguire. Let's start in the morning. Take me from then all the way until this morning."

The detective was following protocol and obviously didn't believe Korbin. Why would he? He must hear all kinds of excuses and lies from people he had to question for crimes.

"I woke up at about eight, made some coffee. Watched some television for a while, and then went to meet a friend at the Laughing Grass Pizzeria."

"What time was that?"

"Two in the afternoon."

"What friend did you meet?"

"Collette Hamilton." He explained that she was worried about Damen hurting her and that they had made plans to meet back at the restaurant this morning, when he'd help her get out of town. He checked the time. He wasn't going to make it now.

"She came to you for help?"

Did that seem strange? "Yes. We're friends."

"Romantic friends?"

"No."

"Has this Damen Ricchetti been violent with her before?"

"I wasn't aware of his abuse until she told me yesterday." But he explained how Damen had been behaving differently, leaving out why.

"Why did she go to you for help? Why did she need *your* help? I guess I don't understand why she couldn't leave on her own."

"She trusts me. And she's afraid of Damen."

"What were you going to do to help her?"

"I found her a place to stay where she'll be safe for a while." He didn't mention the fake ID. "And I'm going to give her some money."

"She knew you had money?"

. He nodded.

"Please respond verbally for the recording."

"Yes, she knows I have money. Look, I need to get out of here so I can help her."

The detective stared at him for a long moment. Korbin hoped Collette's knowledge of him having money would provide enough of a motive for her to come to him for help.

"What do you do, Mr. Maguire?"

"I have a degree in computer science, but I'm not working right now. I have a trust fund."

The detective nodded, watching him again. "After you left the restaurant…which one did you say it was?"

"The Laughing Grass," he said. "Pizzeria."

"Don't they sell pot there?"

"They don't sell it, but you can bring your own and smoke it in a private room. As long as you're a member of their club, it's legal."

"Do you smoke pot?"

Was he trying to establish something about his character? "No."

"Did you smoke some pot yesterday?"

"No."

Korbin suffered another of the detective's stares. "Where did you go after you left the restaurant and what time was that?"

"Around three. I went straight home. I did some internet searches on places for Collette. A place to rent. And I withdrew some money for her."

"So you did go out last night."

"No. I stopped at my bank on the way home."

"But you just told me you went straight home."

"You can check with my bank. I was there shortly after three." He gave the name of his bank. "After I got some cash for Collette, I went home."

"And what time did you finish searching the internet?"

"About eleven. Then I went to bed."

"The hit-and-run occurred at 2:21 a.m. A thirty-year-old man was crossing the street with the walking sign lit. He wasn't doing anything wrong."

"Someone stole my car," he said. "And I think it was Damen." He'd been home and hadn't heard him break into the garage and drive away with it. Damen was the only person he knew who could do that.

"Can anyone confirm you were home all night?" The detective ignored his claims, the raisin creases of his forehead deepening as he fixed impassive eyes on him.

"No."

"Has Ms. Hamilton ever filed charges against this Mr. Ricchetti?"

"Not that I'm aware of. She told me he threatened to kill her. She's afraid of him."

"And since you're such a nice guy you agreed to help her?"

Korbin didn't respond to that, but his fear for Collette's safety was another matter. "Please. Either let me go so I can check on her, or have someone go check on her for me. Damen might have hurt her." He should never have let her go back to her house alone. He should have stayed with her and taken her home with him.

"If you're so worried about her, why didn't you notify the police after she came to you?"

In Korbin's line of work, going to the police was never an option. He hadn't even considered it when he'd met Collette. "I guess I thought she should be the one to do that." And he hadn't thought she'd be in too much danger.

The detective sighed and leaned back against the chair. He studied Korbin a while, not believing him.

"Witnesses got your plate number after the hit-and-run. We found the car abandoned not far from the scene."

"It wasn't me driving."

"They described a man who looks like you."

Damen had dark hair but wasn't as tall. Three inches shorter.

"Wasn't it dark at 2:21 a.m. in the morning?" Korbin asked.

The detective didn't respond. He had to realize that would make a difference. No one could positively identify him without any doubt.

Another detective entered the room and motioned for

the other to come to him. He did and listened to the man. Korbin couldn't make out what was being said.

A moment later, the other man left and the detective returned to his seat.

"There's no evidence of a break-in at your home, Mr. Maguire." He looked at him, waiting for an explanation.

Korbin had none.

"Your security system is operational. There's nothing broken. No fingerprints."

Damen must have found a way inside. Copied a key. Taken a garage door opener. Something.

"Why don't you tell me what really happened?" the detective said.

"I have. I didn't kill anyone. My car was stolen and I think it was Damen who did it."

"Why would he do that?"

He couldn't say it was because he'd refused an illegal hacker job. "He must have seen me meet with his girl-friend." That had to be it. Korbin hadn't looked closely on his way inside. It was only after he'd realized Damen was becoming violent that he'd paid more attention. Damen could have seen him go inside to meet Collette. He may have even sneaked inside. Spied on them.

"And in a jealous rage, stole your car and deliberately ran a stranger over so you'd be charged?"

"Yes. Check the car for evidence that he was in it." Damen would have worn gloves but maybe there'd be other evidence.

"He's your friend. He could have been in the car before this."

"I wasn't driving the car. It wasn't me."

The detective didn't respond. No one would believe he wasn't the one driving his car. But the detective began to show signs of doubt. Or maybe he just didn't have enough on him yet. The evidence hadn't been fully analyzed. Korbin now had a taste of what it was like to be falsely accused. At all costs, he had to prove his innocence, or Damen would have his way and Korbin would spend time in prison.

Korbin was released on his own recognizance and was out by late afternoon. He was worried sick about Collette. He took a taxi home to get his phone and saw that she hadn't called—not even when he hadn't shown up at the Laughing Grass this morning. She wasn't answering her phone, either. He tried calling Damen but he didn't answer. Where was Collette? Was she all right?

Parking his truck outside Collette's house, he jumped out and jogged to her door, knocking several times and ringing the doorbell. When that produced nothing, he used his tool to unlock the door, looking around to make sure he wasn't seen. Going inside, he took two steps in, shutting the door behind him, and saw a lamp and some picture frames broken. And on the other side of the couch, Collette lay on the floor. Blood had soaked the carpet beneath her. She'd been shot and it looked like she'd been dead several hours.

"No." Korbin was light-headed with shock and dismay as he rushed over to her.

He crouched to check for life even though he knew she was gone. Her eyes stared sightlessly up at the ceiling. Breathing out a harsh breath, Korbin bent his head and swore. How could he have allowed this to happen? How? She'd come to him for help and he'd failed her. Damen had killed her. She'd been afraid of him and he'd killed her.

Standing, he picked up a dining room chair and slammed it down onto the floor with a growl. It broke into pieces. The horror of what Damen had done almost made him pick up another.

His wife's beautiful face came to him, engulfing him with terrible grief and guilt. He hadn't saved her, either. She'd died because of his underestimation of Damen. Just like Collette. While ravaging guilt and helplessness gripped him, he vowed to bring Damen to justice.

Returning to Collette's body, he began to search for evidence, carefully checking the area surrounding her and her clothes, all the while not disturbing any of the crime scene.

The gun…

With that sobering thought, he looked for the weapon. It wasn't here. He searched the whole house and didn't find the gun he'd given her.

He went to her computer. She didn't keep it locked, so he easily clicked his way to her email. Not finding anything there, he went through all of her files. In a folder labeled "Resumes," he found an email file with the subject "What's Next?" It was an exchange between Damen and a man he didn't know. Korbin opened it and realized his luck had finally improved. Collette had forwarded an email exchange from Damen's machine to hers. She'd cleverly hidden it in the file folder and deleted it from her email program. If Damen had checked, he'd missed it.

Korbin printed a copy, reading the exchange on the screen. A man named Tony wanted to know if Damen had finished putting together a team and Damen had replied with Not yet, but I'm close. The time the email was sent was a few days after Korbin had refused his request. Tony had replied, You promised me a team. If you can't handle this, I'll have to make other arrangements. What wasn't written there was what Tony would do with Damen if he failed him. You'll have your team, Damen had responded. And the last of the thread was Tony saying, For your sake, I hope so.

With Collette dead, Korbin didn't have to worry about Damen finding out that she was onto him. What else had she known? What had made her keep this email thread? Korbin wished he could ask her.

Wiping his prints from the mouse and anywhere else he'd touched, he left the house, deliberately leaving the email open on Collette's computer so that it would be easy for police to find.

Now he had to get somewhere safe to hide, somewhere he could do some research on Tony Bartoszewicz. And figure out a strategy to take Damen down. Before Damen cost him more than he already had.

Chapter 2

"I'm not using my house as a fortress to protect me from men, Mother." Putting her book down on the table, Savanna Ivy stood up from the cushiony chair in the corner of the loft. Her feet sank into the thick mocha rug as she passed between a love seat and a television atop an antique wood cabinet. A log railing allowed a view of the living room below. She saw through the gabled windows and under exterior lights that it was snowing harder now. Her mother had interrupted a really good book on a stormy evening.

"You went there on purpose," her mother said.

"I live here."

"On purpose," her mother insisted. "Your reclusiveness worries me."

Camille Ivy didn't like it when Savanna went into her hermit modes. She couldn't surprise her with her celebratory family visits. Tucked deep in the woods just south of Wolf Creek Pass, Savanna's log home was on seventy-five rugged acres in Colorado's southeastern San Juan Mountains. In winter, she was frequently snowed in.

She went down the open stairs and into her living room, passing a white leather sofa, love seat and chairs with nail-head trim on a mosaic rug in dark green and black. A beautiful alder wood buffet and wine cabinet were behind the sofa and against the wall.

Beside the large gabled window, the black gneiss rock fireplace rose all the way up to an exposed log ceiling. She had a fire going. Soft piano music played from her stereo, stored in a built-in cabinet where a huge television was embedded in the log wall, off for now.

The sun had set an hour ago. It had been snowing all afternoon and the news had forecast another storm the next night, a much more severe storm. A blizzard, they were saying. Savanna couldn't wait to spend the day cooking and reading.

"You need to talk about it, Savanna," her mother said in her silence.

"I like living alone, Mom. There's nothing wrong with me. I'm okay. How many times do I have to tell you that?"

"You shouldn't be alone right now."

Another man had broken her heart and she was in the grieving process. "Don't worry about me. I've been through this before. It'll pass."

"That's what worries me." Then her mother sighed. "You and Autumn. You're both so independent. At least she's around other people when she travels, and she found herself a decent man."

That came with a sting Savanna had trouble pushing

away. Savanna had thought she'd met two decent men, but they'd turned out to be liars.

After a moment, her mother said, "I'm sorry, honey. I didn't mean that the way it came out."

Savanna wished her mother would stop talking. "It just hasn't worked out for me yet. It is what it is."

"You bought that mountain home after the first one."

Savanna didn't argue. Her mother thought she was hiding here, burying her heartache and protecting herself from any more. Maybe she was. She felt better here than anywhere else. That had to count for something. If her mother preferred to think of her remote mountain house as a fortress, then it was a fortress. The only way in was a long and winding dirt road. Either that or on a snowmobile, or a pair of cross-country skis or snowshoes, or horseback. And when it snowed as it did now, no one was getting in and Savanna wasn't getting out. She needed this time to herself. Being alone and isolated rejuvenated her.

"You need to get out more. Be with other people. Socialize. It's not good for you to be pent up in your house with nothing else to do than think."

"I have plenty to do here. And I'll come see you in spring."

"Don't be a smart-mouth, Savanna Ivy."

"I'm not. The way it looks outside, it *will* be spring by the time I get out of here.

In her mother's long silence, Savanna added, "Do you really think all I'm doing here is obsessing over my ex-boyfriend?"

With that her mother breathed a laugh. "No. Your hobbies are keeping you busy, I'm sure. And you always were a solitary girl. I just hate to see you hurt."

"I'll get over that. And I will come and see you this spring."

"Okay, honey. You've managed to somewhat calm me." And then she asked, "Did you plow your road?"

So her mother could come to visit? Savanna could hear her thinking it.

"No."

"Are you going to have it plowed?"

"Sometime. When I need to get out of here, I'll have it plowed." Until she was ready for visitors, she was grateful for the snow.

"Oh, Savanna."

Savanna laughed lightly. "Would you like me to host a family gathering here?"

"You know I'd love that, and you also know I prefer spontaneity. But you take your time. Just call me often so I know you're okay."

"I will. Love you, Mom."

"Love you, too."

Savanna pressed the off button on her remote phone and stared out the gabled window, entranced by the falling snow. Maybe she'd have her road plowed later this week. One night with her family wouldn't be so bad. Except for all the questions.

She was about to start dinner when she saw something. Soft lighting reflected on the glass. Leaning closer, she saw headlights shining through the heavy snow. A truck. It wasn't moving. Who would come to see her during a snowstorm? Were they lost? A vehicle not moving in this weather would put anyone inside in real trouble. If they stayed in the truck and ran out of gas, they'd freeze, and if they tried to walk through the snow, they might not make it to her door without snowshoes. She watched for several more minutes. Whoever was out there was well and truly stuck on her road. There had to be at least two feet on the ground.

Going to the front entry and into a large walk-in closet where she kept every imaginable necessity for navigating snowy terrain, in several varying sizes to accommodate her large family, Savanna geared up in her under- and outerwear and put on some boots. Meeting a stranger or strangers on a remote, snowy road had its risks. She was a single woman all alone in unforgiving wilderness. Stuffing a container of Mace into her pocket, she left the warm coziness of her house and stepped into the fifteen-degree air.

Snow pelted her face as she made her way to the barn. The four-car garage was attached to the house and the heated barn wasn't far from there. She employed caretakers who did most of the work, but they were off for the weekend. She managed everything on her own when she had to. She preferred it that way so that she'd be self-sufficient whenever she needed to be. Savanna, like most of her siblings, did not depend on others to take care of herself.

Inside the barn, she saddled a big gray Oldenburg stallion named Gandalf. He was built for the rugged terrain of the San Juan Mountains. With sturdy legs and lots of stamina, he was also a beautiful animal, sort of like a giant version of a Friesian. She had a stable full of Oldenburg horses. They were her favorite horse for their strength, versatility and personality.

The horse nickered as she led him outside, eager for the exercise he anticipated.

Climbing onto his eighteen-hand-high back, Savanna gave him a gentle nudge with her heels. The stallion began to walk through the deep snow, occasionally having to leap.

Savanna squinted as the three-quarter-inch snowflakes fell. Every once in a while the wind gusted and she could barely make out the edges of the road. She followed the wood crossbuck fence with copper post caps that ran all the way down the road to the highway. Seeing the truck, she looked for signs of a person. There was too much snow on the truck to tell if anyone was inside.

Gandalf whinnied and tossed his brawny head, tugging at the bit as though eager to run for the new adventure that shone a light on him.

Savanna spotted the figure of a man trying to shovel the tires of his truck free from snow. A lot of good that would do. What did he think he'd do once he dug himself out of the ditch? Drive a few feet and get stuck again? Four-wheel drive or not, this snow was deep enough to stop anyone. She really wasn't in the mood for company. Putting her annoyance in check, she committed herself to helping someone in need.

He quit working when she neared. At the truck, she halted the big horse. He was a giant of a man. Probably six-four. She amended her earlier assumption. This guy could probably have walked through the deep snow all the way to her house.

"Are you lost?" she asked.

He stepped through the deep snow and stopped next to her. "I made a wrong turn."

"Where were you headed?" Her neighbor ran a yurt touring company on his ranch. He'd converted his eight bedroom house into a bed-and-breakfast. Maybe he was trying to find it.

"A friend of mine has a cabin near here."

She looked through the snow at his truck. There was no one else inside. "Who?"

"Julio Chavis."

The name sounded familiar, but she hesitated. Gandalf stomped his foot and snorted, eager to be moving in the heavy snow.

"It's his vacation home," the man said.

Savanna patted Gandalf's neck as he stomped and snorted again. "Are you alone?"

"Yes."

Why would anyone come up here to be alone? Recalling her conversation with her mother, she realized that may not be so unusual. Besides, she knew of a man who owned a cabin two miles up the highway from her road and across from the yurt touring lodge. She'd never met him. He rarely came here; at least that's what Hurley over at Lost Trail Lodge had told her.

Reluctant to open her home to a stranger, she looked at his truck again, buried to the top of the wheel wells in snow. He wasn't going anywhere tonight.

"Do you have a plow?" he asked.

Returning her gaze to him with a frown. "No. I hire out for that."

"When will you hire out to plow it this time?"

He seemed as annoyed as her, wishing she'd have kept her road passable.

"I can have someone out here in the morning."

He nodded with a grim line to his mouth. He wasn't keen on being stuck here. He'd rather be at his friend's cabin. Alone. She could relate to that.

In her silence, he twisted to look back through the falling snow. "It wasn't as deep through the trees. Should have turned around in there." He tipped his face up to the sky. "It's worse than I thought."

"Common for this area." She contemplated him some more, Gandalf shifting his feet with another snort. Well, there was nothing else that could be done. "Get your things and climb on. You can stay here for the night."

"Maybe if I could use your phone."

And do what? Call a cab? "No one will come out here tonight, not in this storm."

After a few seconds of internal debate, he went to the truck and retrieved a duffel bag, then turned off the engine and locked the vehicle.

Rather than take her hand, he grabbed the saddle horn and propelled himself up onto the horse's back behind her.

Gandalf pranced through the snow and then leaped into a trot, his gait smooth and belying the deepening snow.

Turning her head, she asked, "What's your name?"

"Korbin Maguire," he answered. He had a deep, gravelly voice that tickled her senses and caught her off guard. "And you are?"

Still grappling with her reaction to him, she squinted against snowflakes and said, "Savanna Ivy." Had his voice changed because of a similar reaction to her?

"Nice to meet you, Savanna. I'll thank you in advance for your hospitality."

He sounded more professional now, as though he'd checked himself. "Well, I couldn't leave you out here in this storm."

"I would have hiked up to your house. Would have been a workout, but you wouldn't have had to ride out in this."

"Gandalf loves a good ride." She patted the stallion's neck.

"He's a big horse."

"That's why I bought him. He's well suited for these mountains."

They both had to turn away from a gust of wind that pelted them with snow.

"How long is this storm supposed to last?" he asked.

"At least tonight. Another storm's headed this way after that. A bigger one."

They reached the barn.

"Isn't this one big enough?" Korbin asked as he dismounted.

Savanna climbed off after him and led Gandalf through the corral gate. Korbin closed that while she opened the barn door. When they were all inside, Korbin shut the door. Instant relief from the billowing snow made Savanna sigh. Other horses nickered and snorted and moved in their stalls with the new activity. During the day, their outer doors were opened to individual corrals with enough room to move around.

While she pulled off Gandalf's saddle, Korbin surveyed the barn. It was a nice barn. Savanna would make no fuss over that. Money had not been a factor when she'd built it. If she was going to have horses in this climate, they would be safe and comfortable.

"Where's the spa?" Korbin teased, grinning.

And oh, what a hot grin that was. Savanna stopped brushing Gandalf to stare. She had noticed how in-shape he was back on the road, but he'd removed his hat and unzipped his jacket and she could see more of his face. What had begun with the sound of his voice now sparked into a tickling sensation.

This was how she'd fallen for her last two boyfriends.

That initial attraction. Masculine, handsome face. Eyes she could melt into. Then letting her guard down. Trusting a little too much.

Snapping out of her trance, she looked around at the other five stalls, heads of varying colors poking out to observe them. Just because he was handsome didn't mean he was worth exploring. She had to get better at that—not letting her guard down too soon.

Turning back to Gandalf, she finished grooming him, ever aware of Korbin. He'd sensed her reaction, and it wasn't to his joke about spas. He said no more.

Going to a cabinet at the back of the stable, she reached into a basket of fresh carrots she kept there and took out two. Korbin waited at the stall, watching her feed the horse the treat.

"What do you do?" she asked. If they were going to be spending the night together, they might as well get acquainted.

When he didn't immediately answer, her wariness sprang up. She looked at him.

"I'm a computer scientist," he said. "Currently between jobs."

Why had he hesitated? Had he contemplated lying? Was he lying? Why would he lie about being a computer scientist?

"What kind of job did you have?"

He seemed to think first before he said, "Systems engineering."

"Were you fired?"

"No. I left. I'm taking a break for a while."

Why did he feel he needed a break? The same reason he needed to spend time alone in remote wilderness? There was something about him that made her wary, the way he hesitated before answering her, why he was alone up here.

"What about you?" he asked.

She began to understand his earlier hesitation. How much was she willing to reveal about herself to him?

Savanna petted Gandalf's nose, who had finished his treat and stuck his head out of his stall. His soft nose and the loving blinks of his big brown eyes soothed her. "Nothing right now." She paused. "I was a motivational speaker, but not anymore."

"Taking a sabbatical, too?"

Despite his charmed grin, she didn't respond. That was a topic she did not feel like discussing. She'd only recently decided to stop speaking about positive thinking. And she'd told no one in her family about that. Jazzing others up with positive energy used to give her positive energy, and then she realized this was who she was. A loner. Not the interesting person she personified in front of an audience.

Leaning forward to kiss the soft fur of Gandalf's nose, she turned and walked for the exit.

Korbin picked up his bag and followed. Back out in the snowstorm, Savanna was aware of his glances as they trekked through the deep snow. Then his attention shifted to the house. Big, golden logs jutted out at the corners, except at one end, where the turret rose like a sentinel. Made of black gneiss like the chimney, the color and texture contrasted beautifully with the logs.

Korbin closed the door behind him, taking in the open walk-in closet filled with winter gear. "You must have been some motivational speaker."

When would he get the hint that she wasn't going to talk about that? She hung up her jacket and removed her boots and snow pants. Now down to her base layer, she ignored Korbin's appreciation of the close-fitting material, a floral-patterned white thermal top and matching tights.

He was in wet jeans.

"Would you like me to dry those?" she asked.

"Sure."

She looked up at him watching her. "I'll show you to the guest room." Turning, she led him into the living room, seeing how he missed no detail. Upstairs, they passed her loft and went down a hallway.

At the first door, across from a full bathroom, she stopped and flipped on the light switch. Lamps on each side of the bed illuminated tan walls and the cushiony white comforter with soft green throw pillows. Sheer drapes hung parted over two windows on each side and a dark square iron decoration in a sun-like shape hung above the bed.

When he nodded his thanks with one more sweep of his gaze over her thermal underwear, she closed the door and went to her master bedroom, this one bigger. Although the walls were the same color, a painting of a mountain meadow in fall hung above a king-size bed covered in reds and yellows, and there was a balcony where she planned to do a lot of reading in the summer. Going into her oversize walk-in closet, she changed into some spandex pants and a flannel shirt. Leaving her room, she passed his still-closed door and went back downstairs to wait for him, unable to explain her sense of foreboding.

In her large kitchen, she went to the phone stand and looked up her neighbor's number. There was no cell service up here.

Holding the phone to her ear, she walked into the living room while the phone rang a few times. Then Hurley answered.

"It's Savanna."

"Are you okay?" he asked.

"Yeah." At least, she hoped so. She glanced up to the railing that exposed the loft and hallway and the still-closed guest room door.

"It's snowing pretty good out there," he said.

"Yes. A man got stuck on my road. He told me that he was on his way to that cabin across from your lodge. Have you heard anything about that?"

"No. Chavis keeps to himself. I've only met him a few times. Why? Are you worried?"

"No." She relaxed a little. Korbin had said the man's name was Chavis.

"How did he end up at your place?"

"He took a wrong turn and got stuck on my road. I didn't have it plowed."

"I bet you aren't happy about that."

Hurley knew her well enough to know she liked her isolation. Most people who lived up here did. They weren't city folks.

"I'll manage." She looked out the gabled window. Heavy snow falling under outdoor lights didn't have the comfort value it had before she spotted the truck on her road.

"You sure you're okay? Robert and I can ride over on snowmobiles. You can stay the night here."

"No." Savanna felt trapped in other people's houses, and she'd especially feel that way now. "I'll be all right."

"If you're sure…"

"I'm sure. He's harmless enough."

"All right, then. I'll call Mike and have him out there first thing tomorrow morning to plow your road."

"You're too good to me."

"I'm a phone call away, Savanna."

She smiled. "I know. Thanks, Hurley." He was about ten years older than her and married to a sweet woman who cooked with the skill of an executive chef.

Hanging up the phone, she put the handset down on a side table next to the sofa. Straightening, she turned and her body jolted. Korbin stood there. She hadn't heard him come down the stairs.

He'd changed into a long-sleeved soft-gray henley and distressed denim jeans. His feet were bare. Back up at his face, she was drawn into his ghost-gray eyes. Messy, thick black hair was cut to about an inch and a half, and stubble peppered his jaw. He had an unnerving way about him. More than his size, an eerie mystery shrouded him.

"Feel better now that you've checked up on me?" he asked.

Was he insulted? No. She saw that he was teasing her.

"I promise I won't bite," he said.

"Okay, but I might." She smiled but the message was clear. She *would* bite if he got out of line.

Although he didn't smile or grin, his eyes showed his humor—or was that shrewdness? "Then we're both safe."

She went to the stereo. Shutting that off, she turned on the television. The channel was set to a local station. The news.

Korbin appeared, walking slowly, observing as he had before, missing no detail. He picked up the remote from where she'd set it on a side table.

"Do you mind?" he asked.

She shook her head and he changed the channel to

something on the wilderness of China. She sat down on a white leather chair, debating whether she should call Hurley back and ask him to come pick this man up and take him to the lodge.

"What's a young, beautiful woman like you doing living in the mountains all alone?" He sat on the other leather chair. "What are you? Twenty?"

"Thirty-three. You?"

"Thirty-eight."

"Where do you live?"

"Is this where we get to know each other?" he asked, now with a slight grin.

She didn't think he was flirting, just keeping it light. "I've never had a stranger in my house before."

"I live in Denver. I bought a house in Montana, but I don't go there much."

Two houses? Why Montana? And why didn't he go there much? "Not married?"

"Not anymore." His terse answer and the dousing of any sign of humor alerted her to something amiss. With his arms on the rests, he tapped his palm against one in agitation.

She didn't push him further. She understood the need to avoid those types of subjects. "Are you from Montana?"

"No. I grew up in North Carolina."

Work must have brought him to Colorado. She suspected the house in Montana had something to do with the woman he'd married.

"Your family lives there?" she asked.

"My parents. I'm an only child." He looked at the television but she could tell he wasn't paying attention to the program.

"What's it like being an only child?" Savanna asked. "I have seven brothers and sisters."

His brow raised and he whistled, his mood lifting.

"It's a miracle any of us got any attention growing up."

"How do families manage with that many kids?" he asked.

Delighted that he didn't recognize her name, Savanna almost didn't tell him. "Jackson Ivy is my dad. They managed just fine."

"Jackson Ivy?"

He seriously did not know her father? Savanna's jaw dropped open as she gaped at him. "You don't know who Jackson Ivy is?"

"No. Should I?"

"Well, if you watch any movies you should." But then again, why should he? Why did anyone have to care about the producer of a movie they watched?

"He's an actor?"

Savanna started laughing. "No. He's a movie producer. Did you see *The Last Planet*?"

"No, but I've heard of it. That's your *dad*?"

She laughed again, softer now. "Yes."

"Your parents live in a mansion in California. I caught a documentary about that once." He stared at her as though she were an alien now.

"Changes the dynamics, doesn't it?" Although she joked, she was actually quite serious. All of her brothers and sisters dealt with this in one way or another.

He only continued to stare at her.

Savanna began to feel uncomfortable. What was he thinking? That he'd struck gold? If he owned two homes he had to have money. She didn't know what computer engineers made but it must be decent.

"My dad founded Maguire Mercantile," he finally said.

Stunned, Savanna stared back at him while the significance of that sank in. Maguire Mercantile was a Fortune 500 company, a well-known leader in ranch and farm supplies, but their Maguire outerwear was popular with anyone. Mountaineers. Skiers. School kids. You name it. They were experts at keeping people warm and dry.

"Wow," Savanna breathed. "Your dad might be richer than mine."

His deep laughter made her laugh with him, and then she became aware of other things. His big body relaxed in her white chair, legs open, broad shoulders and strong arms. A giant package of *yum* right here in her living room.

"Were you dreading telling me who your dad was?" he asked.

"Yes." She was still smiling.

"I always dread telling women who mine is."

She related to him on a level that sent her guard up. She felt as though she were sliding down a slippery slope with nothing to grab a hold of.

"Growing up, I felt like Richie Rich. I love my parents and they're good, loving people, but they're a couple of rich snobs."

"You watched the documentary on my parents' mansion," Savanna said. "Mine are, too."

"Yeah, but your mother seemed so down to earth. That's why I remembered it."

"She is all about the family. But she isn't innocent of showing off her wealth. Her parties are embarrassing sometimes."

He chuckled. "I stopped going to the ones my parents held after I turned eighteen and left for college. I couldn't stomach seeing them act different than when we were at home together."

The camaraderie they shared was amazing and began to make her uneasy. "Do you see them often?"

There was that hesitation again. "Not as often as I should."

Why not? She decided not to ask.

"You?"

She supposed it was only fair that she answer that question. "One of my mother's favorite pastimes is surprising her children with visits. She usually gathers up as many of the other family members as she can before arriving unannounced with food and beverages. It's either that or we all meet at the family home in Evergreen. It's a more central location than the mansion in California."

"It would be hard for her to surprise you here."

"One of many amenities of this place." She met his eyes and couldn't look away despite the inner warnings ringing in her head.

She stood up. "I was going to make dinner when I saw your headlights."

"Can I help?"

He must be hungry. "No. Make yourself at home." She met his eyes a moment longer, wondering if she should have extended that much of a welcoming invitation.

Before going into the kitchen, she glanced once more out the window where the snow piled higher by the hour. How long would this man be stuck here with her? On the surface he appeared to be good and honest. But what secrets would she find he harbored…and why?

Chapter 3

Korbin wandered Savanna's living room, glad the storm would give him some reprieve from police. The expensive furnishings were homey and inviting rather than a statement of wealth. He still reeled over the revelation of who her father was. Rarely did a woman surprise him the way Savanna did. He'd have never guessed she came from big money, and found it more than a little refreshing. He'd spent his adult life working to remove himself from that lifestyle. Savanna clearly had been successful in doing so. Although she had impeccable taste when it came to her home.

At the gas fireplace, he touched the stone that rose up to the ceiling. Polished smooth, it was a mafic metamorphic rock, probably a hornblende gneiss. When he wasn't hacking computers, he was a voracious reader, and geology was a hobby of his.

Growing more curious about the woman who'd chosen such a rock, he investigated further, going into a turreted dining area off the living room. Bright outdoor lights illuminated heavy snowfall through the panel of tall windows.

Leaving that, smelling Savanna cooking something on the stove, he saw her standing there, head bent and concentrating on what she was doing. The flannel shirt didn't cover her rear in those tight spandex pants, and he could tell she wasn't wearing a bra. Her feet were bare in the warm house, toes sinking into the rug before the stove.

As his intrigue mounted, he decided it was best to control where that would lead. Instead of letting male instinct take charge, he walked down a hallway that extended between the kitchen and living room to familiarize himself with the layout of the house in case he needed an escape route. There was a large main bathroom on the left and across from there was a bedroom-size library. Bookshelves filled every wall except where two tall, narrow windows looked out to the front. A closed laptop sat on an old library table, wood chair pushed in underneath. Two brown patterned wing-backed chairs were angled in front of one bookshelf. Korbin checked out a few of the titles, taming the excitement that she loved to read as he did. Savanna had a varied taste in her fiction and had an impressive collection of nonfiction. How to make pottery. History of trains. Ancient civilizations. And several biographies, one featuring her father.

Leaving the library, lest the building interest take him over, he heard something sizzling on the stove and went into the only other room on this level. A wood bench with a pottery wheel on top was in the center of a large sunroom. Solid white French-style windows kept sound and cold outside. There was a double door next to a five-piece sea-grass seating arrangement on one side of the room. Good to know. The other side was a work area. Against the wall was an antique dresser with rows and columns of small drawers and white knobs. It looked like an old card catalog storage cabinet. On top was a metal rack from which a few strands of earrings, necklaces and bracelets hung, some beaded, some with colored and designed glass pendants. Sliding one of the drawers open, he found individual beads. Next to the cabinet was a work desk, with a partially finished necklace with a stone pendant waiting for the next impulse to create.

Savanna made jewelry along with her pottery. And that wasn't all. Along the far wall, windows ran above a long counter, a sink with a farmhouse faucet and a stove on one end, trays of cooled candles on the other with some work space in between. The cabinets below were left open and the shelves were filled with pots, wax and wicks, oil-based dyes, scents and a variety of jars and bases. A closer look revealed materials to make soap as well.

He turned to go back to the living room and saw Savanna standing at the entrance, long dark red hair in a ponytail and those amazing eyes fringed by thick lashes. Her plump lips and petite, sloping nose made her all the more of a man magnet. She seemed uncertain as to how she felt about him invading her personal space. It sort of dimmed his sparking attraction.

"You have quite a few hobbies," he said, covering his fascination.

She looked at him a moment longer. "Dinner is ready."

He followed her back to the kitchen, where she'd set up sturdy paper plates on the kitchen island. She'd already dished out pork chops with sautéed fruit, red onions and banana peppers on top and some kind of salad.

Savanna opened the microwave and brought over a bowl of steaming mashed potatoes. He didn't care if they were out of a box.

He looked up at her and smiled his thanks.

She smiled back. "I wasn't expecting company, least of all a hungry man."

"I wasn't expecting to *be* company." But here was as good of a place to hide as any.

While he piled potatoes onto his plate, she put a glass of water in front of him and sat next to him, putting down a bottle of sparkling water. She began slicing her pork chop and ate daintily and slowly, frequently glancing over at him and occasionally taking a swig from her bottle of water. Most people who drank that stuff put it in a glass. She drank it like a beer. He almost chuckled.

"You like living alone, don't you?" He said it more like an observation.

She put her water down and smiled. "What gave me away?"

"You seem—" he glanced down at the bottle of water "—set in your ways. In a good way." Was he digging himself a hole here?

"Well, when you make it to my age without getting married, it's bound to happen."

Unable to stop himself, he said, "I find it very hard to believe you've never been married."

She put her fork down. "Well, I haven't."

He watched her drink some more water, uncomfortable with him, not trusting in the least. "Why not?" Someone as beautiful as her wouldn't stay single long. Or was her remote address an issue?

Setting her water down, she looked at him. "It didn't work out."

"So there was someone serious?"

Instead of answering, she picked up her plate and took it to the sink.

Korbin followed. The more evasive she was the more her mystery made him think of more questions. He put his glass down on the counter and his paper plate on top of hers while she made washing forks and knives take longer than necessary.

"Why did you quit motivational speaking?" Did her relationship that didn't work out have something to do with it?

With an unappreciative glance, she took the paper plates to the trash can inside a cabinet door. Then she leaned back against the counter with her hands draped over the edge. Her flannel shirt stretched over her breasts, drawing his eyes. The material was too thick to see much detail. Taking in her long, slender legs, he all but drooled over the apex of her fit thighs.

When he finally looked back at her face, he met the fiery blue of her eyes.

She had some secrets of her own, or subjects that were off-limits.

"Sorry," he said.

"I was engaged once," she said. "He found someone else who had more to offer."

He hadn't expected her to answer and suspected she hadn't, either. Their building curiosity was mutual, it would seem.

"Was he blind or just stupid?" he asked.

That softened her. A tiny smile poked the corners of that succulent mouth. "Both, I'd have to say."

"Did he lose interest after you showed him the pre-nup?"

The way she blinked said it all. He'd guessed right.

"I've had that happen to me before."

Instant warmth transformed her face when he said that. She breathed a laugh and smiled at him, straight white teeth flashing. He almost forgot what had brought him to her deserted road. This pull between them was getting strong.

He didn't ask her if she loved the man. Obviously, she had. And obviously, she'd stopped speaking about inspirational things because of it. Did her hobbies fill the void left behind?

"You said you were married once," she said. "Did she sign a prenuptial agreement?"

He supposed he should have seen that coming. "No. I never asked her to." Niya had looked like a blond-haired Barbie doll but inside she'd been the genuine article. She was the kind of woman who didn't know how beautiful she was. Korbin had to tell her all the time, or she wouldn't believe it.

They had struck it off so well that Korbin had put off telling her about his parents. She'd grown up in a small Midwestern town in a working-class household. She had one brother. When he had finally told her, she'd been disappointed. She'd been angry with him for keeping it a secret. She hadn't spoken to him for a week afterward. He'd never had a reaction like that from a woman, and it had made him love her all the more.

He'd pursued her relentlessly. Called. Stopped by the house she rented with another student. At last she'd agreed to see him again. He'd been forthright and honest with her in all things from then on. They'd fallen madly in love. It was unreal.

And then…

"I'm sorry," Savanna said. "I don't like it when people ask me about my engagement and…" She didn't finish. "I shouldn't have pried like that."

And what? What had she been about to say? If he asked, he'd be prying the same as she had. And then he'd be obligated to reveal more of his own past. That made his mind up. Talk of Niya was best avoided.

"What other hobbies do you have?" he asked instead.

"Come on." She started for the kitchen entrance. "I'll show you."

He trailed her through the living room to the stairway. Underneath the upper-level steps, more led to a basement. At the bottom, a huge rec room opened. There was a bar and a huge television with theater seats. Shelves on both sides of the TV were full of movies and video games.

Savanna passed that, then turned on a light that illuminated the other half of the room. But the light didn't come from above, it came from a miniature town set up on a big table. A train track wound its way around, crossing a river and going over a road. There was a hill of houses overlooking the town. All of the buildings had lights and there were even stoplights that worked and cars that followed another track around town.

"You did this?"

"A little at a time."

"You're like a boy." He laughed. "This is great." He walked around the table. There was even a mine.

After studying every detail of the setup, Korbin saw her watching him with a soft smile. She loved how he appreciated this.

"You'd be a bad fit for city life," he said. "You wouldn't have time for all of this."

She shook her head. "No."

But he sensed she'd rather share it with someone. "Do you ever plan to have kids or are you too much of one yourself?"

"I'm too much of a kid myself," she said. "I make a better aunt than I would a mom."

He could see that about her. "I feel the same way, except I'm an only child."

Sharing the growing connection between them, the moment heated up. Her eyes batted and lowered and she clasped her hands in front of her.

With the *choo-choo* of the train, Korbin stepped closer. Something deep in him warned to resist this, but desire overruled. Reaching out, he took her hands, coaxing her to unclasp them and then pulling her slowly to him. One step. Two. And then she was against him. She put her hands on his chest and looked up, in a spell that had fallen over them both.

He didn't give her time to react. Didn't give himself time to think. Just kissed her. Soft at first. Gentle. Warm. And then the very thing that had him in awe over her rolled into a ball of flames.

She made a groaning sound and the next thing he felt was her fingers raking through his short hair. He gave her more, and the fevered kiss compelled him to wrap both his arms around her, hands gliding down her slender back to her rear and pressing her against his growing hardness. She had to feel it through those thin pants.

This wasn't supposed to happen. More than the reason that had brought him here, he still felt beholden to someone else.

Slowly, with unease building, he pulled back. She looked up at him through half-opened eyes, luscious mouth plump and wanton. She'd felt exactly the way he'd imagined. And more. So much more that foreboding crept into his unease. He felt as though he would betray Niya if he allowed this to go any further.

The smoke began to clear. Her eyes grew more aware. Abruptly she stepped back.

"I'm sorry," he said. "I don't know what made me do that." Angelina Jolie lips…tight pants…braless breasts…

"Uh…how about a movie?"

"Sure." A really loud, action-packed movie with no sex in it.

The next morning, Savanna stretched with a languorous moan. She'd just had the most wonderful dream.

Korbin's big, strong body on top of hers…a big, hard erection igniting her flesh…

Her eyes popped open. Springing to sitting position, she cursed and wiped the hair off her flushed face. She was ready for him and he wasn't even in here! Would she fall so easily for yet another man, only to lose him later?

Appalled, Savanna flung the covers off her, took a long shower and stayed in her room for a little longer. All the while, his kiss kept taunting her. So did the way he looked at her after the action thriller they'd watched. They'd walked upstairs and at his bedroom door, temptation to stay in her bed had begun to burn in his eyes.

She could have stripped naked for him right then. Hell, she could have stripped naked and pushed him into his room. Instead, she'd forced her feet to back up until she was able to turn and go to her room, where she'd looked at him as she closed the door.

Sleep had come much later. Now it was coming to 10:00 a.m.

Dressed in jeans and a gray wool sweater, she finally went downstairs.

Korbin was in the kitchen with a cup of coffee, reading one of her books. The television was on in the living room, tuned in to a weather channel that was talking about the blizzard on the way for tonight.

He looked up when he heard her. His eyes flared with heat before he stopped the reaction. Shutters came down and emotion vanished. He was guarded, cold. Stopping his attraction. Where had that come from? Did he regret kissing her last night?

That part of his past he couldn't talk about must be why. Instead of thinking twice about entertaining any romantic possibilities with him, she should take his lead and put a stop to this right now. Going into another high-risk relationship wasn't on her adventure radar. High-risk because there was too much uncertainty. The next man she got involved with, she'd get to know very well first. As in, it would be months before she slept with him, not weeks as she'd done before.

The sound of a passing snowmobile had both of them looking outside. The sky was overcast, but it had stopped snowing.

Hurley rented snowmobiles, but his property was far enough away that no one ever rode this close. The trails were several miles away.

Savanna went to the back patio door. She saw nothing, and the sound faded.

"I hope they aren't lost," she said.

When Korbin didn't respond, she looked at him. He

stared at the window, brow low and creased. It bothered him that a snowmobile had driven so close to her house.

"What's the matter?" Once again she felt a strange sense of foreboding come over her. Something about him caused it. Why?

"Nothing." He stood up and went to the front door, opening it and searching outside. Then he closed and locked the door and went to the garage. When he made sure that was locked tight, he returned to the living room.

He was acting weird.

A sound from the sunroom stiffened Savanna. She remembered that she'd left the door unlocked in there. Looking at Korbin, she saw he'd realized that along with her.

An instant later, a man wearing a black ski mask and winter outerwear appeared with a pistol. The shock of the sight rendered Savanna frozen. He fired the pistol at the same time Korbin pushed her into the kitchen, putting her behind him just as the man rushed in after them.

Savanna stepped backward as Korbin grabbed an island stool and threw it at the man. While the man stumbled, Savanna ran out of the kitchen through the other entrance. She flattened her back against the wall, breathing hard, looking around for a weapon. She spotted the phone on the side table. Hearing Korbin fighting the stranger, she ran to the phone and then back to the wall for cover, ducking as the man fired again. Bullets struck her cabinetry and Korbin leaped into the living room, taking cover with her.

They had to get out of here.

"This way!" Savanna ran for the front entry.

She stopped short when the man in black emerged from the other kitchen opening, aiming his weapon and blocking their escape. She waited in horror for him to shoot.

Korbin moved so that she was behind him. "Don't shoot."

Savanna wasn't going to wait for the man to start firing his gun. Picking up a bottle of wine from the buffet and wine cabinet, she hurled it at the man. He ducked and the bottle shattered against the wall.

Korbin charged forward and punched the stranger hard enough to knock him down. He fell to the side, partially in the kitchen.

Savanna ran to the front entry and took cover there, lifting the phone. There was no signal. The line was dead. Not that calling the police would do much good. How would they reach them in time with all the snow on the ground?

Oh, God. What were they going to do?

Dropping the phone, she heard Korbin fighting the man again. Peeking around the corner, she didn't see them. They were in the kitchen. A loud crash told her something had just gone through her patio door. Another gunshot rang out, followed by a few smacking punches, and then the two men crashed to the floor in the kitchen entry. Korbin had the intruder's wrist in his grip, keeping the gun aimed upward. The intruder twisted free but Korbin hit his face and then kicked the gun from his grasp. It clattered to the floor. Savanna ran to pick it up just as the man pulled a knife from a holder on his boot. He lunged at Korbin, who jumped back to avoid being cut.

Savanna moved to stay out of his way and saw the other man run for the broken door. Korbin didn't chase after him.

"Let's get out of here." Korbin took the gun from her

and guided her into the entry, looking back to make sure the man didn't follow.

"Who was that?" she asked.

He put his back to the wall near the doorway. "We can't stay here."

"Why not? That man is out there."

"There's a lodge across from Chavis's cabin. Let's ski there," Korbin said, gesturing to her closet full of gear. "Get dressed."

Savanna kept everything in here anyone might need for cold weather. "You, too." She handed him long underwear that was still in the package. Korbin stayed by the door with the gun. The house was quiet.

"Maybe we should stay here," she said. "I think he left."

"Your back door is broken. He'll come back. We should go somewhere safe."

Korbin had a good point. If the man returned, he'd be able to get inside. But would they be any safer out in the wilderness? It was a long way to Hurley's lodge.

"He's on a snowmobile," she said.

"We'll hear him. We have to get away from here," he said.

"Why? And why did a man show up in my house shooting at you? What's going on?" Was he on the run from something?

Korbin looked at her as she handed him a jacket.

"Was that a cop?" she asked.

"No."

"Who was it, then?"

He shrugged into the red-and-black Descente breathable jacket. "I don't know."

Wondering if he was lying, Savanna found long underwear and a lightweight fleece. "But you know why he's after you." The man had to be after him. No one would come after her.

Next she found a breathable jacket and snow pants but didn't dress. That feeling of foreboding intensified. Instinct urged her to stay in her house. She could board up the window with extra fencing that was piled outside the stable.

"Get dressed, Savanna."

She threw the garments she held onto the floor. "I'm not going anywhere with you."

After peering out from the entry to check if the man had returned, he said to her, "You have to."

"No, I don't. You brought that shooter into my home. It was peaceful until you got here."

He stared at her. "This involves you, too, now."

The sting of shock froze her. "How?"

He hesitated, much the same as he had when he'd first gotten stuck on her road. "He saw you. You're with me. That means you're in danger."

Just because he'd seen her? "Why was he shooting at you?"

"Get dressed, Savanna. I don't have time to explain right now. We have to get as far away from here as we can." When she only stared at him, he urged, "Please. Just listen to me. And trust me. I'll keep you alive. I promise."

"I'll keep myself alive by staying here."

"What if he comes back here?"

Her face grew cold with dread. "Why would he do that?"

"Savanna…"

She stared at him as she began to see his point. She

might not be safe here and she would be at Hurley's. Get to Hurley's. That's what she had to do. She quickly dressed and then slipped her feet into ski boots. Putting a pair of boots in front of him, she went back to the closet and threw him a hat, gloves and goggles. A backpack came next. Korbin caught it and slung it over one shoulder and then caught a transceiver she tossed at him last.

The sound of crunching glass, as though someone had stepped over some in the kitchen, galvanized her into faster action. After slinging her own pack onto her back and securing her transceiver, she picked up two pairs of mountain skis just as a loud crack of a firing rifle deafened her and took a chunk out of the doorjamb inches from Korbin's head. He fired back and ran after her out the front door.

The intruder had a rifle now!

Shaking, frantic for air, Savanna shoved her booted feet into the skis, Korbin doing the same beside her. She skied toward the trees, looking back to see the man with the rifle appear in the front doorway. He saw them skiing away but didn't fire. Instead, he disappeared back into the house. With sickening dread, Savanna knew he'd go for his snowmobile. He'd track them down and kill them. The faster they reached Hurley's the better. The only problem was that a straight line to Lost Trail Lodge was over a fourteen-thousand-foot mountain. Assuming they could stay hidden from the gunman, they would have to ski miles of rugged terrain. Even if they took the shortest route, she didn't think they'd make it before the next storm hit.

Tucking the gun into a pocket of his jacket, Korbin started skiing in the direction of the lodge. Savanna skied ahead of him. He didn't know the way. She did. And the safest. This was dangerous avalanche country.

Snowcapped peaks were hidden under building clouds. Pine and blue spruce trees sagged beneath the weight of snow. A blanket of smooth white powder stretched before her to the edge of the trees. She headed for a path that led to Hurley's yurt-touring trails.

Finding the trail, she skied to a stop and looked back at her house. From here it looked peaceful. Leaving tore at her.

Korbin skied to a stop beside her. "Let's get moving."

She looked at him with doubt before skiing ahead of him through the trees. The sound of a snowmobile made her push harder. The man would easily find their tracks and follow.

A few minutes later, the sound faded and all she heard were their skis swishing through the snow.

At the base of the hill, she stopped. Climbing would slow them down. So would the weather. The wind had begun to blow, lifting fresh powder off the surface.

Savanna searched through the trees and listened for the snowmobile, briefly meeting Korbin's eyes before moving on. The trail reached an avalanche chute. Korbin stopped, looking up the steep slope and not skiing across. After the heavy snow, the danger was high right now.

She skied out onto the slope, traversing it carefully until she made it to the trees on the other side. Korbin followed and they picked up the trail again.

At the top of the slope, Savanna heard something moving in the trees. She stopped to scan their surroundings.

Korbin did the same. It was probably a deer or branches falling under the weight of snow.

"How much farther to the lodge?" Korbin asked.

"We won't make it there by tonight."

His gaze shot to her. It was already midafternoon and snow had begun to fall.

She explained about the mountain. "Crimson Morning is the closest yurt to my house and the farthest from the lodge. We have another hard climb and then it's mostly downhill from there to reach it. We should stay at Crimson Morning tonight and try to make it to the lodge in the morning."

"What do you mean, try?"

"It's going to take us another two hours to get to Crimson Morning. Maybe longer in this weather."

He looked ahead at the trail in consternation. As an experienced skier, he had to know it took roughly an hour per mile to ski in this terrain, and another hour for every thousand vertical feet. Longer in bad weather.

"How far is the next yurt after Crimson Morning?"

"Silver Plume will take us another two or three hours."

"Then we ski to Silver Plume today."

Savanna tipped her head back to observe the sky. "That could be dangerous." Wind carried heavier falling snow down upon them. She'd rather play it safe and stay at Crimson Morning.

"It's a risk we have to take."

She met his look. Whoever had shot at him and why must have him worried. It had her worried. It upset her calm world and thrust her into a frightening unknown. People shot at her brother Lincoln, not her. Well, Autumn, too. What was it with their family? They seemed to be living their very own action movie.

The snap of a twig made her jerk to her right. There was no sound of a snowmobile. The man who'd attacked them couldn't walk through this snow. It was too deep. Had he taken a pair of skis from her house?

Korbin pulled out the gun and aimed into the forest. She looked in that direction but saw nothing. Then a figure moved among the trunks. A mountain lion prowled forward and stopped when it saw them.

Savanna's heart slammed in her chest, but she remained still and quiet.

Korbin didn't fire. He waited. A gunshot would alert the man after them of their whereabouts. One good thing about the snow is that it would soon cover their tracks. The big cat's head faced them, studied them and then sprang into an acrobatic run through the forest in the opposite direction.

He turned toward her. Calm. Full of secrets. Different from the man she'd spent an evening with, showing off her train set and watching a movie. Handling a gun was not unfamiliar to him. What was he hiding?

Crimson Morning came into view. Korbin had taken the lead and they'd made good time. Savanna showed no signs of tiring, but he skied to a stop in front of the yurt. No other skiers were there. The lodge had likely held off any tours until after the storm.

Korbin looked for signs of the shooter. He hadn't heard the snowmobile, which could mean he'd taken to skis for quieter stalking.

He looked at Savanna. "Are you okay to press on?"

She nodded. She must feel better about the time they'd made getting here. Korbin loved that about her. She hadn't asked him about the gunman, either. Getting to safety was the top priority, but he knew she was thinking about it. He'd have to explain it eventually. She was a tough woman, albeit in a slender, feminine body.

Korbin skied past Crimson Morning and began another climb. A feeling came over him about halfway up the mountain. Had he heard something? They were in a clearing. He looked into the trees and didn't see anything. But then a slight movement just upslope caught his eye. As soon as he spotted a black hat poking up above a fallen log, the explosion of a rifle echoed off the mountainside. The bullet splintered a tree trunk beside him. Pieces of bark hit his jacket.

"Get down!" he yelled, scrambling on his skis to take cover behind the tree.

A second gunshot cracked. He heard it hit the snow near his feet. He leaned his shoulder against the tree and checked on Savanna. She'd crouched behind another tree not far from him, gripping her poles, eyes wide with terror, breath misting the air, giving their position away.

Korbin pulled out the gun.

Another gunshot erupted. The bullet tore through his backpack, giving his body a jerk. If he tried to peer around the trunk, he just might get a bullet in the head for the effort.

The shooter had a clear shot. All he had to do was wait for them to move. Damen. Korbin had known it was him as soon as he'd heard the snowmobile back at Savanna's house. He had followed him here, maybe even predicted where he'd go. He had a snowmobile, a pistol, a rifle and skis. He'd planned well. Korbin had to predict his next move. But how? He and Savanna would have heard him if he'd ridden this far. Unless he'd ridden to this point and waited for them, knowing they'd try to seek help at the lodge. Korbin wouldn't have thought Damen was smart enough to pull something like this off. And his biggest question was why? Why come after him? Why try so hard to kill him?

He looked for a way to escape. The trees where they had taken shelter weren't thick. Just on the other side, another clearing offered a possibility. There were two drawbacks, however. One, the trees were spaced wide enough to offer little protection, and two, the clearing over there was an avalanche chute. But if they could reach it and ski away...

Spotting something that would serve as good cover, he looked toward Savanna and whispered harshly, "When I start shooting, ski for that boulder."

She jerked her head, spotting the boulder, and then nodded at him.

Korbin stuck his poles into the snow and eased the pistol beside the trunk. Aiming in the direction where he'd seen the hat, he fired and then sprang into motion after Savanna started skiing. He skied hard to the next tree, where he fired again. His bullet hit a fallen tree trunk where the hat bobbed down and out of view. Korbin skied the rest of the way to the boulder, joining Savanna there. When Damen kept firing, Korbin fired back until the gun clicked. No more bullets.

As soon as he tossed the weapon aside, a distinct rumble began high up on the mountain.

"Avalanche," Savanna murmured, fear giving her voice a tremor.

"Get away from the chute." Korbin looked over the boulder. He didn't see the hat anymore. Damen had gone to take cover, probably hoping they'd die in the avalanche. Which they very well could. The trees weren't thick here. It was a small cluster that divided chute. They were right in the middle of the avalanche path.

"Get back into the trees!" he shouted. It was the best chance they had.

In an instant, the rumble was upon them. Korbin was flung forward and bashed into a tree. A white cloud engulfed him and he heard Savanna scream. He wrapped his arms around the trunk and held on. Snow ripped down the mountain, splintering trees and crashing with a deafening roar.

Seconds later it was over. The avalanche reached the valley and went silent. Korbin looked for Savanna…and didn't see her.

Chapter 4

She screamed long and loudly. The snow engulfed her. She closed her eyes and mouth to keep it from packing there. Both her skis ripped off her feet, twisting one of her knees painfully. She tried to remember everything she learned about what to do if caught in an avalanche.

Keep her head in the uphill direction. Wait until the momentum slowed. Swim for the surface while the snow was still mobile. Create a breathing space.

Even if she were buried as little as one foot, her chances were slim for survival. If she were buried for more than thirty minutes her chances grew lethal. Only one in four people lived through an avalanche if they were buried in one at all. If the asphyxiation didn't kill her, the cold would.

She wasn't ready to die...

Each second felt like an eternity. The snow began to slow. She tried to swim upward. When the snow began to slow and stop, she moved her hand up to her mouth to create that life-saving breathing space. Her gloved hand touched her lower lip. She wiggled her fingers. Good. A small pocket of air. Now if Korbin could find her...

The snow hardened like cement around her body. She tried not to panic.

Korbin hissed a curse.

Moving swiftly, he threw off his backpack and retrieved a shovel and collapsible probe pole. With the side of his ski he kicked the backpack across the snow, careful not to let it slide downhill, wanting to mark the area where he'd last seen Savanna. It would provide a reference point if he needed it during his search. Immediately he turned his transceiver to receiving mode; it would be the only hope he had of saving Savanna's life.

Something he couldn't do for his wife. Something he couldn't do for Collette. Dead women were stacking up in his life.

Well, he'd be damned if he'd let another one down.

The transceiver Savanna wore would still be set to send a signal and his would pick it up when he was close to her. He heard only static now, but he pushed himself into motion and skied down toward the toe of the avalanche. Once there, he removed his skis. Most of the time the bodies were found at the end of the slide. Korbin tried to control his morbid thoughts.

The bodies.

Hearing a snowmobile, he spotted it emerging from the trees. He crouched behind a mound of clumpy snow until the sound grew fainter. Then he stood and resumed his task while he kept watch for the snowmobile. Had Damen seen Savanna being swept away?

Damen was determined to kill him, and now probably Savanna, too. And Korbin had a good idea why. He must have seen the email he'd left open for police at Collette's home. Police hadn't found it because Damen had gotten there first. He'd seen what Korbin had uncovered.

Seeing and hearing no sign of Damen, he put all of his attention into finding Savanna. Maybe Damen had assumed Korbin had suffered the same fate. Maybe he'd run out of ammunition.

Using a grid pattern, Korbin began to search for a signal from his transceiver. The avalanche was moderately sized, with the crown of the slide stretching across the topography at the base of the slope. In seconds he picked up a signal and stopped every few paces in order to determine from which orientation it was the strongest. When the signal faded, he knew he had passed her. He marked a line in the snow. Then he headed back in the same direction he'd come until the signal faded again. He marked another line in the snow.

Walking to the midpoint of his imaginary bracket, he oriented himself toward the strongest signal and adjusted the sensitivity of his receiver, turning it down to catch differences in strength more efficiently. He walked at a right angle to his original line until the signal began to grow weak, repeating the same method as before. When he was at the midpoint of his second imaginary bracket and found the strongest signal for the second time, he again walked at a right angle.

Finally, he pinpointed the area where he thought Savanna was buried. He checked his watch. It had been more than ten minutes since she had fallen with the slide. With shaking hands, he extended his collapsible probe pole and began sticking it into the snow. Five more minutes passed before he hit something. He estimated her depth and began to dig. Careful not to force it into the snow so hard that it would harm her if he struck her, he worked diligently.

All the while, haunting images of Niya suffocated him. Her bloodied body. Her cold lips as he breathed air into her lifelessness. Pumping her chest, refusing to let her go.

The shovel revealed clothing. He threw the shovel aside and dropped to his knees to dig with his hands and find her face. His heart raced and his breathing filled the air in great billowing puffs. He exposed her chest and dug higher. Collar. Hair.

Face!

"Savanna!"

She broke through the last layer of snow, gasping for air and looking dazed, reaching for him. A new thought came to him that kept his adrenaline up. Hypothermia.

Dragging her out of her white grave, he laid her on the surface of the snow and unzipped his jacket, then hers. He pulled her against him and used his body heat to warm her.

She tried to bring her arms between their bodies in an attempt to warm them as well, but he wouldn't let her. Her limbs would have been the first to plummet to dangerously low temperatures in the snow, and if they were warmed first, chilled blood would be driven to the core of her body. If that happened, it could kill her.

When she relaxed underneath him, he knew she was getting warm. Lifting his head, he looked down at her. She was breathing normal now, her eyes calm.

"Thanks," she said.

"Anytime." He grinned and got off her.

She sat up and looked around, grateful to be alive. "We should have stayed at Crimson Morning," she said in a light tone. Humor diffused how close she'd come to dying. But she meant what she had said.

Did she think Crimson Morning would have been safer? "That shooter might have found us there." He stood and extended his hand, which she ignored, then stood on her own and said, "Let's get to the next yurt."

Keeping an eye on her, watching for signs of injury, he started to look for her skis. One of them was right next to where she'd been buried. The other took some searching.

"Are you sure you're okay?" Korbin asked when they were under way again. If she wasn't, she'd still have to ski to Silver Plume. They were closer to that than Crimson Morning.

"Yes. I'm fine."

She'd probably be sore and bruised, but it could have been so much worse. Korbin still struggled with shaking off the memories of Niya. Why had they hit him then? They hit him often but usually he could put them out of his mind. Not so today. Today, they tormented him. Maybe that was because he'd saved Savanna and hadn't been able to save Niya and as usual, guilt riddled him.

Wind whipped snowflakes against the balaclava that covered Savanna's face and spotted her goggles. They'd had to stop to check a compass several times, and skiing against the wind had slowed them down. Beside her, Korbin bent his snow-caked body to remove his bindings. It had taken them two hours longer to get here through the storm. She was cold and sore everywhere.

It was dark now, which had made getting here even harder. Korbin hadn't said much. Not that talk would have been easy with all the other challenges. Grimness had settled over him. At first she thought he was worried they wouldn't make it to Silver Plume. But it was more than that.

Sticking her skis in the snow beside Korbin's, out of sight from any passersby once the storm cleared, Savanna marched through the snow to the yurt door. Up under the overhang, she found the built-in container open on the top and retrieved the key. Hurley had told her where he kept spares at all of the yurts.

The octagonal yurt had two windows in front, but the wood panels were shut from the outside. Hurley had prepared them all for the blizzard. A wood-burning stove was in the center, with two twin-size beds underneath a cramped loft, two uncomfortable-looking chairs and a love seat to the right, and a kitchen with a small island on wheels. There was even a bathroom with a composting toilet and shower in a small enclosed room, the door next to the kitchen cabinets. There was no electricity. The yurt was dark. Savanna fumbled around until she found a flashlight in a kitchen drawer.

In a trunk at the foot of one of the beds, there were camping lanterns. While Korbin lit a fire in the wood-burning stove, she put three of the lanterns out, one in the kitchen, one in the living room and one between the beds.

Within thirty minutes the yurt began to warm. Savanna removed her hat and jacket. She'd be stuck with sleeping in her base layer.

Going into the kitchen, she began to scrounge for something to eat. They'd burned a ton of calories today and she was starving. Hurley kept the yurts stocked with a lot of canned and boxed food. Ordinarily he'd charge skiers who stayed here, but the main reason he kept them stocked was for emergencies like this.

"Your choice of canned chili, canned mac and cheese, canned enchiladas, or tuna with noodles and creamy broccoli sauce," she said.

"How about all of it?"

She glanced back with a grin and then took out both boxes of creamy broccoli noodles and two cans of tuna. Korbin took two kettles outside and came back in with heaping piles of snow.

Savanna started the gas stove. Each of Hurley's yurts came equipped with a propane tank. She'd boil one kettle for drinking water and the other for the noodles. Retrieving a frying pan, she emptied the tuna into that and prepared the sauce mix. While she did that, Korbin went to get more snow so they could take showers. There was no running water because it would freeze, so all water had to be brought in.

A half hour later, she filled their plates with the steaming noodle mixture and made two cups of tea. She joined Korbin at the small square table. Hunger kept them quiet for a while, but Savanna noticed that Korbin frequently drifted into thought. He'd been like that ever since the avalanche. And before that he'd seemed to be hiding something. This was a different silence, though. Not hesitation, not reluctance to say too much.

He must be worried about the shooter catching up to them. They'd been careful to make sure they weren't followed, and Korbin had told her he saw the shooter driving away on his snowmobile. They were safe for now, but the danger still loomed. His drifting attention hinted to something more akin to sorrow.

"You've been awfully quiet since the avalanche," she said.

Drawn from another faraway memory, it took him a moment to respond. "We had to get to this yurt as soon as possible."

The weather wasn't the entire reason. "You're still quiet."

"A lot on my mind."

His curt reply was more of an evasive tactic. He didn't want to talk at all tonight.

Well, she did. He had some explaining to do. "There's been a lot on my mind, too," she said. "Like why did a man break into my house and start shooting? He must have been after you."

When he didn't respond, she asked, "Do you know who he is?"

"Yes."

That was all she got out of him. He owed her an explanation. He'd almost gotten her killed.

"Who is he?" she asked.

Gone was that ruminating look and in its place came shrewdness she'd seen in him before. "Someone who's in a lot of trouble."

Whatever that meant. "What's his name?"

"Savanna, it's best if you—"

"Tell me." She was getting impatient.

"It isn't safe."

She lifted her eyebrows. "And that was?" She motioned with her thumb toward the door of the yurt.

After a bit, he sighed. "His name is Damen Ricchetti. He was a friend of mine until he got into something he shouldn't have."

"What something? Can you be more specific?"

With a resigned blink, he finally said, "I found out he was into some black-market business." When she started to ask what business, he held up his hand. "I'll tell you all I can."

All he felt *safe* in telling her.

"I learned the name of a man he's been in contact with," he said. "I read a revealing email exchange. He and another man discussed a business arrangement they had made together. There wasn't much detail but I have the name of the man he was communicating with. Damen doesn't want me to know the man's name. I didn't think he'd come after me and try to kill me with what little I discovered. That I didn't see coming." He paused. "I didn't see a lot until recently." He looked at her. "But no more. I'm going to end this. Damen isn't going to hurt anyone else."

By his vehement conviction, she believed him. But something didn't add up. "Is that why you were on the way to the cabin?"

"Partly, yes."

Partly? There was more? He was withholding the whole truth. He'd come here to hide. That much she was sure of now.

"Is Damen a computer scientist like you?" she asked.

He grinned along with a cynical laugh. "No. He barely graduated from high school."

"What does he do for a living?"

When he hesitated, Savanna suspected he was choosing his words carefully.

"He's a con artist."

That surprised her. He'd told her. "And he's your friend?"

"Not anymore. He ripped off wealthy people who

made money by taking advantage of others. Executives of pharmaceutical companies who hide bad results of testing. Banking executives who get bloated bonuses. Unethical entrepreneurs. It was a game to him. He'd find their weaknesses and plan a way to rob them. Somewhere along the line he lost his scruples. Anyone is a target now. Including me."

She took in his big form, light gray eyes assessing, seeing how she'd react to this. He was imperturbable. Matter-of-fact. But his honesty touched her and some-how made what he said all right.

"Did you work with him?" she asked. Con artist…

Again, he hesitated. His eyes blinked. "Sometimes."

Only when hacking was required? He helped his friend steal from wealthy people they'd deemed immoral. Did that make the theft okay? She had trouble with that. She had even more trouble with how she almost justi-fied it along with him.

She was attracted to him—a thief. He put an appeal-ing twist on his purpose, but that didn't change the fact that he'd helped his friend steal.

It was best to keep things casual with him. She wasn't over her last love. She wasn't ready to take on another one, especially a six-foot-four hunk who should frighten her rather than make her yearn to get naked with him.

Unsettled, Savanna took his empty plate and hers to the kitchen. They were paper so all she had to do was throw them away. She went about cleaning up the light mess, leaving the drinking water in the kettle in case either one of them needed some later. All the while she couldn't pinpoint the source of the feeling that he wasn't telling her everything. He'd been honest, but there was more. More under the surface.

So immersed in thought, she didn't notice him come up behind her until his hand rested on top of hers, stilling her wiping motions. She'd cleaned the counter long enough. It was an automatic action while her mind spun.

She looked up at him while he put his hand on her waist and turned her to face him. The intimate way he touched her and the hard energy of him lit her up inside. All she could do was melt in the clarity of his eyes.

"I won't let anything happen to you."

He said it with such certainty, and yet, how could he know? Was he that sure of himself? He didn't try to convince her he wasn't a bad guy. He had to realize she'd wonder, and yet he didn't make excuses. She both respected him for that and built up her defenses. Her heart was still vulnerable. Maybe she'd always be vulnerable when it came to men. She had no tools to protect herself from falling in love. She needed to learn to develop them. Until then, men who posed any kind of threat to her had to be rejected.

While her mind reasoned that way, her body had other ideas. When he lifted his hand and brushed his fingers along her cheek, she flushed with desire. He turned her on that easily. A look. A touch. His nearness. This did not feel safe. She sensed the same in him, reluctance no match for the passion they generated.

Powerless against the spell of this mysterious love drug, she didn't fight him when his fingers moved beneath her chin and he gently raised her head. She was a rapt observer as he lowered his mouth to hers. Maybe he was an observer, too, a puppet to the seductive strings that tugged them.

Soft and slow, he kissed her, withdrawing every once in a while as uncertainty gained momentum, only to fall into the spell again. The sultry play of kisses built to parting of mouths. He kissed her harder.

She slid her arms around his shoulders, dissolving into him as he pressed her body against the kitchen counter. A tiny part of her warned not to let this go any further, but the movement of his head as he took her mouth for another kiss sent her to a steamy land of temptation.

He lifted her and put her on the counter. She opened her legs and gripped his butt and tried to pull him against her. The only thing that mattered was the desire to feel his erection where she needed it most. She wanted to crawl inside his skin. Be one with him, with his strength, his mind. Everything.

He was almost there. To that place she yearned to go with him. If he'd just touch her more. Finally, he gave in and moved his hips closer.

Yes.

A shudder racked him and he dragged his mouth over her jaw to her neck, where he went still. She started to search for him with her mouth. But his lack of response gave her time to realize what was happening. What was about to happen.

She stiffened as Korbin stepped back, the gray of his eyes drilling her with a fevered stare. He was leaving the choice up to her.

Except she couldn't decide what to do next. She was too confused.

It was enough to cool her passion. She slid off the countertop. How could she have no control when he kissed her? Why couldn't she stop him?

Because she didn't want him to stop....

When she gathered her wits, she asked, "What happened between you and your wife?" She had to know.

As she anticipated, that stiffened him and he stepped back, his passion calming with hers. Was it guilt she saw take him over?

But he seemed to understand why she asked. If this intimacy continued between them, she needed to arm herself with what she was up against.

"She died. A year ago."

Died.

Not divorced. He'd suffered a terrible loss. Just the look in his eyes convinced her. He'd loved her. Disappointment crushed her. That and self-reproach. She had to learn to listen to her reasoning and be disciplined enough to follow that reasoning. The best way to accomplish that was to arm herself with knowledge. The more evidence she had on his state, and how that state made him a bad choice, the more empowered she'd be to control her feelings.

"What was her name?" she asked.

"Niya. I met her in college, when I started my PhD."

He had a PhD? She followed his rugged form over to the wood-burning stove, sexy and masculine and made for the outdoors. Sitting on the sofa, she watched him add more wood to the fire.

"She graduated with a degree in English and got a job teaching middle-school kids," he said. "I always thought she was too normal for me."

"Why too normal?"

After closing the stove door, he turned to her, still crouched. He didn't have to reply. He'd helped his friend steal. His wife was an innocent schoolteacher.

"How long were you married?"

"Eight years."

That was a long time. "Did she get sick?"

Korbin stood and came over to the sofa, sitting down beside her with a heavy sigh. "No."

"How did she die?"

He stared ahead without answering. She doubted he'd spoken to anyone about this. But if she hadn't been sick, how had she died?

"Was it an accident?" she asked, trying to help him in what must be a painful thing to talk about.

After several seconds he finally said in a low, pained voice, "Yes. She shouldn't have died. She had so much life in her."

Grief racked him. Instead of reaffirming her need to keep a distance, she felt great empathy for him. His loss. After a year he hadn't made much progress.

"You must have loved her," she said, needing to hear him say it, to prove to her that he was too broken for a new relationship, one with her, another person who was too broken for one.

He gave a brief nod. "I would have spent the rest of my life with her."

There it was. He couldn't have chosen more convincing words. Although grief had a way of elevating the deceased to divine heights, Korbin had loved his wife as fully as a man could.

She averted her gaze, finding the glow of fire through the glass of the stove comforting.

"She was nothing like you," he said.

Both that he continued to talk and what he'd said surprised her. She turned back to him.

"Oh?"

"She depended on me for a lot of things and never wanted to be left alone."

Savanna depended on no one and loved being alone. "Maybe that's why men never stick around."

"It would take a strong one."

Like him.

Thinking that her fiancé had ruined their engagement because he wasn't strong enough to handle her independence was a lot better than feeling unloved. She'd loved her fiancé and she'd loved someone else after him. Neither had loved her.

"Being alone doesn't bother me, but I could be alone with a man." The way they were right now. She couldn't stop these thoughts. He was strong enough for her, and she was alone with him. She watched him realize the same in the way his regard softened toward her.

"I think you would depend on someone if you were ever given the chance," he said. "There's a difference between depending on someone out of need and depending on them as part of a team."

"Is it safe to depend on you?" she asked.

As her meaning sank in, his softness faded and he became unreadable. He was too damaged to be part of any team. He was a lone wolf. Like her.

"Right," she said. "I've had my heart broken. I don't need it broken again."

His eyes never wavered from hers and she could see he understood but could say nothing to alleviate her fears. And why should she expect him to? They'd only just met. This was about her own insecurities. Her weakness. One she hadn't had before she'd met her fiancé. She'd like to get back to that place. Fearless. Full of adventure. Korbin gave her plenty of adventure, but it wasn't the kind she had in mind. He was dangerous for her, and not only to her heart.

Chapter 5

Where the hell was Damen? Demarco Ricchetti stuffed his phone into his pocket with a hard sigh and rang the doorbell of a small, run-down ranch home in a bad part of Denver. His twin brother had started acting strange several months ago. Some would call him arrogant. Reckless. Maybe even stupid. As his twin, Demarco would say he was all three and more. But he was also a product of his upbringing. Their dad had always favored Demarco. He was the one with all the brains. The ambition. The women. They were fraternal, not identical, and Damen got the bulldog looks. He was shorter than Demarco, stockier, and had acne scars. Demarco had smooth, youthful skin and a physique that attracted countless women.

He was sure Damen's low self-esteem had kept him from excelling in school. Demarco went to college. Damen barely made it out of high school. He did have his redeeming qualities, though. Despite being unpopular and last in their dad's pecking order, he loved Demarco and would do anything for him. They had a special bond, the kind he couldn't really describe. It was just there. They knew each other's thoughts. They were one.

Demarco didn't like thinking that it was pity that made him overprotective of his brother, but he was afraid that was the reality. But Damen seemed to be headed down into a cesspool of his own creation and Demarco didn't want to be flushed along with him. He was torn over doing what he'd always done, or turning his back on his brother for the first time in his entire life. He hadn't talked to him in days, and ever since the news broadcast of his girlfriend's murder, he kind of needed to. Why hadn't his brother called him? The murder of the woman you loved wasn't something you didn't share with your twin brother.

It wasn't like Damen to avoid him. They talked every day, mostly by text. But he wasn't even answering those. And he'd bet the news that police were looking for Korbin Maguire in connection to a hit-and-run was no coincidence. It was all very bizarre but had to be related somehow.

Demarco was about to knock when the door opened to an average-height, dark-skinned man.

"Hey, Demarco. Come on in." Baxter "Bear" Brown stepped aside. In this part of Denver, Demarco had to be careful about what he said and did. With a glance around, he stepped into the house.

Bear was Damen's business partner; at least that's what Damen had called him. When Demarco had asked if he was getting into trouble again, his brother had joked and said, *"only a little."*

Demarco now knew that it was far more than a little. He was sick with it.

"I'm looking for Damen. Have you seen him?" Demarco moved deeper into the living room and faced Bear.

"Not in a few days. I've talked to him, though. He went up to Wolf Creek."

That immediately sparked an alarm. "Why did he go there?"

"He didn't say. Vacation, I guess. Or just to get away and clear his head. After all, his girlfriend was just killed."

No, Damen did not go there to get away. There had to be another reason, and it popped into his head right then. "He went after Korbin Maguire. Korbin has a friend who owns a cabin there."

"No way, man," Bear said in surprise.

There weren't many other places in Wolf Creek that Korbin could go, and as long as no one told the cops, it was a great place to hide. The only reason he knew about it was that Korbin had taken Damen hunting one year and Damen had talked about it.

"He was pretty busted up over his girlfriend. Maybe he went to cap him. Finish him off."

So, his brother had told Bear that Korbin had killed his girlfriend. "What did he tell you about her murder?"

"That he saw Korbin leaving Collette's house. That's what he told the cops. Now Korbin is their prime suspect."

He'd actually told the cops Korbin had killed her, or alluded to it. If Korbin had been at her house at the time of the murder, he'd look guilty.

"Where was he when he saw Korbin?"

"He didn't say. He just said that he found her dead after that."

Demarco smothered a scoff. Found her dead. He was probably the one who killed her.

"He cared for Collette. He told me he was going to ask her to marry him. If somebody killed my sweetheart, I might go after him, too."

Demarco refrained from saying there had to be another reason Damen went after Korbin. "That's what worries me."

"Yeah. Damen can be dangerous. You have to watch him, but Korbin—" Bear shook his head "—I wouldn't go up against a guy like that. Damen might be the one to get hurt."

Korbin did have a formidable reputation. Demarco was afraid that he was innocent and Damen had framed him. Korbin would be no match for a gun.

Damen was a jealous man. And he was especially jealous of Korbin. He often complained about him, but never cut him out of his life. Korbin was good at what he did, that's why. Damen was more interested in making money than the way he felt about Korbin. Maybe he'd caught Korbin with Collette and sought revenge. And then something else had happened. He and Collette argued and things got out of hand? Whatever the reason, Damen hadn't intended to kill her. And it made no sense for him to go after Korbin, not when he'd already set him up for murder. So what was going on? What was his brother up to now?

Demarco saw movement in the kitchen to his left and had to stop a physical flinch. On the beat-up wood table were piles and piles of money. Wads of cash that someone was dividing.

"Business must be good," Demarco said as nonchalantly as he could muster. As Damen's twin, the criminals who now worked for Damen trusted Demarco. They assumed Damen told him everything, or they wouldn't have let him in the house while they were counting the proceeds of a drug deal. Damen dealt drugs, but not on this scale. From the looks of it, he'd hit the big time.

"Damen got that Sinaloa dealer to work with him," Bear said. "Things are going to change for him. For all of us. We're very happy to be working for him."

Demarco could just bet. Money like that would be a great motivator.

"I won't keep you," Demarco said.

"You going after Damen?"

"Yes." He grinned. "Keep him out of trouble again." As always.

"All right, man. Hey, if you see him tell him we got the first payment, okay?"

"Sure."

Demarco left and cursed in his car. He didn't want anything to happen to his brother, but was it wise to involve himself in any of this? How far would he go for him? Not having an answer and feeling deeply obligated and compelled to save his brother, he called his wife, preparing himself for her reaction. They had a nice life together. He made a good income with his antiques and estate auction house. She didn't have to work and stayed home with the kids. Their life was so different from Damen's. Normal. Law-abiding.

"Honey, I have to go to Wolf Creek tonight."

"What? Why?"

"I found Damen."

"So call him."

"I've been trying. He isn't answering." He explained about the cabin, only telling her that Damen had gone after Korbin for allegedly killing Collette.

"So you're going to try to stop him? Demarco, this is getting crazy. Don't go there. Come home."

"I have to go."

"He could get you killed."

"No, he won't. I'll call you when I get there."

"Why can't you just let him be?" she said. "You're too protective of him. You enable him, do you realize that?"

Yes, he sure did. "I have to go, honey. I have to stop him from hurting anyone. I have to at least do that." His wife was sheltered and didn't understand Damen the way he did. "I'll be all right."

Finally she relented and he drove toward the mountains. Even as he still reeled from the prospect of Damen being capable of killing someone.

The weather was horrible and Demarco berated himself for not checking first. He was amazed the highway was still open, but certain it would be closing soon. He could barely see the road. He passed a sign and couldn't make out what it said. It was some sort of lodge. The map he'd looked up on the internet showed one close to Julio Chavis's cabin. Ten minutes later, he spotted a turnoff. The road hadn't been plowed yet, but his Jeep Grand Cherokee handled it just fine. Plus, in the trees it wasn't as deep. The road wound up an incline, and then the trees opened to a clearing big enough to fit a log cabin. There was light glowing from the front window and smoke drifting up from the chimney. Either Julio was here or his brother was. He'd put in a wager that it wasn't Julio.

Getting out of the Jeep, he flipped up the hood of his

jacket and turned his head from the wind as he hiked up to the front door. It was locked, so he had to knock.

He watched the curtain part at the front window and recognized his brother. The door opened. Damen stood aside, gaping at him in shock, a gun in his hand and lowered at his side. Like him, he had signs of gray in his dark hair and had blue-green eyes, but his looked green in the sunlight when Demarco's looked blue.

"What are you doing here?" he asked as Demarco entered, stomping off snow from his feet and shrugging out of his jacket.

"You weren't answering your phone."

"So you drove all the way here?" His brother put his gun down on the table and Demarco sensed his tension. He wasn't glad to see him. That signaled that a big hidden agenda was at play here.

"It's not like you to avoid me."

"I wasn't avoiding you." He walked into the small living room where a glass of dark alcohol on ice waited. Damen was drinking by himself.

"How did you find me?"

"It wasn't hard." Demarco sat on the chair across from him. It was quiet in the cabin except for the crackle of fire and wind blowing outside. "I stopped by Bear's. He told me."

Damen sipped from the drink. "I'm going to have to talk to him."

"Why? Don't you want me to know where you are anymore?"

His brother eyed him in a way he never had before, with suspicion and growing annoyance. "I'd have called you if I did."

"What are you doing up here, Damen?"

"I have a little business to take care of." His eyes lifted and he looked all around the room as though he could see outside. "This storm is causing a delay."

"What kind of business?" Demarco wanted his brother to tell him. That way he'd know where Damen felt he needed to lie. If he lied at all. He hoped he'd still trust him, and then maybe he could talk some sense into him. His long silence didn't bode well. He was forming a lie.

"I came here to find Korbin and tell the cops so that they can arrest him."

Demarco steepled his fingers and stared at his brother, fighting for calm. "You didn't come to kill him?"

The low, deep laugh that came from his brother was foreign to him. Soft. Calculating.

"I'd love to kill him," Damen said, delight in his eyes.

"Over Collette?" Demarco asked. It was all he needed to say.

Damen's whole face contorted into rage, which he quickly masked by taking his drink and sipping harshly, then putting the nearly empty glass down with a *thunk*. He looked away.

"Is she the reason you're here?" He was a lot smarter than his brother. And always careful not to let on to that knowledge.

But real grief flashed on Damen's face and disarmed him. It's what always happened. His less fortunate brother strummed his sympathy chords. He had loved Collette. But he'd believed Korbin was taking her from him and he'd snapped. A true crime of passion.

"What would you do?" his brother asked, the one he'd grown up with, the one who could sucker him into anything, draw him into his problems. The way he was doing now without even trying. Why couldn't he live without breaking the law?

Demarco lowered his eyes.

"If your wife had an affair, what would you do?" his brother asked, earnest and sincere. Emotional, though. The angry kid. It lurked underneath.

Crossing his knee over his leg, very professor-like, Demarco said, "I wouldn't kill her."

"Do you think I killed Collette?"

Still the professor, he said, "Did you?"

He knew this would trip up something in his brother. Damen would know Demarco was suspicious.

"No," he said, growing wary. "Why did you ask me that?"

"I want to know."

"You think I killed her?" Damen all but yelled. Then he smoothed his reaction. "Do you think that, Demarco?"

Uncrossing his legs, Demarco stayed neutrally somber. "I think you're really upset that she's dead."

His lower-IQ brother missed his slightly sarcastic tone. "I am."

"What happened?"

An angry scowl stormed his brow. "I saw him leaving her house."

There was the lie. Or maybe it wasn't a lie, but Korbin hadn't killed Collette.

"He was with her when I wasn't there. Collette and I were going to move in together." His anger intensified. His fist clenched and he pounded his knee as he growled, "I was going to *marry* her."

Demarco waited for him to calm down. When he had marginally done so, he said, "And that's why you're here? Revenge?"

As though directed in a movie scene, Damen produced a remorseful face and a few grunting sobs. No tears. Not the real kind.

"Why didn't she love me? If she'd only have loved me," he sobbed. Insecure, desperate.

Demarco let him go until he eased off the show and blinked several times between shadowy looks to him. Each fake display knifed him with unbelievable shock.

After dealing with feeling that he was less than everyone else, comparing himself to others and not feeling as though he measured up, he'd finally broken. His reaction was no longer positive. He no longer tried to persevere. He was fighting back now.

"You don't believe me?" Damen asked.

No more sniffles. He observed Demarco with an aloofness that he'd never seen before.

This was where Demarco had to be careful. Damen didn't know what he knew, and if there was any hope of saving his brother from further destruction, he had to reach him. Somehow.

"Why did you come here, Damen?"

His brother slammed his short glass down, splashing what little remained. Demarco hadn't been aware that he'd had the glass in his hand. He met his brother's angry face. Damen's breath reeked of alcohol.

"I told you! I saw him. He killed her!"

"Do you really believe that?"

"I *know* he did."

Disappointment and the dagger-sharp hurt gripped him. Damen was lying. To him. How could he help him if he didn't trust him?

Demarco leaned forward, elbows on his knees. "Why didn't you call me?"

"Because I knew you'd try to talk me out of it. Isn't that why you're here? You want to stop me."

"From doing what? Are you going to kill him?"

Damen shot to his feet and walked unsteadily to the bottle of booze on the kitchen counter. Demarco followed, watching his brother fill the glass.

"When did you start drinking like that?"

Damen didn't answer, just faced him and took a drink.

"You're dealing drugs and drinking too much and now you're contemplating killing someone. What's going on with you, Damen?"

"Maybe I'm tired of trying so hard to be like you."

He was never like him, and Demarco wasn't aware that he'd been trying to be. What he was saying was that the only way he knew was the illegal way. He thrived in that environment.

"Why don't you come home with me? Forget this madness. You can stay with me and Cora until you figure out something to do. Just as long as you stop doing the drugs and drinking, and for God's sake, don't kill anyone…" He'd almost said, "anyone else."

His brother stared at him for a long moment. For a second or two he thought he'd reached him.

"I give you permission to stop trying to help me, Demarco. You've been there for me my whole life, and I appreciate that. More than you know. But I have to make my own way, don't you see?"

"Yes, but you can't make your own way breaking the law." He stepped forward and took the glass from him before he took another drink.

"That's what I do, Demarco. I've been doing it for years. I'm good at it. For once, I'm good at something you aren't." He took the glass back and gulped the entire contents.

"You're going to end up in prison." Or worse. "You won't get away with it much longer."

"Why? Are you going to turn me in?"

Demarco just looked at him. He could turn him in. He could cast doubt on Korbin's guilt.

"I can't protect you if you keep going on the way you are."

"I'm not asking you to. I never asked you to." He slammed the glass down. "I think you should leave."

"Damen, please. Listen to me. Don't do anything stupid."

That was the wrong thing to say. His brother's face darkened with the insult as he perceived it.

"Just get out of here," Damen said.

"Come with me." They'd have to stay at that lodge he saw on the way here. The stormy roads were too bad.

"Get out!" Damen roared. "You think you're so much better than me. Well, not anymore. I'm doing things my way now!"

"You're making a mistake, Damen."

With a roar, Damen shoved him. He stumbled back but caught his balance. Damn it. He was going to make his brother listen.

Charging, he shoved Damen and sent him crashing into the table. Chairs tipped over as his body fell.

"You're coming with me." Demarco bent to lift his brother off the floor and then threw him toward the door. "And you're going to straighten your life out if I have to institutionalize you!"

"You'd do that, too, wouldn't you?" He scrambled to his feet. "Mr. Perfect that you are." He crashed into him.

Demarco slammed against a wall and couldn't block Damen's punch to his stomach. Bent over, he was kneed by Damen next. He staggered away from the wall and blocked another punch, but missed the next to his face. He fell backward onto his backside. Tasting blood, he watched his brother breathing hard, his hair a mess, his eyes bloodshot.

When he didn't come after him again, Demarco climbed to his feet, holding his stomach. *Screw this.* He went to his jacket.

"What are you going to do?" his brother asked.

Wincing as he put his jacket on, Demarco only looked at his brother, a stranger to him now. Then he turned and left.

Chapter 6

The blizzard still raged into early afternoon the following day. Korbin had ventured out to open one of the wood planks over the window so he could see the snow. All that had done was cake the window in snow. He turned to see Savanna playing a game of solitaire. They'd started with a game of chess last night and another this morning, followed by a few card games.

She really was the type who needed to stay busy. And for her, the best "busy" was entertainment or crafts. He'd fallen into the sight of her animated face, her smiles and the happy, contented glow in her impossibly blue eyes. Her occasional laughs.

Too much time was passing. He had to get off this mountain. Get what he could on Damen and then prove his innocence. Not reveal things about himself that he never revealed to anyone. His wife's death. Had he ever spoken of her like that to anyone? No. It hurt too much.

He'd almost confessed everything to Savanna. All the details of Niya's death. Almost. Her evasiveness about her fiancé stopped him, and he was at odds with himself over why.

Maybe because he never did talk about his wife. He kept it bottled up. While some would argue that wasn't healthy, neither was the agony of her absence, the effect of it. Savanna buried her pain just as he did. They were silent sufferers. Savanna's preference not to air her torment had enabled him to do the same. But there was a nagging realization that Savanna, someone who understood his struggle with loss, would listen with a sympathetic and nonjudgmental ear if he chose to unload some of his burden. And perhaps she could unload some of hers, because he would know to only listen and not push for too much information. He had a feeling they could help each other. Did she sense the same?

Korbin harbored more than Niya's death, though. His pain included Niya's daughter. Fallon Ellgard was from a previous relationship and refused to talk to him. He'd tried several times after Niya died. He'd succeeded only once before the funeral, when Fallon had accused him of killing her mother. She'd stood far apart from him at the service, and he hadn't forced his presence on her. After trying a few more times after that, he'd decided to give her some time to get over her mother's death.

There was too much burden. Niya. He couldn't seem to let go of her. Didn't want to let go. She was taken from him too early. His life had fallen apart after that. At least, that's how he felt. Would he ever be able to reach her daughter? Would she ever forgive him? He needed her to. Maybe then he could begin to get past Niya's death. Until then, he had a fierce obligation to remain loyal to

Niya. Betraying her was unthinkable. Women had tried to lure him and failed. While he couldn't say Savanna was trying to lure him, she had come closer than anyone in succeeding. What made her so different? Maybe it was the wealth they had in common. And their heartaches. Regardless, he'd steer clear of the temptation. Aside from honoring Niya with his loyalty, he didn't think he ever wanted to feel the way he had for her again. He'd had his one true love. He didn't need another.

If he could walk away from Savanna now, he would. Instead, he was stuck in this yurt. Though spacious for a yurt, it was still confining.

Korbin went over to her and sat at the table where she had all the cards spread, satisfied smile soft on her mouth. She only glanced up at him before resuming her concentration.

Solitude really did suit this woman.

"You could stay here all winter, couldn't you." He stated rather than asked.

That brought her look up to him, where it stayed. Then she scanned the interior of their snowy lair.

"I might run out of food." Her gaze hit the window. "Not water, though."

"Why do you like it so much?"

She shrugged. "I've always been that way. Although, my mother seems to have forgotten that. She thinks I moved here to get away."

"And you didn't?"

Placing the card she held down onto the table, her happy contentment faded. This was not something she freely spoke about. Her personal affairs were tightly guarded secrets. He didn't think she'd answer.

"Yes, and no. I went back to my roots, that's all."

"After your fiancé called it off?" he asked.

And again to his amazement, she answered. "Yes, except he didn't call it off. I did."

He could see the breakup had been very painful for her. "Sorry." She'd told him that he'd found someone else.

She leaned back against her chair and stared across the yurt.

"How did you catch him?" he asked.

She turned back to him. "What makes you think I caught him?"

He shrugged. "Lucky guess."

Picking up the card again, she tapped it on the table. "He ran a kids' play center, you know, the kind that have all the inflatable jumpers and bounce castles. He met the mom of one of the kids. One night he didn't come home when he'd said he'd be there and he wasn't answering his phone. So I drove to the jump center. He didn't even lock the front door. I walked right in, even though it was late and no one else was there. He was in his office with her. Going at it."

She turned her head, the pain of memory sticking with her even after all this time.

"They didn't even know I was there," she said. "About an hour later, he came home and I called off the wedding. That was seven years ago."

And she still wasn't over it. "He never knew you caught him?"

Slowly she shook her head. "He asked why. I just told him I thought I loved him but I realized I didn't." She got a faraway look. "He wasn't even upset. Not that I expected him to be."

"You loved him."

Now she lowered her head, letting go of the card and putting her hands in her lap.

"Still love him," he said.

Now her head jerked up and she looked at him. "No. Not anymore. I did love him, yes. I loved him very much. It took me a long time to get past him."

"Then why are you still so upset about it?"

She averted her gaze. "I keep wondering the same thing. I guess it's because I don't understand how a man can ask a woman to marry him and then so easily end up with someone else."

"It's probably the same reason that sort of thing happens to me. They're in it for money until they realize money isn't enough."

"I suspected he wasn't totally in it for me. He was always annoyed whenever I talked about my family or we had to go to a gathering. I think he felt threatened. He had a thriving business and made decent money, but nothing compared to my dad."

Korbin nodded. "Was he the last man you've been serious about?"

To that he received a closed look, much the same as he'd received when he'd first arrived. "Why are you asking me all of these questions?"

"Because I'm curious. And I know what a struggle dating can be when you have rich parents." He also knew all about loss.

Her eyes lowered as though she were trying to hide the smile that threatened. After a moment she looked up. "There was someone else, but it wasn't as serious. We saw each other for a while, but we never talked about marriage. He was a lawyer in Denver. I thought we hit it off, but I was wrong. That ended a few weeks ago." She kept meeting men who wouldn't commit.

"Well, you just might be as jaded as I am."

She exhaled derisively. "You're probably jaded more."

"I don't like thinking I'll be alone the rest of my life, but I can't say losing Niya didn't change my perspective."

"Yeah. I get that. I'm still on birth control even though I know I'm nowhere near ready for another relationship. I guess I don't trust myself with men anymore."

He chuckled, finding it much too easy to talk to her.

Smiling back, she met his eyes and saw into them a little more than he liked.

"Is it ever not fresh?" she asked.

She hadn't asked for herself. She may have gotten over her fiancé enough to move on, to try again to find that special someone to spend the rest of her life with, but it was him she doubted. His wife's death would always be fresh.

Digging Savanna out of that avalanche had brought everything back in vivid color. He could smell, taste and feel every second of the memories that were dredged up about Niya's death.

"Not for me," he said. Best if she knew now he was no better than the last two heartbreakers she'd wasted her love on.

He felt too much of a kinship with her to even consider starting anything that might hurt her again.

Damn. Now he'd need something to pass the time.

"Let's play something else." He gestured to the cards.

Savanna put a card down on the table and watched Korbin. His questions earlier should have made her feel interrogated, picked apart, but she'd sensed his need to know. Why had he? Their chemistry had him as ruffled as her. He'd surely had women who'd tried to tempt him before, but Savanna *had* tempted him. She felt it in his kiss. Now he was backing off.

Wasn't she? Savanna didn't see herself getting serious over someone any time soon. Isn't that how he was? It struck her as sad. And then…necessary. For both of them. She began to wonder, though. Was he ruined for any other woman? Was she ruined for other men?

"What?" he asked.

Realizing she was staring at him, she sent her attention back to the game. "Nothing."

"You cocked your head at me."

"I did?" She played another card.

"What were you thinking?" he pressed.

She watched him play a card and then decided to forge ahead. "Can I ask you a personal question?"

He chuckled. "It's my turn."

He had asked her some personal questions, too. She smiled. "I was just wondering how many women you've been with."

He leaned back on his chair, perplexed. "Been with? As in…" He twirled his finger to indicate she wasn't sure what. Whoopee?

"Yeah. Since your wife died." She played her turn.

"I didn't sleep with anyone," he said.

She should be happy to hear that. Instead, that revelation bred anxiety. His loyalty to his wife was impenetrable. Whether he remained faithful even after her death out of love or guilt, his honor was intact. What woman would earn a worthy place in his heart? It seemed an impossible feat. He wasn't ready to love again. She'd seen it in him many times. The guilt after he kissed her.

How many affirmations did she need before she stopped toying with him? Toying with the possibility of sleeping with him? Or more. How could she be certain anything would develop from that? His devotion to his wife would prevent him from letting a night of passion build into anything more than that. A night of passion.

There was no denying they had passion. But what about love? Did she have it in her to take that kind of gamble again? And did their passion hold that much of a promise? It felt that way to her, but what about him?

"I should learn from you," she muttered.

"What was that?"

He hadn't heard her.

"Never mind." She wished she hadn't said anything.

"No, tell me."

"I said I should learn from you. The way you abstain."

"Are you saying you're easy?" He teased, but this was a major topic for both of them.

She didn't return his humor. "Not sexually."

There was no mistaking her meaning. She trusted too easily in the men she fell in love with. In that respect, yes, she was easy.

"You're not easy if you fall in love," he said, serious now.

"I'm no good at picking men." He'd be another bad choice.

"I've never looked at it that way. Picking someone. It just happens."

She looked away. Had it just happened with her fiancé? No, she'd chosen him. But the one after that…him she hadn't chosen.

"Either way," she finally said, "I always lose."

He studied her as he digested that comment, which

was simple truth to her. She wasn't insecure. She'd lost love twice. A fact. What wasn't fact yet was whether she'd lose again.

"I suppose, then, that we have something in common in that regard," he said.

"Do we?" Had he guessed the source of her curiosity?

"I believe that's why you asked me if I'd been with anyone," he said.

Caught, she joined him for a long stare, communicating without words the understanding of how it felt to have love taken away. Possibility hung in the air, as well. This uncommon attraction between them. This bond they had. Understanding each other. Falling into a mystical abyss of feeling.

Uncomfortable, Savanna scooted back her chair and stood. Leaving him there with the game, she went to one of the beds and removed her clothes down to her base layer, long thermal tights and matching top.

With her back to him, she didn't hear him come up behind her. His hand slid over her hip to her abdomen, drawing a startled breath from her. Then he stepped closer and put his head down beside hers.

"Let me show you something."

What was he going to show her? Sweet temptation burned through her. She didn't resist when he eased her to face him, pulling her against him. Savanna inhaled another surprised breath and didn't have time to recover from the feel of his hard body so close to hers. Heat swept her away. He sank his fingers into her hair, tipping her head back without tugging too much.

His gaze drifted over her face, twin flames licking her features.

He put his mouth on hers.

Savanna stopped breathing and she stared up at the detail of his eyes while fire roared through her. He angled his head, sliding his mouth over hers. She parted her lips, unable to stop herself, and he took the hesitant surrender. His tongue brushed hers, his hand holding her head to him. He pressed harder, asking for more. Demanding. With a sound of want she had no control over, she let him have all of her.

He sank into a deeper kiss with a groan that fanned her desire. She slid her arms over his shoulders and let herself forget how little she knew him. She dragged her eyes closed to sensation.

He ravaged her mouth with sensuous kisses, tasting, delving, taking her tongue in a deep and erotic dance. She lost herself in him, gave herself over to the feelings he stirred in her. She caught her breath when he warmed a fevered path down her neck, only to find that she needed even more air. She arched her back as he neared her breasts, felt them rub against his chest.

Then he stepped back. No longer did his mouth work magic on her. She stumbled to catch her balance without his arms around her, staring at him as coherency returned.

He'd only been showing her something.

"Why did you do that?" she asked, struggling to calm her racing heart and the thrilling flutter that still tingled.

"We have that in common, too," he said, voice gravelly from desire. "I think you know that."

What was he suggesting? That they go with it and see where this went? What about his devotion to his wife? Was he capable of loving anyone else that way?

She doubted he'd go the rest of his life without ever finding someone he could at least live with for companionship. But the takeaway for her was she'd risk more than she was willing to in order to find out if she could be that woman.

She'd rather be single than live with a man just for companionship. And if he turned away from love to be safe with a companion and nothing more, he'd die a lonely man.

"Don't do that again," she said.

"Why? Because your heart was broken?"

Needing her own space, she went into the bathroom. She shut the door and saw that there was plenty of water in the bucket sitting on top of the on-demand hot water system. Removing her clothes, she turned on the shower and stepped into the stall. Putting her face under the stream of water, she hoped the soothing warmth would ease her inner unrest. But the unrest came from an unsatisfied sexual need. She wanted Korbin. Did she want him physically or was her heart entangled, as well? If he kissed her again, she'd find out, because there would be no stopping what would follow.

As though hearing her thoughts, Korbin opened the bathroom door. Savanna's heart slammed faster. He was coming into the bathroom? While that shocking revelation both excited her and filled her with dread, he opened the shower door.

Turning to face him, she leaned against the wall. "What are you doing?"

Korbin's heated gray eyes took in every detail of her wet body and then stepped into the shower. "I've had a broken heart, too."

He was as afraid as she was. But he was ready to take a chance. With her.

"Korbin…" Was she ready to take a chance on him?

"Let go, Savanna."

She barely knew this man, but that only intensified her desire. How much would it mean if they had sex? She'd loved the last two men she'd been intimate with. This wasn't about love. Not yet. It certainly was about the possibility of love. But tonight. Now. This early in their relationship. It was not about love. No. This was about abolishing fear.

When he moved closer and put his hands on her breasts, she lost all of her air and any resistance with it. Flutters chased through her as he caressed her. She ran her hands over his forearms and up to his biceps as he moved his hands down her rib cage, to her waist and then back up. Water splashed over his shoulder and back, dampening his hair. He was a vision.

Then he lifted her, holding her against the wall. She felt his hardness and wrapped her legs around his hips, closing her eyes as he kissed her, the spray of water making for a slick, sultry joining.

He dragged his mouth down her neck and then went down to take one nipple and then the other. Savanna dug her fingers through his wet hair and watched him. When he raised his head, she kissed his mouth, his cheek, then trailed her tongue over his brow. She kissed his cheeks, each of them alternatively, then found his lips, seeking something, anything that would assuage this raw need.

When he entered her, she sank down onto him, feeling him stretch her soft, ready flesh until he buried himself all the way. He was bigger than any other man she'd been with and moved gently at first. She hooked her arms over his shoulders and urged him to give her more. With a groan, he withdrew on a velvety slide and pushed into her harder. They found a rhythm.

"Oh…" She found his hot gaze and ground on him, closer and closer to oblivion.

"Yes," he breathed.

She shattered from her core outward.

Only after the explosion of ecstasy settled did she realize he'd peaked with her. That, and the water had run out and it was getting cold in here.

Savanna trembled, and not all from cold. She breathed through parted lips, head resting against his. Vulnerable. Uncomfortably so. She felt as though her whole being was exposed to a stranger.

Hadn't that been the idea? Stranger sex to heal from past hurts? She quickly discovered it wasn't going to work.

Korbin kept her on him as he stepped out of the shower. Snagging two towels from an open shelf, he carried her into the yurt. Warmth from the stove helped, but goose bumps rose all over her wet skin.

At one of the beds, he lowered her down and then followed onto the mattress. He wasn't finished with her. A little panicky feeling made her stiffen and put her hand on his chest. Lying beneath him, she saw a reflection of her mood in his look. Unsettled by what had occurred, awed and more than a little disturbed by the power of it. That was the only thing that stopped her from asking him to get off her. He was in this with her.

But any more of what they'd had in the shower and she'd be in trouble.

"Korbin, I—"

"Shh." He kissed her mouth briefly and then began to dry her hair.

She watched his face as he worked, muscles relaxing. He dried her everywhere. The towel rubbed her skin, a lover's hand, his hand, guiding it. After a while, Savanna took the towel from him and treated him to the same ministrations. His big arms caged her as she dried his back and shoulders. All the while, his gaze never left hers. More long minutes passed. She rubbed his hair last. Fascinated by the messy end result and the sexy, rugged planes of his face, she let the towel drop unheeded to the side of the bed.

She felt his rippling muscles against her body, smelled his clean skin and saw passion in his eyes. He dipped his head and kissed her, a tender melding that stirred her own passion. He began to harden but didn't do anything about it, just kept kissing her, seducing her with warm, erotic play.

His hands moved over her skin without a towel now, an artist sculpting soft, wet clay. Down the side of her breast, her waist and hip, and her thigh and then back up again. One muscular arm held him over her. She ran her hands over his chest and shoulders and then his waist when his hips began to push his erection against her.

A little of that vulnerability returned. She tensed and began to close her legs, bringing her hands back to his chest.

Taking her lower lip between his teeth, he nipped gently and then made love to her mouth as though to apologize for the sweet torture. Meanwhile, his hand slid down to her inner thigh, an intimate touch that disguised his purpose. He eased her leg back open, reaching to the back of her knee and holding her there while he penetrated her. Expert lover. Marauder. He made her so hot.

Crushing his mouth to hers, he kissed her hard while he moved inside of her. Holding himself deep and then withdrawing, his thrusts started slow and then built force. She cried out with a powerful orgasm.

Afterward, Korbin held her against him as he lay on his back. She curled on her side and sleep eluded her for hours. She would not be the same after this night. All those things she used to say in her motivational speeches about relationships gone bad zeroed in on her. What was positive about sleeping with a hacker wanted for a hit-and-run and murder?

The next morning, Korbin led the way to the lodge. The blizzard had moved on last night. The yurt had been half buried and he'd had to shovel to clear the front door. It had kept him busy and that had spared him from facing Savanna. He'd woken before her, having not slept much. Neither had Savanna. He'd listened to her toss and turn as much as him.

Getting ready to leave the yurt, they'd exchanged brief, sheepish glances. He marveled that she felt like him. Both of them struggled with the consequences of sex. It had meant more than he'd anticipated, and he was sure Savanna felt the same. Although he felt more guilt-ridden. She probably felt regret.

What had made him think he could sleep with Savanna and not feel he'd betrayed his wife? He hadn't thought. That's what had happened. Now he was angry with himself.

He kept a fast pace all the way to Lost Trail Lodge, a log structure bigger than Savanna's but just as tucked away in the forest. There was little activity outside. The sun had peeked out from behind clouds on and off all morning. And at nearly two in the afternoon, they were beginning to thicken again.

He loved the snow, but he wished it would lighten up for a day or two. He couldn't afford to be stuck at Savanna's house—or anywhere else with her. His desire for her only added to his anxiety over clearing his name. That and all the thinking he'd done about Niya, both before he'd slept with Savanna and now, the morning after, had taken its toll.

"Boy, am I glad to take these off," Savanna said as she stuck her skis into the snow near some others. He could hear the tension in her voice. Was it because she suspected he regretted sleeping with her? Regret wasn't the word to describe how he felt. No, that was pure guilt and remorse. He didn't regret the phenomenal sex he'd had with her. He just felt like a dishonorable ass for giving in to the temptation when he wasn't ready.

He stuck his skis into the snow beside hers. "Are we going to be able to get a ride out of here?" He walked beside her toward the entrance.

"Why? Are you in a hurry to get away from here?"

What she really meant was *from her*. He stopped and faced her. "I'm in a hurry to stop Damen from killing us both."

She studied him closely, not believing him. "Hurley will let us use his truck." She pointed to a parked Chevy crew cab and started walking again.

Hurley opened one of the thick, wood double doors. He had on tan Carhartt overalls and a long-sleeved thermal ivory shirt.

"I sure am glad to see you," he said to Savanna, then shifted a look to Korbin.

Hurley was around six-one and sinewy with muscle. He must have given a lot of ski tours, and the lodge must have required constant maintenance. He worked hard and his body showed it.

"Sheriff said you had some trouble over at your place," Hurley said.

Korbin stepped up to the door with Savanna. "How did the police know there was trouble at Savanna's?"

Hurley held the door to allow them to pass. "Someone tried to pay you a visit."

Savanna stopped before him while Korbin entered. "Who?"

"Your brother. The sheriff just got here. They're in the dining room."

Korbin looked at him. Sheriff? Here?

"Which one?" Savanna asked.

"He said his name is Macon."

"Macon is here? He was on a movie set. How'd he get here? And why?"

Movie set? Her brother was an actor? Not surprising since their dad was a producer.

Hurley motioned for her to go inside. She entered the lodge ahead of him and then turned to face him as the door closed.

"When did he arrive?"

"About three hours ago." He walked toward them. "He couldn't call police from your place so he drove to the nearest phone he could find."

Hurley's. Lost Trail Lodge. Where were the police now? He turned to face the spacious lobby with plenty of seating before a river-rock fireplace. A huge red mosaic rug covered the pinewood floor and elk heads hung from log walls, their dead, glossy eyes staring.

"I'm sure the sheriff would like to talk to you," Hurley said.

"Good." Savanna started toward the wide opening leading to the dining area and then stopped and looked back at him when he didn't follow. She'd already begun to sense something was wrong. That he wasn't being completely forthright. Well, he wasn't. For good reason. But what choice did he have?

He started walking. When he reached Savanna, she eyed him suspiciously.

"Does talking to police make you nervous?" she asked, low enough for only him to hear. Hurley had already entered the banquet room.

Korbin didn't respond as he entered the cavernous room with her. To the right, several tables took up half of the room. To the left, the sheriff sat with a tall, russet-haired man in a brown leather seating area before another enormous fire, river rock rising to the exposed log ceiling. Light from the gabled window sparkled on shelves of liquor behind a long bar.

They stopped talking when the three of them approached.

Savanna's brother shot to his feet and rushed over to her. "Where have you been?" He embraced her.

Korbin stopped beside her, Hurley to his left.

"Skiing," she said.

"Your house…" He surveyed her as though making sure she was all right. "The door was open and it was a wreck. The back door was broken. The heat was running and it was still cold in there. I've been going out of my mind imagining what must have become of you."

"I'm all right."

His face eased of tension and he rubbed her arms up and down. Tall and lean with chiseled features, he looked like an actor.

When Macon looked at Korbin, Savanna turned.

"Macon, this is Korbin Maguire," she said.

"Are you the reason Savanna is in danger?" Macon asked.

"Someone is trying to kill him," she said, sounding as though she were defending him. Was she?

"Kill you? Who?" Macon asked.

Korbin looked toward the sheriff, who just now rose to his feet. Gray hair peeked out from under his beige cowboy hat and deep wrinkles fanned out from his eyes. He stopped before them.

Korbin saw no sign that he recognized him. "His name is Damen Ricchetti. He's involved in cyber crimes and is into something big right now." He explained what he'd told Savanna.

"What is the name of the person this Mr. Ricchetti doesn't like you knowing?" the sheriff asked.

"Tony Bartoszewicz." Korbin spelled the name for him. "I don't know anything about him, and Damen came after me to keep me from doing so." He turned to Savanna. "I made a wrong turn in the storm."

The sheriff finished writing down the name and then looked up at Korbin. "And this Mr. Ricchetti is the one who broke into Savanna's house?"

"Yes," Korbin said.

"He shot at us," Savanna said. "We were forced to ski into the wilderness. The yurt saved us." She looked up at Hurley to send him her silent thanks. He gave her an answering faint smile.

Macon eyed Korbin in a way that made him uncomfortable. He wasn't buying the story. For an actor he was sure street-smart. Maybe he suspected there was more to it. Well, there was. A lot more.

"How well do you know Mr. Ricchetti?" the sheriff asked.

"I thought I knew him very well. We've been friends for more than ten years."

"Can you give me his address?"

Korbin did.

"And how about his place of employment? You said he was into cyber crimes."

"He runs a contracting company. He employs information technology types."

"What's the name of his company?"

"DR Consulting." It's what he filed his taxes under.

"And you haven't noticed anything different about him?"

"He's been distant. Doesn't talk as much as he used to. But nothing significant. It wasn't until I discovered his association with Tony that he became violent." All of that was true. He only left out the fact that they both illegally hacked the wealthy. He glanced at Savanna to see if she'd reveal anything. She stared at the sheriff's notebook but didn't say anything. Her gaze lifted and met his.

The sheriff tapped his notebook with his pen. "What brought you up here?"

Savanna's eyes shifted to the sheriff. Yes, that was a good question, wasn't it? Korbin fumbled with a reply.

"I needed a few days alone."

The sheriff studied him a while and for a moment he thought he'd ask more questions.

"I'll pass this along to the authorities in Denver," he said. Korbin felt his suspicion. He felt Macon's, too. And Savanna was becoming agitated. She folded her arms and had a cold demeanor now. He'd have to tell her everything.

"We finished up at your house," the sheriff said to Savanna. "I had my deputy arrange to have your window boarded up. It should be safe to go back there. There's a mess to clean up, though."

Savanna nodded, awkward and revealing.

A glance at Macon confirmed he'd noticed, too.

"You should have the patio door replaced as soon as possible," the sheriff said.

"I will."

"And I'd recommend upgrading your security. You're remote and that sometimes deters most, but in this case..."

"Yes. I'll do that. Thank you."

Savanna had an appearance of a woman who needed protection and taking care of, but Korbin had seen for himself how misguided that perception was.

The sheriff tipped his hat at them and then walked toward the lobby with Hurley, the two going into a conversation about an upcoming local event. Small-town talk. The sheriff would do some checking on him, but by the time he figured out he was a suspect in a murder and a hit-and-run, Korbin hoped to be long gone.

"I think you should come with me, Savanna," Macon said.

That interrupted Savanna's consternation as she, too, had watched the sheriff leave. "Aren't you up in Vail working on a movie?"

"Yes, but you shouldn't be here alone."

"She isn't alone," Korbin said. He doubted a movie star had what it took to protect her, and wouldn't have the time, either. No. Korbin wasn't about to let her out of his sight.

"If it wasn't for you, she wouldn't be in danger."

"But she is in danger," Korbin said. "Damen might go after her now that he's seen her with me. He'll assume she knows what I know. I can keep her safe."

Macon turned from his sister to face Korbin. "Really. And how do you propose to do that? What makes you so sure you can keep her safe?"

He didn't ask something stupid like, *What makes you so sure you can?* He might be an actor, but Savanna's family had money. They could protect her.

"It's like you said. If it wasn't for me, she wouldn't be in danger. I feel obligated."

"Well, I officially absolve you of all obligation."

Savanna sighed hard then, swatting her hand in the air to vent her frustration. "Would you stop making decisions for me? Both of you."

Leaving Korbin staring in stunned silence, she marched toward the lobby.

"Is she considering sticking with you?" Macon asked, incredulous.

Korbin didn't answer. He followed Savanna to the lobby, glad to see the sheriff had gone. He stopped before Savanna and Hurley, who stood near the front desk waiting for them.

"Savanna…" Macon started in again.

"Macon. Stop. I don't need you to protect me. I don't need anyone to protect me."

"That's not what I saw when Damen broke into your house," Korbin said.

"Just come with me, Savanna. I'll drop you off in Evergreen."

"I don't want to go to Evergreen," she snapped.

"There aren't many who can tell Savanna what to do," Hurley said with a grin. "I've offered to help her on many occasions and she usually refuses. Nicely, but a refusal nonetheless. Folks up here tend to be that way. We like our isolation."

"Yeah, well, so do criminals." Macon eyed Korbin. "As we've seen."

Savanna stepped up to Macon, taking his hands. "I'll be all right. I'll do what the sheriff suggested. Get a security system. I'm not running away from my life."

"What about him?" Macon thumbed toward Korbin. He was close to his height.

Savanna rolled a slow glance toward him. "He'll take his trouble and go away."

She meant more than Damen. After last night, she was pulling back, ruling him out as a potential love interest. He should be relieved. He wouldn't have to face all the turmoil and confusion having feelings for Savanna invoked. But something shifted inside him. He was relieved, but regret was stronger—regret that he'd never see her again. Regret that she'd be out of his life for good. And a question as to whether letting her go that way was wise…or right.

"Mom's going to have a fit," Macon said. "She won't stand for this."

"She'll have to." With a disgruntled breath and a shake of her head, she turned to Hurley, who had emerged from a storage closet behind the front desk carrying two pairs of winter boots. Korbin and Savanna were still in ski boots. The man sure thought of everything. That had been obvious with how well equipped the yurt had been.

"What's with her?" Macon asked.

Korbin saw how perplexed Macon was. More than Korbin's character had him wondering.

"She seems upset about something."

Korbin didn't offer an explanation and hoped Macon would just drop it. He didn't.

He scrutinized Korbin. "Is something going on between the two of you?"

"Someone shot at us."

"No." Macon kept eyeing him suspiciously. "You two have something going on. Is that why she won't go with me? She'd rather be with you?" When Korbin said nothing, inwardly squirming, Macon said, "You were alone for a long time. A night at her place. The yurt..."

"Nothing's going on between us." Nothing he was willing to discuss, anyway.

"What's your story, Maguire? What weren't you telling the sheriff back there?"

If he hadn't told the sheriff, what made Macon think he'd tell him? As guilty as he appeared, some information had to be withheld. For now.

"If you get my sister hurt, I'll have to do something about that."

Again, his acting profession didn't mix with this glimpse of a man who delivered threats that had to be heeded. Korbin had the distinct impression that he was capable of retaliating to avenge his sister. Where had that background come from? Korbin doubted even his family was aware of this side of him.

"As soon as I know more, I'll be the first to tell the police. You have my word," Korbin said.

"How do I know your word is any good?"

"You don't." He met the other man's gaze and watched him digest the truth of that statement. Macon didn't know if his word was any good. He'd have to trust him. Or not. But Korbin's message was clear. He'd given his word and he intended to keep it.

Macon gave him a pat on his shoulder. "Take her home. Let her decide what she wants to do."

Korbin nodded once. He wouldn't force Savanna to do anything she didn't agree to. He walked over to her. She'd put on the boots and was waiting for him.

Taking the pair Hurley had for him, he removed the ski boots and put those on.

"Thanks for all your help," he said to Hurley.

"You take care now." He handed Savanna some keys.

"I'll take you to your truck," Savanna said to Korbin.

"I'll meet you there," Macon said. "I have to go get my things from my room and make a couple of calls first."

He'd make sure Korbin took her there. Korbin would do the same if he had a sister and something like this had happened. He followed Savanna out to Hurley's truck. Before she reached the driver's door, he stopped her.

"I'll drive."

She didn't protest and climbed up into the passenger side.

"You should stay with me, Savanna," he said as he began to drive.

"And continue this charade? No, thanks. I'll take my chances with a new security system. And don't forget, my dad is really rich."

Her frustration came from sleeping with him. He wasn't going to broach that topic now. So she could afford security personnel if she decided to go that far. All right. He had a control problem going on here. He'd lost two women he should have been able to protect. Savanna was not going to be the third.

He didn't argue. Just drove the short distance to her road. Moments later, he spotted his truck—and the swarm of other vehicles up at her house, unmarked Denver detective cars.

"What's going on?"

Somehow the police had tracked him here, and the sheriff hadn't yet been informed. Korbin braked, glanced over at Savanna's questioning face and then did a U-turn. She wasn't going to like this.

Chapter 7

"Are you kidding me?" Savanna held on as Korbin slid out onto the highway.

He raced as fast as he dared up the icy road. Now wasn't the appropriate time to explain everything to her.

"What are you doing?"

Just then a black Escalade passed going the other way. Savanna watched it, and Korbin saw her brother in the driver's seat. He didn't notice them.

"Stop this truck!" Savanna twisted to look for her brother, but Korbin saw in his rearview mirrors that he wasn't slowing to turn around.

Spotting the turn to Chavis's cabin, he took it. The road had recently been plowed. There were other cabins in the area. The first turnoff was Chavis's. Korbin drove up the driveway, protected by a thick forest of trees. In the clearing, he stopped.

Savanna sat on the other side of the truck, a fiery beauty full of temper.

"Take me home. Now."

"Just come inside. I'll explain everything."

"I don't want to know any more about you. The fact that you just ran from police is already too much."

"I talked to the sheriff," he said.

"Only because you *had* to."

"Come inside, Savanna. If you still want me to take you home after I explain, I'll take you."

She stared at him, debating.

He opened the driver's door, taking the keys with him and surveying the small clearing. She must think he had some redeeming qualities, because she got out and trudged through the snow to the door of the cabin, which was a lot smaller than hers and not as nice.

Inside, they stomped snow off their boots. The cabin was oddly not chilly. Korbin went to the thermostat and checked the heat. It was set at about seventy degrees.

Savanna waited in the middle of the room, the rustic kitchen behind her. Light from the front window touched dust in the air. Moose-patterned log furniture in the living room and bulky wood side tables had been chosen by a man. Savanna eyed everything as though ticking off a list of feminine accents she'd add, or maybe things she'd get rid of. But that lasted all of ten seconds. Then she turned her expectant gaze on him.

Korbin went to the fireplace, crouching and holding his hand out. It felt warm. Someone had turned up the heat and had a fire. They weren't alone.

Creaking floorboards brought Korbin up and moving toward the hall. Damen appeared with a pistol. He aimed at Savanna.

Ignited with rage, Korbin turned and as Damen began to swing the pistol toward him, he knocked Damen's hand. The gun fired and took a chunk out of the wall.

Savanna screamed while Korbin took Damen down to the floor. No way was he letting this man get the upper hand on him again. He squeezed Damen's hand and bashed it and the gun against the wood floor. Wrestling Damen's kicking legs, he blocked a punch and jabbed his fingers into the other man's eyes, eliciting a shout from him. The gun fell out of Damen's hand.

Korbin grabbed the gun and aimed it at Damen's head as he climbed to his feet. Damen blinked rapidly and rubbed his eyes, sitting up and trying to see. Swinging his foot, Korbin clocked him in the head, sending him falling backward, unconscious.

Disarming the pistol, Korbin went into the main room where Savanna crouched behind the kitchen island. Seeing him, she rose. Korbin put the gun on the island and stuffed the magazine into his front pocket. Savanna's breathing was fast and shallow. Her body trembled.

"Are you all right?"

She nodded shakily.

Korbin brought one of the kitchen chairs into the living room and then went out into the garage, where he found some duct tape and an extension cord.

Back in the cabin, he saw that Savanna still stood near the kitchen island. She watched as he dragged Damen to the living room and lifted him onto the chair. Damen groaned.

"What are you doing?"

She must be in shock or something. She could see what he was doing. "Tying him."

Working faster, Korbin wound the extension cord

around Damen's body, making sure his arms and legs were securely bound. He used duct tape to wrap around his ankles and wrists, double assurance he wasn't going anywhere.

Slowly, she moved toward him. "He was going to shoot me."

He straightened and looked at her. "Yes."

Confusion and fear and abating adrenaline kept her face slack. "Why?"

Damen's head rolled and began to lift.

Korbin helped him out by gripping a handful of hair and yanking his head back. Damen met his eyes groggily. As it dawned on him that he was bound, awareness of his situation came into his eyes.

"What don't you want me to know about Tony?" Korbin asked.

A sick clown smile curved his lips. "I can't wait to see you rot in jail."

"I thought you wanted me dead."

Damen lowered his head and tested the binds at his wrists and ankles.

"A little hard to kill me like that," Korbin said. "Some friend you turned out to be."

"You've been getting too righteous, Maguire. I should have seen this coming a lot sooner than I did."

"What? That I wasn't going to do your bidding anymore?"

"You didn't have a problem with it before."

"Well, I do now. How did you find me?"

"When you didn't show up here, I used Chavis's snowmobile and backtracked your path. That's how I found your truck. Got stuck, did you? Lost in the storm?" Damen chuckled and glanced over at Savanna. "Well, you always were lucky with the ladies. Or did you plan to stumble upon a beauty like her? Did you know I'd look here for you?"

Savanna sent Korbin a sharp look that questioned the validity of Damen's claim.

"I didn't know you were coming after me until you started shooting," Korbin said. "Tony must be someone important to you if you're willing to kill to keep him a secret."

The clown smile faded. Damen didn't like that much. Whatever his association with Tony was, it was a dangerous one.

"You should have left Collette's computer alone, Maguire. Why did you think to look there? I never did. I didn't know she was getting suspicious of me. How much did she find out? Is that why the two of you met?"

"You set me up for that hit-and-run." He hadn't explained any of this to Savanna, and she was absorbing all of it with a good amount of speculative confusion.

"You and Collette were conspiring against me."

"No," Korbin said. "What did you think was going on with us?"

"Were you sleeping with her?" Damen asked, emotion darkening his eyes. "Were you with her the night before you met her at the restaurant?"

Collette must have succeeded in avoiding him that night. "No. I never slept with her."

"She liked you." His mouth and eyes contorted with a sneer. "She talked about you all the time. And she said the two of you were friends."

"When did she say that?"

"When I confronted her about the meeting she had with you. I saw you go into that restaurant and meet her."

Had he seen them leave? Korbin had searched pretty thoroughly then, before he'd given Collette the gun. He would have noticed. Damen must have left as soon as he'd seen them get up from the table.

Damen had set him up because he thought he was fooling around with his girlfriend. "You've really sunk to a new low, haven't you?"

"If you didn't sleep with her, you would have. I know you, Maguire. How you are with women."

How was that? He'd been married and after Niya's death, he hadn't seen anyone. Sure, plenty of women came on to him, but he hadn't been interested. Damen was delusional. Jealous. Korbin had suspected as much, and even that the feeling had intensified the longer they knew each other and the deeper into crime Damen fell, but for Damen to act on it? Maybe it was that Damen couldn't control him. He controlled everyone else he worked with, certainly everyone who worked for him. But never Korbin.

"Collette asked me to help her get away from you," he said. "She was going to meet me the next morning and I was going to get her away from you."

Damen's eyes didn't move from Korbin as he considered that. "Well, I guess she got her wish."

That was uncalled for and not something Korbin would let slide by. He punched Damen on the side of his eye, quick and hard, the sound of knuckles against flesh cracking.

Savanna inhaled sharply, not having expected the violent response.

"Tony," Korbin said. "Who is he?"

Damen shook off the dizzying effect of Korbin's hit. "I thought you knew."

"How would I?"

Damen shrugged within his confines. "Bear could have talked."

Bear was one of Damen's thugs he'd recently taken on and part of what had begun to change Korbin's mind about him.

"No. I didn't have time to ask him. Is he involved, too?"

Damen stared up at Korbin for a while, weighing his options, which weren't many in his current predicament.

"Let's talk about this, Korbin. If you let me go, I'll tell the cops I talked to you the night of the hit-and-run. You'll be cleared."

"What about Tony?" And let's not forget Collette's murder. Surely Damen hadn't forgotten that it was Korbin's gun he'd used to kill her. Or had he known it was his gun? Maybe he hadn't. If Collette hadn't told him, how would he have known?

"You have to agree not to interfere in that," Damen said.

"And my word is all you need."

That clown smile returned. "We are friends, Maguire."

"Wrong. We *were* friends. We aren't anymore."

Damen shook his head, lowering it and then looking up at Korbin. "I can't have you ruining my business arrangement with Tony."

"You're hardly in a position to stop me." And, oh, did Korbin ever intend to ruin it.

"Aren't I? You'd rather go to prison for something you didn't do?"

"You've got that confused, Damen."

"Do I?"

"Yeah." He bent to bring his head close. "I'm not the one who's going to prison. You are. Trouble is I need a little more time to ensure that."

"It won't be long before the cops get here. I told them about your friendship with Chavis."

"Good. Because you're going to need them."

"I'm going to need the cops?" Damen outright laughed, a deep, robust sound that ricocheted off the walls.

"Savanna?" Korbin said. "I need you to wait in the backroom. Or outside in the truck. Whichever you prefer."

"Wh—why?"

"Because I don't want you to see this."

Damen's smile vanished. He was beginning to recall Korbin's reputation. This was why no one went up against him, why no one tried to make him do things against his will. Damen should have remembered that. He should have considered the possibility that he'd find himself on the receiving end of Korbin's brand of justice.

"What are you going to do?" Savanna asked. She was a strong, brave woman, but she wasn't accustomed to violence.

"Give us some time alone together, Savanna." His calm tone was both reassuring and a warning.

Savanna looked from Damen to Korbin. "I'll be in the truck."

Savanna started toward the truck, a thousand questions going through her mind. Who was Collette? Who was Bear? And what was Korbin doing in that cabin right now?

The only reason she didn't drive away was because

that man had shot at her. Well, and she didn't have the keys, either. Still punchy and dazed over how close she'd come to dying, she couldn't think straight. What was the right thing to do? Damen had set Korbin up in a hit-and-run accident. What had happened with that? Had someone died? And what's with the woman, Collette? She'd been trying to escape Damen and Korbin had tried to save her.

Everything she'd heard painted Korbin as a hero. He'd jumped between her and Damen when he'd shot at her. He'd saved her. Again.

About fifteen minutes later, Korbin emerged, striding calmly toward the truck as though he'd just left a hair appointment instead of a man tied up. When he climbed into the truck and handed her the keys, Savanna had regained some of her aplomb.

"Is he dead?"

"No. But he'll be in the hospital for a few days."

Just the right amount of time he needed? He'd beaten the man so severely that he'd be taken to the hospital. That's what the police would find when they arrived to look for Korbin. Damen. Beaten to a bloody pulp.

"Where are we going?" She wasn't even sure she was going anywhere with him.

"Denver. I have a friend who can help us."

She didn't even ask to be taken home. She didn't know where she wanted to be right now. But there was one thing she needed to set straight. "There is no *us*."

He paused in clipping his seat belt in the passenger seat to observe her, probably trying to ascertain whether she meant them as a couple or them in this situation.

"There *is* an *us*." He clipped the belt as though that

made everything final. "Damen shooting at you made that a certainty. You're staying with me now."

She jerked the gear into Reverse and turned the truck around. "I cannot believe this."

"I'll make it right."

"Like you did in there?" She jerked her thumb toward the back window, where through the rearview mirror the cabin disappeared as the thick forest swallowed them.

"Collette was Damen's girlfriend," Korbin said. "He killed her after she met with me." He explained everything about the meeting and the hit-and-run and then finding Collette.

Nauseated to discover two people had died before he'd fortuitously found his way to her remote road, Savanna drove white-knuckled, pale and cold.

"Didn't you notice anything off about Damen before now?" There's something wrong with a person who was capable of murdering people. A staged hit-and-run? He had to have noticed something.

"He wasn't always like what you saw in there. I told you the truth about him. And me. We stole from the wealthy. It was a game. Until now."

Now it was no game. Damen would kill to preserve his dangerous association with a man named Tony.

"And yes, I have noticed the change in him before now. That's why I was getting out," he said. "After I found out about Bear…"

She was almost afraid to ask. "Who is Bear?"

"A drug dealer."

She gaped at him as long as she dared while she drove. "You make it sound like you were a member of a street gang."

"It was starting to feel like that."

She didn't know how to handle all of this. Part of her said drive somewhere safe and get away from him. Another sensed he was an innocent man who needed some help.

"I'm sorry about all of this," Korbin said.

She said nothing, unwilling to encourage him or let him think she was going to go along with any of this.

"I would have taken a bullet for you back there," he said. She glanced at him because she heard how much he meant it.

He turned from the window. "I don't want to lose anyone else."

She glanced over at him. Then looked forward at the curving highway ahead.

"Collette was someone special?" she asked.

"Not romantically. She had a rough go as a teenager. That led her to Damen's door. But she was trying to better herself. She was a nice girl, wouldn't have hurt anyone. She deserved more than what she got."

His wife had died. His friend. And a stranger. All because of his association with Damen. All but his wife... or was she included in that stat?

"How exactly did your wife die?" she asked. He'd noncommittally said it was an accident, and she hadn't asked what kind.

It was a long moment before he replied. "She was shot." He turned toward the window again. "A group of men drove by. They were trying to kill Damen, and they got her instead."

Oh, dear God. How terrible! Savanna didn't know what to say at first. But then she began to wonder about some things.

"Why was someone shooting at Damen?"

"I never did get a straight answer, but the police said it was gang-related. That's when I found out Damen was selling drugs. He must have gotten too close to their territory. After they missed him, he sent out his own posse. I didn't know he had people like that working for him until then. I didn't see much of him after Niya died. I was too…"

Grief-stricken.

Savanna felt the sting of sympathy. It stung because it only hammered home what she'd already realized this morning. He wasn't ready for a relationship. She could argue that neither was she, but sleeping with him had been stupid on her part. If she was ever going to succeed in sparing her heart from further damage, she had to start making smarter decisions.

"It took me a while to process everything," he said. "About eight months later, Damen came to me. He asked if I'd help him with a new deal he was working. He said he couldn't tell me any details until I agreed to join the project. That's when I told him I was finished. We had words. I accused him of my wife's death. It was essentially his fault. He got into drug dealing without telling me. My wife and I were not aware of how much danger we were in just by being with him. I was furious with him for that. He tried to threaten me, but backed off."

Going over his big frame, appreciating it too much, she recognized his confidence. She could see how his friend wouldn't try to go up against him. But Damen could make him pay in other ways, like staging a hit-and-run. He'd underestimated what would happen after that, however. Or he wouldn't be lying in that cabin broken and bleeding.

"But he never got over it," she said.

"Damen was always competing with me. I had the college degree. I had a beautiful wife. And he could never control me. He made comments every once in a while. I should have paid closer attention."

"So when he saw you with his girlfriend, he snapped."

Korbin nodded solemnly. "He must have heard her when she called me and followed her."

"Do you think he had your wife killed intentionally?"

His head shot up and turned to her. He'd never considered that. But it was entirely possible that Damen had arranged for a drive-by.

"Those men were part of a gang," Korbin said. "It was in the police report. They were all arrested and sent to prison with varying sentences. The one who fired the fatal shot got life."

She slowed the truck as they arrived in Monte Vista. Brick and stone buildings lined the two-lane road. A car pulled into a diagonal parking space. People walked along the sidewalks on both sides, the late-afternoon sun casting long winter shadows.

"Let's get rid of this truck and get some different clothes," Korbin said. "Maybe some hats."

She supposed she ought to feel like a fugitive. But with Korbin appearing to be wrongly accused, she didn't.

"You want to know what I think?" she asked.

"What's that?"

"I think I was a boring motivational speaker."

When he just looked at her. She didn't explain. She was in a box when she spoke about love and optimism. This was no box. This was real life. Too bad she didn't have a speech to uplift her.

Seeing a clothing store and gift shop, she turned the next corner and parked in a back parking lot. Together they walked to a back entrance to the shop. A bell jingled as Korbin opened the door for her and she stepped inside. He put his hand on her lower back as she walked down the narrow hall. The contact brought back the intimacy they'd shared, firing tingling warmth everywhere.

A woman with curly white hair peeked down the hall from her post behind the counter.

"Welcome to Nelly's. Anything I can help you find?" She was an energetic sixty-five-year-old in an ankle-length plaid skirt with an elastic waist and a white blouse tucked in.

"We'll look around," Korbin said.

The woman turned back to the man at the counter, who was paying for whatever he'd bought that the woman had put into a bag.

Savanna sifted through a rack of long-sleeved shirts, looking up at Korbin as he perused the men's section. Tall, hard-muscled, pronounced jawline peppered with stubble, his sex appeal kept her heated. She had a vivid recollection of that steamy night. Steamier than any other in her life. She didn't think she'd ever spent so much time making love with anyone.

Finding a dark blue waffle henley, she draped that over her arm and moved on to the pants. There was a display of hats on top of the rectangular white shelf. Savanna picked out a pair of black leather ponte pants and snagged a black newsboy hat. There was a small section of shoes and she found an okay pair of black Sorel boots. At least she could get rid of the boots Hurley had lent her. Next, she found a hoodie and headed for the dressing room. All the sizes fit so she removed all of the tags and brought them out with her.

Korbin waited for her outside the door of the fitting

room and extended a jacket to her, black to match her hat. She smiled at the fact that he'd noticed what she'd chosen and then ran her gaze over his new outfit. He'd opted for a black pair of jeans and crew neck sweater. He'd also found another pair of boots. Black, like the rest of his outfit.

"Planning on doing some sneaking around late at night?" she asked.

He grinned. "Can't hurt to be prepared." He slipped on a beanie and she all but melted into a puddle. All the black really brought out the shine of his gray eyes.

Dipping down, he angled his head to reach under her hat and kiss her. It was so unexpected that she had no time to react. But then burning heat turned her tingles into throbbing desire.

When he let her lips go, she had to catch her breath.

"Let's go." The sound of his sexy voice only strummed her nerves more.

He took out a wallet he had in his back pocket and paid cash for their purchases, the white-haired lady eyeing them. Leaving there, Savanna walked beside him as he searched for a place to find a car. They walked up the main street for a while.

Savanna watched him. Sure enough, the guilt settled in. He'd been drawn to kiss her and soon after felt at odds with himself.

"Police," he said.

Seeing an unmarked police SUV approach down the highway, she lifted the hood of her jacket to cover her long hair. The car passed without notice.

"There's a rental car place up ahead," Korbin said.

"We're going to rent a car?"

There was also a bus stop across the street. Korbin

saw it at the same time and they looked at each other in agreement.

But as she walked with him to pay for two tickets, she wondered if she should go find the sheriff instead. She wasn't wanted for anything. The police were looking for Korbin. Did she really want to be involved with this anymore? Did she really want to risk more nights like the one they had at the yurt? With him—a man who'd suffered such great loss. A man who was a criminal whether he'd been falsely accused of the hit-and-run or not. He'd spent a good chunk of his adult life stealing from the rich.

Could she trust him? Could she trust her heart, her future, with a man like him? An instinctive voice whispered, *No.* He'd never said he'd stop stealing from the rich, stop hacking. He drew the line with Damen, but did that matter?

When Savanna imagined taking him home to meet her mother, she cringed. She'd have to lie about his profession. He was no match for her. If she introduced him with the truth, he'd appear nowhere near the type of man her parents expected her to end up with. Or her. Savanna didn't expect to be with a man like Korbin.

But what about her fiancé? And what about the lawyer? They'd both been respectable men. And both had betrayed her. In all his wrong-side-of-the-tracks splendor, Korbin was being honest.

It was that conflict—that confusion—that made her step onto the bus with Korbin.

Chapter 8

Demarco went to answer the doorbell. It was just after dinner and he and Cora had cuddled close on the couch with a movie. He opened the door, expecting a neighborhood kid selling something, and was surprised to see two men dressed in winter jackets and dress pants.

"Mr. Ricchetti?" the one with blond hair sticking out of his hat asked.

They knew his name? He wished he hadn't answered the door. "Yes."

He dropped open a wallet that revealed a police badge. His partner, an older man who wasn't wearing a hat over his gray hair, did the same.

"I'm Detective Harris and this is Detective Gunderman. We'd like to talk to you about Collette Hamilton. May we come in?"

He could hardly say no. Anxious as to why they wanted to talk to him, he moved aside to let them in. "Sure."

He led them to the kitchen.

"Demo?" Cora walked into the kitchen. Her natural blond hair hid the fine strands of gray and her blue eyes still sparkled at forty. Seeing the detectives, she asked, "What's going on?"

He introduced her to the detectives.

"I'm sure you're aware of your brother's girlfriend's murder?" Gunderman said.

"Yes."

"Would you gentlemen like some coffee?" Cora asked.

"That would be nice, thank you," Harris said. Their work shift was probably long from over.

While Cora went about brewing a pot, Gunderman took charge of this impromptu visit. Demarco was sure they used the element of surprise to their advantage whenever they could.

"The reason we're here is we'd like to talk to you about your brother's relationship with Collette and Korbin. As his twin, you may be able to provide us with some information that could help us find her killer."

"I don't see how I can help."

"You may not be aware that something you know could help. That's why we'd like to talk to you."

Detectives were good at this—smoothing things over to get possible witnesses to talk. "Okay."

His partner slid a recorder onto the table. "Do you mind?"

Demarco shook his head and Harris started the small digital recorder.

"You know Korbin Maguire?" Gunderman asked.

"Yes, through my brother."

"How well do you know him?"

"Pretty well, but not as well as Damen does."

"What kind of relationship did he have with Collette?"

"Damen?"

"No, Korbin."

"I wasn't aware of any relationship."

"They weren't having an affair?"

"Not that I know of." He supposed it was possible they'd carried on in secret, but he more believed his brother had been paranoid about that. Jealous of Korbin. "They were just friends."

"Did you see your brother at all the morning after Collette was murdered?"

Boom. There was the real reason they were here. Demarco stared at Gunderman, a moral battle raging within.

Damen hadn't known he'd seen him and he hadn't made contact. "No."

"You don't seem sure," Gunderman said, a seasoned detective who probably knew he was lying.

Cora put steaming coffee cups onto the table and turned her eyes to him briefly. He saw her alarm, although she covered it well. Only someone who knew her would have picked up on it. He'd have to answer to her after these two men left.

"I'm wondering why you're asking me that."

Gunderman's eyes met his steadily. "One of your brother's neighbors said they saw you drive up in front of their house that morning. Around eight-thirty."

Demarco was careful to keep any reaction from showing, while inside he was frantic for something to say. He frequently parked in front of the neighbor's house when he went to see his brother, as he had that morning. "I don't know any of Damen's neighbors."

"Well, they recognized you."

That was possible, since he went to Damen's house a

lot. These detectives must have shown them a picture of him, maybe even his car, and they'd identified him or his car as being the one in front of their house.

"Why were you there?" Gunderman asked. He was so calm, but his mind had to be working with clever speed right now. He was one step ahead of him and Demarco had no way of predicting what else he knew.

Not wanting to walk into another lie, he stuck to the truth. "I needed to talk to him, but I didn't go in."

"What did you need to talk to him about?"

"We had an argument the day before. Twins do that."

"Why didn't you go in?"

"I wasn't ready to face him."

"All right. Why didn't you tell me that when I asked you if you saw your brother that morning?"

"Because I didn't see him." He had, but Damen hadn't known. Didn't that count? It was a way to justify another lie.

When the detective stopped questioning him, he realized the neighbor hadn't seen Damen leave his house, or Demarco follow him. They had only seen him drive up. It had been seconds later that Damen had appeared on his front porch. He stuffed the gun in his pants and got into his car without looking around. He hadn't thought to worry about being seen, as though stuffing a pistol into his pants were the most natural thing in the world. That was Damen, never thinking first before doing.

He escorted the men to the door. There, Gunderman turned and handed him a business card.

"If you think of anything, give me a call. Day or night." His gaze bore into Demarco's.

He closed the door, certain the detective knew he wasn't telling him everything.

Hearing his wife, he turned to see her lean a shoulder against the white-trimmed doorjamb, folding her arms.

"All right." He held up both of his hands. "I did see him that morning."

"Demarco!" Her arms shot down as she pushed off the doorjamb and walked toward him. "You lied to those detectives!" She pointed toward the closed door.

How could he explain? He looked at her, helpless to the turmoil churning in him.

"What happened when you saw him?"

He could not lie to his wife. She was his world. His love. The one person he trusted and had to keep on trusting. But he had to now.

"I was going to go over to his house to talk to him about the way he's been behaving lately when I saw him come out of his house," he said. Her eyes shifted back and forth, looking into his as though trying to decide if she believed him.

He didn't tell her about the gun. She was worried enough.

"If you know something that could help police…" Cora said.

Images of Damen as a kid rushed him. Then Damen in high school. And after. Had there been a progressive decline in positive behavior? Demarco couldn't get his perception of Damen as a kid out of his head. There were still glimpses of that soul in the man. The good Damen was in there somewhere.

He rubbed his face, moving from the front door to the living room. The movie Cora had chosen still played. Movie night was ruined.

"Do you think he killed Collette?" Cora asked.

"Damen doesn't know what he's doing."

"If he killed someone, that doesn't matter. Do you think he did it?"

"No. I don't know." He was so torn up inside. *No, Damen. Why did you have to do it?* Or had he? "I don't know for sure if he did it or not." It was desperate hope.

She moved closer, angling her head and forcing him to look at her. "There's something you aren't telling me."

"I don't want to find out he did it."

She ran her hands down his arms. "Demarco, you know I love you. I also know how close you are to Damen. But if he killed that girl, you have to tell the police. You have to think about your life. And me. Our life together. I've watched you bend over backward for your brother so many times and he never notices. Why do you go out of your way so much for him?"

"He's my brother."

"Yeah, but…I get the twin thing…but…"

"He's never gotten a fair shake. I just need to help him any way I can." Seeing her eyes go rounder with apprehension, he said, "If he did kill Collette, I'll get him a lawyer. I won't cover for him. But if he didn't kill her…" He had a sick feeling. Damen had killed Collette. How much longer could he deny that?

"Call that detective, Demarco."

He looked at his wife, imagining what it would be like to turn his own twin brother in to the law. "And tell them what?"

"Whatever you aren't telling me."

Just then the phone rang. Glad for the interruption, he went into the kitchen to answer.

"Mr. Demarco Ricchetti?" a man's voice said.

"Yes."

"We found your contact information in your brother's

phone. He's been admitted to the Pagosa Springs Medical Center. He's stabilized for now, but he's not conscious."

Shock paralyzed him for a second. "What happened to him? Is he going to be all right?"

"I'm not sure. They just asked me to call and notify his family."

How had Damen ended up in a hospital? Had he gone after Korbin? He must have. And Korbin had sent him to the hospital. "What happened to him?" he asked again.

"I'm not authorized to discuss that on the phone, sir. I can only tell you that he's in serious condition and is stabilized." The man went on to tell him which room he was in.

"I'm on my way. Will you tell him that if he wakes before I get there?"

"Yes, sir."

When he hung up, he saw Cora looking concerned in the kitchen entrance.

"It's Damen. He's in the hospital. He's okay but he's unconscious." He didn't explain that it had in all likelihood been Korbin who'd put him there. "I have to drive to Pagosa Springs."

He watched her struggle with reasons why he should and shouldn't go. Damen was hurt and needed someone right now. But how much of an alliance should Demarco risk?

She came to him, putting her hand on his upper arm. "Do you want me to go with you?"

Thinking of all the trouble his brother was in, Demarco said, "No." He leaned down to kiss her mouth. "I'll go alone."

"Demo, what if he did kill Collette?"

He smiled softly in an attempt to reassure her. "Damen

won't hurt me." Recalling how his brother had punched him, he thought twice about that. The strike had broken the skin inside his mouth, but hadn't left a mark on his face. Cora didn't know, and he wouldn't worry her.

"Are you sure?"

"Damen's gotten himself in some kind of trouble and I don't want you anywhere near it."

Her expression relaxed. "Okay."

Demarco went upstairs to pack, thinking how wrong anyone was who said twins had a special connection. He had no feeling whatsoever that Damen was hurt. He also was beginning not to care. Damen had been making a pretty messy bed for himself, and he was lying in it now.

Chapter 9

Disguised in their new outfits, Korbin led Savanna into Julio's Mexican Cantina on a charming street corner of Wheat Ridge, Colorado. Minutes from downtown Denver, it had a small-town feel in the middle of the metropolitan buzz. He searched the area for signs of surveillance. If Damen had told police about Julio, they'd be keeping an eye out for them. He spotted a car in the parking lot with two people inside. They didn't notice them. The passenger was busy eating a taco. He had his hands full.

Korbin glanced over there every so often as he and Savanna walked to the entrance. Inside the vestibule, he looked back through the glass. The two men hadn't recognized them.

Stepping into the entrance, he guided Savanna through a throng waiting to be seated. The restaurant had been featured on a dining network television program. Tourists and residents flocked here for their spicy green chili and giant burritos. Savanna stepped up to the wood-planked wraparound porch beneath a western gabled roof.

"Your friend owns this?"

"Yes."

At nearly seven, there was a wait. Korbin gave a false name and asked to see Julio.

Savanna didn't doubt their wait was about to get much shorter when the hostess smiled at her. "Are you Savanna Ivy?"

"Uh…"

"You are!" She laughed her delight and put her hands to her face.

"Could we have a private table?" Korbin asked.

"Of course. Oh my God. I can't believe we have a celebrity here! You're here to see Julio? How do you know him?"

"Table?" Korbin said, impatient.

"Oh, of course. I'm sorry. You probably don't want to cause a scene."

Korbin glanced at the others crowding the lobby. They all stared. So much for not being noticed.

The hostess grabbed two menus and led them into the dining room, seating them in a corner booth in the dim bar area. All of the stools were occupied, and conversation, laughter and clanking dishes blended into a harmonious roar.

He watched the hostess whisper to a waitress, who glanced their way and then nodded with a few words. Business carried on as usual.

Korbin relaxed. For now.

Savanna took a menu from their waitress, who met her eyes but revealed no sign of recognition.

A few minutes later, the waitress appeared with waters. Instead of asking for their order, she put a magazine down in front of Savanna. Seeing it was a copy of an entertainment issue with a picture of her standing with her sisters Autumn and Arizona, she realized she was about to be asked for an autograph. The photo was taken at a Hollywood cocktail party her parents had thrown.

"One of the cooks asked if I could get you to sign this," the waitress said.

Not many asked her for an autograph. Her father was the producer, not her. Taking the pen the woman removed from her apron, she asked for the cook's name and scrawled a greeting to him and his family before signing her name.

"He's been wanting this for a while," the waitress said. "He thinks you're the most beautiful of the Ivy women."

Korbin had to agree that she was beautiful, but was all of this attention due to her face being splashed all over the news in association with a supposed criminal? The public loved a good scandal.

"Tell him thank you for me," she said awkwardly.

"Are you ready to order?"

Savanna ordered a smothered burrito with spicy green chili.

"I'll have the same," Korbin said.

The waitress jotted down the order, glancing frequently at Savanna as though dying to say something.

"I read about your latest breakup," the waitress said. "The lawyer? Is it true he was married?"

Korbin turned sharply from another check of the restaurant and saw how uncomfortable Savanna was over this confrontation. She hadn't told him much about her second heartache. In fact, she'd downplayed it. But now this waitress was asking her about it and she was reacting as shaken up as she'd been over her fiancé.

"It is hard for us to keep anything private."

The waitress noticed her stiff response and backed off. Sort of. She kept her demeanor and tone light. "Well, someone will come along. And he might be sitting next to you." She winked at Korbin.

Did she think he might be Savanna's next try at love? He exchanged a glance with Savanna, who was equally uncomfortable.

"I'll go get Julio." The waitress took the menus and with a smile, retreated to the kitchen.

Moments later Julio appeared. Unlike the waitress, he wasn't smiling. No doubt he'd heard the news. Korbin hadn't told him why he needed his cabin, only that Damen had gotten him into some trouble and he needed to get away for a while to sort things out.

"Korbin."

Korbin reached up to shake his hand and Savanna scooted over to make room for him on her side.

He took the seat. "When you phoned I had no idea you were in that kind of trouble, Korbin."

"I was set up," he said.

"You're their prime suspect."

Catching Savanna's anxious look, he explained to Julio about his meeting with Collette and giving her his gun. He was afraid that Damen had used it to kill her.

"Police haven't found the murder weapon," Julio said.

Korbin hoped they never would.

"Why did you have a gun?" Savanna asked.

He heard her concern, her conflict over being with

him and his shady background. "I bought it after I told Damen I wasn't going to work with him anymore."

"So you carried it with you to the restaurant?"

"I carried it everywhere."

"Do you have money?" Julio asked.

Relieved his longtime friend believed him, Korbin said, "I withdrew plenty of cash when I left for Wolf Creek."

"Then you'll need a place to stay. I'll deny letting you in, but you can stay in one of my apartment rentals. It's between tenants right now. I've also stored a car in the garage there. It's a surprise sixteenth birthday gift for my daughter."

"I don't expect you to do that, Julio."

"Well, I'm doing it. You've always been there for me. I know you are a good man. I can't stand by and watch you be sent to prison for crimes you didn't commit." He dug into his pants pocket and pulled out a set of keys. "I expected you to come and see me after I heard the police were searching my cabin."

"Thanks. I'll make it up to you."

Julio waved his hand. "No need. I'd expect the same if I was ever in a jam. If you didn't come here for help, why did you? I can't imagine it was just to say hello, not in the midst of all your trouble."

"Your brother-in-law is an FBI agent."

"Yes."

"I need you to ask him to get a background on someone." Korbin took out a piece of paper where he'd written Tony's name.

Julio took it and put it in his pocket. "Should I have him call you?"

"Sure." Julio had his number.

In the bar area, a news broadcast began.

"More on the hunt for fugitive, Korbin Maguire. Police have tracked him to a remote area near Wolf Creek Pass. Wanted in connection with a fatal hit-and-run and the murder of Collette Hamilton, Maguire's car was found abandoned following the hit-and-run and he was seen leaving Hamilton's home that same night."

The screen switched to a recorded clip of Damen saying he saw Korbin leave the building at the time of the murder.

"Ricchetti found Hamilton's body and called 911," the newswoman said. "He is not considered a suspect in the case."

Korbin sat stunned as he heard that piece of news. Damen hadn't seen him leave Collette's house. Collette had been dead long before he'd arrived there. Police may postulate that he had enough time to kill her. And Damen's claim to have seen him leave the house supported that theory. But what about motive? The police weren't saying much to the press. Damen had likely told them Korbin was enraged that Collette was going to marry him. A love triangle turned fatal.

The newswoman went on to announce the latest breaking news. "A startling twist has developed on this story. Police are now speculating whether Maguire has kidnapped Savanna Ivy, one of producer Jackson Ivy's daughters. Savanna lives in a remote area of Wolf Creek where Maguire's truck was found stuck in snow. A local sheriff spoke with Maguire and Ivy after they claimed to have escaped a gunman on skis, a gunman Maguire named as his longtime friend, Damen Ricchetti. But yesterday evening police found Ricchetti badly beaten and unconscious in another cabin where Maguire is believed to have been hiding. Police aren't commenting on the case, but the Wolf Creek sheriff said it was possible that Ricchetti went after Maguire for killing his girlfriend..."

"It won't be long before police come here to question me," Julio said, standing from the table. "You better go. I'll get your order ready so that you can take it with you."

"Thanks, Julio."

Julio patted his shoulder once when Korbin stood. "I'll be in touch."

"Don't use your own phone to contact me," Korbin said, turning to Savanna, who was slow to get up from the booth. She seemed unhappy about the things she'd heard on the news.

Taking her hand, he kept it until Julio came back with a bag containing their food, then led her out of the restaurant, careful to watch out for police.

Savanna was quiet all the way to the apartment, and Korbin didn't broach any subject of his guilty appearance to the general public. His life was on the line. If he couldn't prove his innocence, he'd be sent to prison. He didn't have much time.

The apartment was in south Denver. Korbin instructed the cab driver to drop them off several blocks away, as he'd done when they'd gone to Julio's.

Savanna walked beside him in her melancholy.

"Why didn't you mention the lawyer before?" he asked to get her thinking of something other than him killing Collette.

The fact that she wavered with doubt irritated him, but he had to understand. Damen claimed to have seen him leave the murder scene, which, of course, he had, but long after the murder, not at the time of death.

"I did," she said. "I said it didn't work out."

"No, I mean about him going back to his ex-wife."

She kicked a rock on the sidewalk, sending it skipping along. "I didn't feel like it."

Yep, she was hurt by the lawyer. "Did you catch him, too?"

"Are we almost there?" She started walking faster.

"Did he know you caught him?"

Glancing over at him again, she took a while before answering. "I flew to Denver to surprise him. When I arrived, his ex-wife was there. She was in a robe and they both looked like they had just gotten out of bed—at three in the afternoon. He admitted to seeing her and said that was the first time they'd been intimate since before their divorce."

Korbin saw her curl her hand into a fist at her side.

She had felt strongly for the man. Twice she'd been hurt in the same manner.

"Every time I think I know a man, I discover I didn't know him at all," she said.

She must have serious doubts as to whether she knew him or not. They hadn't meet each other long ago, so that was normal, but how long would it take her to trust again? She'd opened her heart to trust the lawyer and he'd betrayed her as her fiancé had.

For some strange reason, that made her safe to him. She'd been wounded and wouldn't give her heart so easily to the next man she fell for. He felt safe being with her, safe to let his guard down, safe to give love a try. As that feeling swept over him, heavy dread sank in his stomach. He'd never considered that it would be possible to replace his wife. But what if he could? What if he fell in love again?

Picturing his wife's face came with a familiar stab of guilt; he withdrew from that contemplation.

A police car appeared on the street.

Korbin considered ducking out of sight but that might be too obvious. He stopped walking and faced Savanna, who spotted the police car with widening eyes.

Pulling her to him, he said, "Don't be afraid."

She resisted with her hands on him. "I'm not afraid."

"Then make it look good."

With his arms slipping around her, holding her tantalizingly close, he kissed her, watching her wary eyes ease into passion.

As he listened to the police car drive by, he felt Savanna relax in his arms. It didn't take much to fuel their desire. Enticed to kiss her for real, he angled his mouth with hers and pressed for more.

A homeless man walked into the alley behind Savanna, barely giving them a glance as he passed. The sound of traffic and people faded away.

Moments later, the urgency of getting to the apartment overruled and he managed to pull back. Savanna looked up at him with sultry blue eyes that he'd so loved losing himself in when he was making love to her. He was back there with her now. Temptation began to build again. He moved to kiss her once more. But she let out her breath and stepped back.

He kept his feet planted where they were, when everything in him urged him to take her back into his arms. He bargained with himself that if he took her to the apartment, they'd have the entire night alone together, where he could taste her the way he had in Wolf Creek.

Brushing her hair back from her shoulder, she started walking. He walked with her, the passion cooling and the significance of the way Savanna made him feel becoming reality. How terrible was it for him to compare her with his wife? They were nothing alike, and he was afraid he could fall for Savanna a lot harder than he'd fallen for Niya. He didn't welcome how he also began to suspect that Niya's death had exaggerated his love for her.

They reached the apartment and Savanna waited while Korbin made sure no one saw them go up the stairs to Julio's vacant unit. It was pretty nice. Not terribly big, but it would do for a safe haven, one only Korbin needed.

Savanna wondered again what she was doing with him. Why didn't she just leave? She could call Macon to come and get her. He'd take her to Evergreen where she'd be safe. Safer, probably, than she was here.

Thankful that Korbin left the television off, she went up to take a long bath. For an hour she soaked with her thoughts.

Kissing Korbin was like a drug. Was her brain in an altered state with him? She'd sensed the way he'd withdrawn after that. He needed to keep his distance from her, too. After kissing her, some reminder must have struck him. He must have started thinking of his wife. Murdered by a gang member.

Why hadn't he told her that after Damen had started shooting at them? He'd procrastinated until he was forced to tell her. Did that mean he was guilty? He'd kept secrets from her. Big secrets. Secrets that would send him to prison.

He could be guilty.

He could have driven the car in a hit-and-run. He could have killed Collette. And Damen could have come after him for it. Damen had made that comment about

Collette getting what she deserved, but he could have just been taunting Korbin. And Korbin had been focused on Tony. He'd kept grilling Damen about the man.

What if there was more going on than she could see right now?

Why would Korbin offer to help Collette if he planned to kill her? And what motive would he have?

Savanna could be missing key pieces of information that only Korbin would know. Or he could be telling the truth…when he was forced to reveal it.

Sighing, sinking low into the water, she asked herself if it was worth staying there to find out. Wouldn't it be best if she left, removed herself from this dangerous adventure and never saw him again? Maybe it was the dangerous adventure that drew her. Korbin was exciting. Her fiancé and the lawyer had not been exciting. They had fit her motivational speaker persona, not this brave woman who championed a fugitive,

Climbing out of the tub, she dried herself, depressed that she couldn't make up her mind. She'd never felt so indecisive in her life.

Dressing in a pajama set, she left the bathroom. Korbin sat reclined in a chair, facing her, the gas fireplace going beside him and no other lights on. He'd been deep in thought, brooding. Fighting the fact that he kept kissing her—and she tried not to remember the other thing they did—when a big, loyal part of him resisted that?

She went into the kitchen, seeing city lights through the window. She had to hand it to Korbin's friend. He'd given them a safe place to go for the night.

Opening the fridge, she realized she hadn't eaten all day. The food Julio had packaged up for them was in there. She took it out, noticing Korbin had already eaten.

She put the Styrofoam container into the microwave and turned for something to drink. Bumping into Korbin, she jumped back and he took a step back. Awkwardness over the contact affected them both.

"I was just…getting something to drink."

"Oh. Here." He opened the fridge and she leaned to take out a bottle of iced tea that was in there. The apartment came furnished, and that included some nonperishable items.

"I'm thinking about going to Evergreen in the morning," she said. "I realize you have this issue over protecting me, but my father has security really tight there."

He straightened from retrieving a bottle of water from the fridge. "We've been over this."

"That isn't the only reason I want to go."

The microwave dinged, sparing her from the hardening look in Korbin's eyes. She took her smothered burrito to the table and sat facing the city lights. The bath and the view worked well to calm her frazzled thoughts. Had she just made a decision? If so, she was very proud of herself, bad-boy craver or not. Korbin's lovemaking hadn't completely robbed her of self-respect.

Korbin sat at the table with her, setting the water bottle down.

"It won't happen again," he said.

She swallowed her bite and looked at him. "What? Kissing? Sleeping with each other?" She didn't try to bridle her sarcasm.

"Only if that's what you want."

And if she wanted it, he'd be happy to oblige?

She set down her fork. He was ruining her dinner. "Korbin, that is what I want. When you kiss me, I want kissing and sex. Don't you get that?"

He blinked with building desire. "Yes. I do get that."

His desire stirred hers. "It isn't fair for you to keep seducing me."

"I won't. I told you, it won't happen again."

"How can you be so sure?" When they were alone together, nature took over. She watched him realize the same.

Finally, he said, "Because…I have other reasons for refraining."

"You feel like you cheated on your dead wife." She said it more like an accusation. Maybe she said it to hurt him. Maybe he needed to hear it.

His eyes stayed on hers a moment, and then lowered with the trueness of the assessment.

"I'm sorry," she said, immediately contrite. "I'm mostly mad at myself for not taking more time to get to know you. I thought I could…be bold and…give you a try. You know, sort of like test-driving a McLaren."

He half grinned. "I'm comparable to a sports car?"

"Not comparable. I can't drive fast. That was the analogy." She picked at her food.

When she looked up, he was fighting a bigger grin.

"What?" He better not tease her about this.

"We can drive slow from now on. What's your speed? Minivan or Subaru?"

She almost let go of a laugh. "A golf cart."

After chuckling from deep down, he leaned forward and slid his hand over hers. The touch revved up her unreasonable lust for him.

The traces of his grin faded and after he held her gaze a while, he said, "I don't want to hurt you."

He couldn't have chosen a worse thing to say.

She pulled her hand out from under his. "But you will, Korbin."

"No. I'll respect your wishes."

"You'll try."

He had no comment to that. He couldn't refute it. He'd try, but he wouldn't succeed. The temptation was too great for them both. And now that they'd sampled how hot it was between them, any opportunity for more would be that much harder to resist. She didn't trust herself, much less him.

"I'm going to stay in Evergreen for a while," she said.

A worried energy lit his eyes and he tried to reach for her hand again. "Savanna—"

"The security is impenetrable there. You don't have to feel responsible for protecting me."

"Yes, I do. I got you into this mess."

"And you can get me out of it while I'm in Evergreen."

The intensity of his eyes didn't diminish, but he understood what she said. It was a logical solution.

"Savanna, I…"

The loss of words didn't need to be found. She could feel what he meant to say but couldn't.

"You don't have to explain," she said gently. "You lost the love of your life and it's difficult for you to move on to someone else. But you have to let me go, Korbin. I can't stay with you. Not with how much…how we…" She couldn't describe the powerful connection they had—or she had. Most likely she was alone when it came to the strength of how she felt when he was inside of her, when he kissed her. Touched her in any way.

"Don't be afraid," he said.

Why did he keep saying that? "I'm not. I'm being practical. You aren't ready for this."

"Are you saying you are?"

It had been only a few days since he was stranded on her road. She looked out at the city lights, needing them to calm her and the confusion milling around her heart.

"No, you aren't," he said for her. "We both aren't."

She turned back to him. "That's why I should go."

"I want you to stay. With me."

"Why? Do you want to keep engaging the way we have and see where we end up?" She didn't think she could do that.

After a slight hesitation, he said, "I'd be willing to give it a try."

Although he said the words that could placate her, the way he said them did the opposite. He sounded anxious, uncertain.

"I can't have a sexual relationship with you anymore."

He sat back against the chair in defeat. Seeing that hurt more than she anticipated. Oh. She hated being so intuitive. She was right about him. There could be no doubt now. He hadn't worked through his issues yet. And she wouldn't be the rebound girl. The one who wasn't quite right. The one who wasn't as right as another woman. No, the man who got her next time would know she was right for him. In every way. And she'd be certain of it. Nothing affirmed her decision to leave more than that.

"It would be more than that," he said. But it came too late, and again she heard his lack of conviction. He might want to believe he was ready for more than just sex, but Savanna could not ignore her instincts.

"You feel guilty every time you touch me. I can't be with you that way. And it's not fair of you to expect me to stay close to you when we both know we won't be able to stop ourselves from touching each other." Having gripping sex. His weight on her, his thickness sliding into her. His ghost-gray eyes full of heat and passion. Her toes curled just remembering. She had to make him understand. "You have to let me go, Korbin. I need that."

For a long time he just sat there looking at her, unable to deny anything she said, hurting her without meaning to. Had she ever turned away from a man for her own good before? No. She'd always held on to the optimism that he'd want her the way she wanted him. Twice she'd been wrong. It could happen again. She had to stick to her decision and go.

"All right, but let me take you," he finally said.

Feeling the burn of tears threaten, she picked up her container of food and put it on the counter. He'd agreed. He knew her leaving was the best thing for them both.

Chapter 10

Macon Ivy unfolded his tall frame from the Denver hotel chair, phone to his ear, waiting for his mother to finish her panicked ranting.

"I'd call Lincoln, but he and Sabrina are in Scotland right now," his mother said. She was trying to solve everything all on her own.

"The police are working this."

He heard her breathing—catching up on breathing, that is. "But kidnapped. My Savanna has been kidnapped!"

"That's what the media are saying. You know how they can be. Maybe it isn't what it seems." Korbin had something to hide, but he didn't strike him as a murderer who'd kidnap a woman. "And Savanna isn't dumb. She wouldn't stand up for him if he wasn't a good person."

"Find my daughter, Macon." His mother began to cry.

He never heard or saw her cry. She was a strong woman. Nothing ever got her down. "You kids are going to send me to an early grave."

He chuckled, hearing her quickly overcome her moment of weakness. "Save the drama for the movies, Mom. Savanna is fine. And I will try to find her." Even though he had zero experience as a detective and the press was camped outside the hotel.

"This is no movie, Macon. Why do my children have to get into trouble all the time?"

"Trouble finds us, I guess."

"Go get her. Bring her to Evergreen. I'm flying there today with your father."

"Are you trying to sneak in another reunion?" In Macon's drinking and drugging years, he'd avoided those gatherings. Now he was beginning to look forward to them.

"Macon. How can you be so insensitive?"

"I'm telling you, Korbin isn't a bad guy. Yeah, he ran from cops and the media are saying he killed two people, but someone shot at him up in Wolf Creek. Someone who is supposed to be a friend of his. There's more going on here."

"Are you sure?"

"Yes." He hadn't been at first, but after thinking about it he was now. "He's innocent. The only thing he's guilty of is falling for Savanna."

There was a long pause on the line. "Really?"

"Oh yeah. You should have seen them together. Something's going on there. They look like they've slept together."

His mother gasped. "Is Savanna not thinking clearly?

Maybe he seduced her and she's fooled into staying with him."

"Mother, stop. Savanna's been through enough with men. She wouldn't be with him if he wasn't worth something." At least, he hoped. Sleeping with someone after just meeting them wasn't Savanna's style. Why had she?

"I'll find Savanna and bring her to Evergreen," he said. And a few minutes later he was able to get off the phone.

Turning up the volume on the television, he listened to a news report on Savanna's alleged kidnapping. Collette Hamilton's murder. The hit-and-run. According to the media, Korbin appeared to have done them both. He hadn't voiced his real concern to his mother. Savanna would be in danger if Damen Ricchetti came after them again. Korbin had put him in the hospital, but wouldn't that just piss him off more as soon as he was released? This Korbin Maguire fellow may not be afraid of that, but Savanna could be caught in the crossfire.

Macon's girlfriend emerged from the bathroom. Slender and fit with long, silky blond hair and blue eyes, she was a vision for the camera. She smiled as she approached in her practiced gait. Placing her hands on his face, she kissed him as though the world were watching. He was getting tired of her. There was no difference between who she was when she was acting and who she was in real life.

Keisha Coulter did a lot of romantic comedies, and Macon felt like he was her leading man. Did she even care about who he was when they were off the set?

She lowered her hands from his face, and he wished she'd stop looking at him so dramatically. "I need to go to Denver."

That earned him a few theatrical blinks. "Why?"

"There's something I need to do." He started to walk to the door.

She followed. "What do you mean? What do you need to do? You're just going to leave me here?"

He turned before opening the door. "You can stay here as long as you like. Or leave."

"What?" That pout might actually be genuine. "What do you mean, leave? I don't want to leave."

"I'm just saying, you can do whatever you want."

"I want to be with you. That's why I came to your hotel. I didn't come here to be alone." She rubbed his chest with her hands, acting again. "How long will you be gone?"

"I don't know. Probably a few days."

She dropped her hands and her mouth dropped open—more drama. No wonder she went through so many men. Probably none of them felt as though she saw them as themselves, only another actor in the scene of life.

"What am I supposed to do?"

"I don't know. Maybe go see your ex." He already knew they were talking to each other. He'd seen a few of their text messages on her phone. Deangelo Calabrese was another guy who acted his way through life. He should have known better than to date the ex-girlfriend of Autumn's ex-boyfriend. Geez, just thinking that gave him a headache. Autumn's ex-boyfriend's ex-girlfriend…

Autumn was living happy as could be in Lander, Wyoming, with her black ops husband and newborn baby. She'd gotten away from the press by getting away from people like Calabrese. Macon should follow suit and do the same with this bubblehead.

"Why would I do that?" she finally asked, no doubt anxious that he was onto her.

"Haven't you been seeing each other?"

"Wh...? No. I mean...we're friends, that's all."

Friends with benefits? He didn't ask. He didn't care.

Suddenly she noticed what he was wearing. "Why are you in jeans?"

"I always wear jeans when I'm off the set."

"Oh." She appeared perplexed for a second.

It struck him then. He didn't want to see her anymore. He'd asked her to meet him here with the intent of sleeping with her, but now it wasn't important. "Maybe it's best if you left, Keisha."

She looked perplexed. "Until you get back?"

"No. I mean leave. And don't come back. I think I'm done with this." He knew he sounded like a jerk, but she wasn't exactly a pillar of morality. She was seeing her ex again, and if he cared about her at all that would have bothered him. The fact that it didn't told him it was time for them to part ways.

After blinking in bewilderment, she grew angry. "Just like that?" She snapped her fingers. "You decide we're finished?"

"You would have come to the same conclusion when you were finished acting this out."

"Acting..." Her brow creased. "I'm not acting."

Maybe not now...

"You're a nice girl, Keisha. It's just not working out for us."

"Oh." She acted out her disappointment, which may or may not be real disappointment. "A-all right." She began going about the room picking up her things and depositing them into her suitcase with furtive glances his way.

No wonder she'd won one of the most prestigious awards in Hollywood.

Turning, he left without another word. Down in the lobby, he met up with his security detail. The lead guard spoke into his radio, getting his driver ready.

Outside, the press was hungrier than usual.

"Have you heard from your sister, Macon?"

"Will your film be delayed because of this?"

"Where's Keisha? Why isn't she with you?"

"Back off," his lead guard, Warley, said, sticking his hand up while two more guards plowed a path for him to the black Escalade waiting for him, door open with another guard standing there.

Macon climbed in the back, looking out at the crowd of cameras and nameless faces of the men and women behind them. While this came with fame and he liked the attention sometimes, now was inappropriate.

"Where to, Mr. Ivy?" the driver asked after Warley sat in the front and another guard sat in the back with Macon.

Macon told him the Denver address.

The driver began to set out, but looked into the rear-view mirror in question. "That's a rough neighborhood. Are you sure you have the right address?"

"It's the right address." Macon didn't look up from checking his email and text messages, but he caught Warley's turn of head.

"Would you mind filling us in on this excursion?" Warley asked.

"Just an old friend I need to talk to for a bit." He'd called Darnell Robbins yesterday and arranged to meet today.

"You have a friend in a rough neighborhood?" Warley asked.

It was a piece of his life he rarely talked about, and wouldn't now, with his security detail.

"Mr. Ivy?" Warley queried.

Macon lifted his eyes, a clear warning.

"We can't protect you if you keep us in the dark."

"You won't have to protect me where we're going." He almost scoffed. If anything, he'd protect them.

Macon ignored his frequent looks. When the driver pulled to a stop in front of a brick apartment building with clothes hanging out on lines in front of some of the upper windows, Macon saw several African-Americans in groups, mostly male. Some sat on front steps, some played basketball in the enclosed court across the street. They'd stopped to take in the Escalade that had appeared.

"You wait here," Macon said to Warley, and then opened the door.

Darnell stood with a group of black men in front of the apartment building. He smiled as Macon approached, shaking his hand and giving him a hard pat.

"Hey, man. I don't have to ask how you been. Big-time actor, huh? I couldn't believe it when I started hearing you were in some hit movies. Whatcha doin' down here, dirtying yourself with us homeys?"

"Hey, Darnell. Thanks for agreeing to meet me. It's been a long time."

"You got my attention, dude. What's all this about Damen Ricchetti?"

"That's what I was hoping you could tell me." He glanced around at all the faces still observing the exchange.

"Ricchetti, huh?" Darnell shook his head as though in awe. Then he looked back at the four other men behind him, who nodded in response, agreeing in recognition and mumbling among each other.

"Big-time drug dealer," Darnell said. "Chased out the other dude who took rank around those parts."

"He doesn't sell here?"

Darnell laughed. "Hell no. A white boy like him? Naw, man, he stays out of my neighborhood. He ain't like you. Catch my meaning, friend?"

"Yeah." What he meant was Damen Ricchetti wasn't trusted here.

"Did you hear that he was hospitalized?" Macon asked.

"Yeah, man. You know he has a twin brother, don't you?"

"No."

"Demarco Ricchetti. Runs an antique auction house uptown. Complete opposite of his brother."

Darnell knew a little about everyone. "What about Tony Bartoszewicz?"

Darnell made a face. "Never heard of him."

Maybe Tony wasn't into drugs. Maybe it was something else. "Thanks, Darnell."

"You want me to look into this Bartoszewicz dude?"

"Sure. Yeah. That'd be great." Macon shook his hand. "Good to see you again."

"Likewise, my man. I'll be in touch."

Macon turned and headed back to the Escalade, seeing Warley watching in amazement. He said nothing as Macon got back into the vehicle. "Julio's Mexican Cantina, please."

"The media's going to be crawling all over that place," Warley protested.

"They're going to be crawling everywhere I go." Except here. Who would guess some of Macon's closest friends were from the dark side of town? While he'd like to shed that part of his past, it was there and not going anywhere. What a coincidence that he and Korbin had that in common.

This time he needed his security guards to get into the restaurant. He had to sign a few autographs before Julio had them brought to the back and into the restaurant office, a cramped room that afforded Macon some privacy. Only he and Julio stood in there, and Macon shut the door on Warley's unhappy face.

"I'm looking for my sister. She came here with Korbin Maguire. You and he are friends?"

"I am sorry, Mr. Ivy. I don't know where they went." He seemed stressed.

Macon cocked his head. "Did the cops fall for that?"

Julio's anxious look said no, they hadn't.

"Well, I don't either. Tell me where my sister is. I don't care about Maguire. I have orders from my mother to take her to our house in Evergreen."

Still, Julio didn't budge.

"Come on. My sister is in serious danger. She's been shot at. Being with Maguire is dangerous for her. All I want is my sister."

"She'll be in danger if I tell you anything," Julio finally said.

"Where is she? Give me something."

Julio shook his head. "Better if you don't know. Famous actor like you. What do you think will happen if you are seen going to her?"

Her whereabouts would be exposed. Damen could find her…or that other guy. He could put Savanna's life in more danger. But could he stand by and do nothing?

Chapter 11

At 3:00 a.m. Savanna left the apartment building. She'd taken just enough cash from Korbin's wallet to get to the hotel where she'd heard Macon was staying. It wasn't difficult to find him with all of his recent fame.

Taking the elevator down to the lobby, she searched for any suspicious characters. Seeing none, she did the same in front of the building. Since getting a cab here might put Korbin at risk, she walked several blocks to a nearby hotel. A taxi was parked at the entrance. She went there and got in, telling him to take her to Macon's hotel.

She had mixed feelings the entire way there. Relief. Depression. It was good and healthy for her to distance herself, but at the same time she couldn't help wondering if they had the real thing. She hadn't felt that powerfully making love with her fiancé or the lawyer. The swell of emotion was behind a wall she'd erected ever since deciding to leave.

Paying the driver, she entered the posh hotel, the nicest in Denver. At the front desk, she asked the attendant to ring Macon's room. It amazed her that she'd gotten this far undetected.

"Tell him Savanna is here," she instructed when the attendant got him to finally answer.

"He said to send you up." The attendant gave her a card. "And to give you a key."

"Thanks." She took the card and rode the elevator to the top floor.

Warley waited outside the door. When he saw her, assured she was who she said she was, he went back to his room. Macon opened the door and took her into his arms.

"Savanna, thank God you're here." He took her inside. "I'll get room service to brew some coffee."

"No. Will you take me to Evergreen?" She needed seclusion. It would be her sanctuary. With any luck, no one would be there. She'd rather go home, but the security was better at the Evergreen mansion.

He put his hands on her shoulders and crouched a little, observing her closely. "What's wrong? Are you all right?" Now he scanned her whole body. "Did he kidnap you like the news said? I didn't think he did, but you look a wreck."

"No. He didn't. I don't want to talk about it." She moved away from him and deeper into the suite. The wall had crumbled some and she felt near tears. She clung to her strength. She'd gotten through this before, she could do it again. She should be good at this by now. Letting go and moving on.

He followed. "Okay. Where is he?"

"I left him."

Moving around her, he angled his head to get another close look at her face. "Are you all right?"

She managed a nod. "I can't talk about it. Will you take me to Evergreen?"

"Yeah. Sure. I'll tell Warley to get everything ready." He went to find his phone.

She listened to him give polite orders to his head of security.

Savanna lowered her head, besieged with the notion that she'd never see Korbin again. Or very likely never. She had to plan for that, anyway. Allowing herself to hope would not only be desperate, it would make her unhappy. *Keep* her unhappy—she was already unhappy. She sat on the sofa, fighting despair. What she and Korbin had was real. But she couldn't have it. She'd lost again.

Macon came to her. "It'll take about an hour." He stood there watching her. "Do you need anything?"

She shook her head.

"Are you sure you're all right?" He sat next to her and her wall fell away. Turning to him, she let go and cried.

Korbin woke to emptiness. He knew she was gone before he checked. He could feel it in the stillness and in his heart. Why had he let her go? Even his will to protect her had failed to prevent her from going. And now that she was gone, he felt a black hole gape inside him, light circling a deep, dark abyss. It was almost like losing his wife all over again. And that unsettled him. He struggled to picture her face. Only images of her bloody body after she was shot inundated him. But he could picture Savanna's face as clearly as though she stood in the room. Why had he let her go? She'd dug the answer out of him.

Savanna was a fine woman. She'd make a fine companion for him. What was wrong with being with her? He did love his wife, and quite possibly always would—the memory of her. Maybe Savanna was right and he wasn't ready to move on. He did feel a mess. Losing someone he loved in such a way would affect anyone like this, wouldn't it? Life as usual wasn't usual anymore. He was displaced, fighting to find his footing again, new footing. He couldn't step where he'd once stepped because the ground had slid away from underneath him.

Meeting Savanna had reversed any progress he'd thought he'd made. And now, in the quiet loneliness of this strange apartment, he realized he hadn't made any progress. No. He'd buried what had happened. Progress would have been if he'd told Damen to go straight to hell after her death. Progress would have been refusing to allow him to attend her funeral services. To even be his friend.

Anger hadn't begun to settle in until after Damen had approached him with a new hacking job. It had taken him a year to get to that stage of grief. Disbelief had held him back for a long time. He hadn't been able to believe Niya was dead. He'd lived in a gray, ghostly realm of existence. Beating himself up with memories of her, of their love, and of her violent death.

Now, as he lay there staring at the ceiling, he couldn't think of her any other way than the day she was shot. Where once her beautiful face occupied his mind day and night, Savanna's had taken her place at the throne of his admiration. It gave him a hollow, wretched feeling. How could he betray Niya so easily? He was torn between finding the new ground he needed to move forward with his life and remaining true to Niya. All he had to do was take that first step. And yet…he couldn't. Because doing so would mean he was walking away from Niya, leaving her behind.

Getting out of bed, he wiped his face in distress and turned on the TV. He was about to get into the shower when he heard a report about Savanna and Macon leaving a posh downtown hotel. He saw her holding up her jacket to shield her face. Macon's security personnel warded off the throng and one of them kept saying, "Sorry, no comment."

As she got into the Escalade he caught a glimpse of her face. She looked beautiful but drawn. Not happy. He fancied that was because of him and not the media crushing down upon her, and then felt terrible for that. She had been right to go. He wasn't ready to move on. He wasn't ready for her.

Seeing her ripped apart his sense of devotion for Niya and plunged him into mucky disorder. Where had these feelings come from? Why did they threaten him so? He felt cornered. Compelled to go after Savanna. Honor-bound not to.

After a shower that he spent mostly lost in thought, he dressed in the same outfit as yesterday. He had no idea what he'd do today. Would he take a chance and go after Savanna or would he fight for his innocence? Why was he still contemplating going after her?

He did have a responsibility to see to her protection. It didn't matter that her father could see to that much easier than he could. He'd gotten her into trouble. He should get her out of it. But that wasn't all of it. Maybe none of it. He wanted her. Plain and simple. Fair to her or not. He wanted her with a ferocity that astounded him.

Despite what his honor told him to do, he looked up the Ivy estate in Evergreen. It showed up on a map.

His cell rang.

"Korbin Maguire?"

"Yes."

"I'm Tennessee Kidd from the FBI. Julio Chavis gave me your number."

"Yes." Korbin felt stiff all over with anticipation. What had the agent discovered about Tony?

"He told me a little about your situation, but not all of it. Not what's all over the news."

Korbin wilted. What agent would help him if he believed what the news said?

"I didn't kill anyone," he said.

"That's what Julio said as well. He said you're being crucified for something you didn't do."

Korbin stiffened again, waiting for the agent to go on. He'd either help him or not.

"Tony Bartoszewicz checks out. I ran every background I could. He's got no arrests. His company is a bit questionable, but there's nothing any cop would raise a brow at. You're a better suspect than him, I'm afraid."

Not the information he'd hoped for. "Why is his company questionable?"

"A janitorial service that doesn't show much profit. Until recently. He's showing a three hundred percent markup in revenue. Could be that it just took some time to get the business up and running."

"Or it could be that he's using the business as a front."

"I found no evidence of that."

And evidence he'd need.

"Why'd you ask to have him checked out?" Tennessee asked. "Julio told me about Damen, but what connection does he have with Tony?"

"That's what I was hoping to find out. They're planning something. I just don't know what. What's Tony's business called?"

"United Janitorial Services. Headquartered in Miami, but he's got contracts all over the US and he's flown to Denver on numerous occasions."

Likely to meet with Damen. "He contracts janitors all over the US?"

"Appears so."

"Can you get me a list of them?"

"The contracts?" The agent sighed. "I don't know. You're a suspect in two homicides. If I help you I could get in trouble."

"I'll get them myself." He'd hack his way to the information if he had to.

"Sorry I can't be of more help. My brother-in-law is a good man and a good judge of character. I'm inclined to believe you're innocent. But—"

"Without evidence, yeah, I know." He was painfully aware of the need for evidence. "Thanks."

"If I find anything that will help you, I'll see that the proper authorities receive it."

He'd hand what evidence he found—if any—to the police, not him. "Thanks again."

After disconnecting, Korbin accepted that he'd never hear from the agent again. But if he did find evidence that would help him, he didn't have to turn it over to anyone. It was good knowing that the agent would. All Korbin needed now was a computer.

In order to do this right, Korbin had to go home and gather some gear. That would be risky. Cops would be watching the place. Although it had been torture waiting until dark with nothing to do but think about Savanna, he had. She consumed him. Memories of his wife faded to the recesses of his mind, and repentance kept him unsettled.

He drove Julio's car to a side street a few blocks away from his house in Lone Tree. The houses were spaced farther apart than average subdivisions, but there weren't any lone trees here. Each yard was impeccably landscaped. He stuck to shrubs and trees.

Nearing his house, he spotted an unmarked car parked on the street. It was too dark to see who was inside, but he'd bet someone was. Out of sight of the car, he made his way to the back door. He used a patio chair to break the window. It was cold out so the men in front had their windows up and hopefully wouldn't hear anything. With a quick glance back at the nearest house, he was fairly sure no one had seen or heard him.

Inside, he saw how everything was displaced and realized the police must have claimed probable cause and gone in and searched his house. His computers—all of them—were gone. Going out to his garage, he saw that his safe had been taken, too.

He couldn't very well go to an internet café and do what he needed to do. Now what?

Leaving his house, he jogged back to Julio's car and got in, undetected. He drove to Damen's house next, finding a hidden key he'd seen him use before. Damen hadn't thought to move it. He hadn't thought Korbin had noticed where he kept it. With a final glance around, he unlocked the front door to get in. There were no cops watching Damen's house. He went to Damen's computer and emailed a clever virus to Tony's main business contact. Someone other than him would likely handle general correspondence. With any luck, he'd be able to hack in tomorrow morning.

Korbin searched Damen's house and found nothing that he didn't already know, no suspicious people he'd been in contact with, no information. He didn't even find any correspondence with Tony, but he hadn't expected to. Damen would be careful about that.

Taking Damen's laptop with him, he left the house feeling a little like Harrison Ford in *The Fugitive*, always staying one step ahead of the law.

Savanna stared out the window of the formal living room, the only place she could find to be by herself other than her room. She wished she was home. She'd arrived at the Evergreen house to find her parents there. That had been a disappointment. She loved them dearly, but she desperately needed to be alone right now.

Rubbing her arms, she wondered how Korbin was doing. The news hadn't reported anything about him today, so he must still be at Julio's apartment. She pictured him there and then herself there with him. With none of this trouble in the way. Without the death of his wife holding him back.

But that's not how it was. He was probably glad she was gone. She was no longer a threat to his elevated worship of his dead wife. Savanna tried not to be a terrible person and be jealous of her, but that irrational part of her wouldn't stop taunting. She *was* jealous. Why did this always happen to her? Why couldn't she have a man she wanted? Why did he always, one way or another, gravitate to other women? Never her. Why? It was hard not to take it personally.

Did she want Korbin? They'd met so recently. Maybe the sex made her believe this was more than it was. Then again, if the sex was that great, then didn't that mean they were a good match? That their relationship was worth a risk? All of that didn't matter if Korbin couldn't let go of his wife.

"Savanna?"

Turning, she saw her mother stop in the doorway, flipping on a light. The sun had set with Savanna standing here.

"Why don't you come and join us for a movie downstairs?"

"I think I'll just go to bed."

Savanna had explained everything to her. Wearing jeans and a soft, long-sleeved knit shirt, her mother's blond bob was smooth and combed and her blue eyes sharp with knowledge.

"You've been through a lot, Savanna. You must feel like you're recovering from a disaster, but besides being chased by police and a gunman, what's got you so down?" her mother asked.

Savanna shrugged, trying to minimize her feelings. "Nothing. Just thinking."

Camille walked over to her and ran her hand down her arm. "You always were my sensitive one, especially with men."

"Mom, don't."

"Well, you were. Have you fallen for Korbin? Macon said there was something going on between the two of you."

Savanna wasn't sure her mother believed Korbin was innocent. Her mother was very open-minded. And she was the kind of parent who let her kids learn things on their own. She rarely intervened. Other than at her impromptu family gatherings.

"No. I haven't known him long enough."

"It's not like you to get close to a man so soon."

"No, it's not." Normally she was extra careful about waiting an acceptable amount of time before certain things happened—like having sex. "What has Macon told you?"

"He said he thinks you slept with him."

Another trait her mother had was that she said whatever was on her mind, regardless of the subject. In this case, sex.

"Mother…"

"It helps to talk about it, honey. Why did you sleep with him so soon?" Her mother rubbed her back the way she had when Savanna was a kid, crying over a scraped knee or something another kid said that hurt her feelings.

"I'm not sure. It just…happened." They were alone in the yurt, trapped by a snowstorm.

"How do you think he feels about it?"

Savanna scoffed. "Guilty. He's still in love with his wife."

Her mother's face fell in distress. "He's married?"

"Not anymore. His wife died a year ago."

"Oh." Camille nodded in understanding. "Well, maybe meeting you will help him get past it."

Savanna didn't see how. It had made him feel worse. "I don't want to be his rebound girl."

"Funny thing about love is that once it happens it doesn't go away and it doesn't matter when it happens. It just does." She patted Savanna's shoulder. "If it's meant to be, he'll come and find you."

Before or after his trouble cleared? How long would that take? What if he was sent to prison? And would Korbin come for her at all? She didn't believe it. She couldn't allow herself that luxury. She'd believed in men before and they always let her down.

"Did you leave because you felt he was too much of a risk? Are you afraid to feel the way you did for your fiancé?"

Savanna faced the window again. Her mother was reading her thoughts.

Her mother moved to stand beside her. "That's a yes if I've ever seen one."

"Mother…"

"You shouldn't let that stop you, Savanna. Aside from his being a murder suspect, if you believe in him, then you should go after him. Don't let fear stop you. If you felt strongly enough for him to sleep with him already, there might be something good between you. Don't let your past spook you away."

She hadn't been spooked with her fiancé or the lawyer. She liked calling him "the lawyer" instead of his name because it made him mean less.

"He's still mourning the death of his wife," she reminded her mother.

"I'm not sure I'd put too much emphasis on that. Everyone needs someone to love. And you said it happened a year ago. That's enough time. You need to learn to let go of your past and move on. Wipe the rejection off your shoulders and press forward without a single glance back."

"Forget my past?"

"The parts that aren't good, yes."

"What if I fall in love and he doesn't love me?"

"Then you feel the pain and you keep trying. Don't shortchange yourself. If you want to find real love, you have to stop shutting off your emotions. Feel them, no matter what the outcome may be."

"Is that what you'd do?"

"As soon as I met your father, I stopped having to do that. But before him? Sure. I was with men who disappointed me. I was hurt. Everyone gets hurt. You have to fail before you succeed, I guess. Isn't that what all the motivational speakers say? Isn't that what *you'd* say?"

Yes, it was. "I don't speak anymore."

"Macon told me. I hope that someday you take it back up. You're a good speaker. You inspire people. When you believe."

"But I don't believe in the same things I used to," she said. "Life doesn't always go the way you want it to."

"No, it goes the way it's *supposed* to."

Meaning, her fiancé and the lawyer weren't meant to be. Her mother had found true love. Savanna had always known that, and now her parents' love was an inspiration. And also a damper on her mood. Would Savanna ever find true love?

"Do you feel like he's the one?" her mother asked.

Savanna lowered her head, not certain what the answer was to that.

"Is it different than the other two?"

Something warm and radiant swelled inside of her. "Yes." She couldn't help beaming with the reply, breathy and flushed.

"Then why the long face? He'll come for you. You wouldn't feel this way if he didn't make you, which means he feels the same way."

"He's already found the love of his life, Mom. And she died."

"Has he been with other women since she died? A lot of men don't wait, you know."

More warmth enveloped her. "No. He hasn't."

"He sounds faithful, Savanna. Like a rare find…if he can clear his name."

Late the next morning, Korbin hacked into Tony's business network. He spent more than an hour going through financial records. It all appeared on the up-and-up, as the agent had said. He studied all the contractors. They all seemed legitimate, contracted to work in corporations all over the United States. There was one in Colorado.

Korbin saved copies of all the contracts on a flash drive anyway. Stuffing that into his jeans pocket, he went to the living room window, thinking of Savanna. She was always on his mind. It was just a question of how close to the forefront of his consciousness she made it.

The apartment phone rang. Korbin went there and answered. It was Julio.

"Have you seen the news?" Julio asked.

"When?" He hadn't had the television on.

"Just now. Breaking news. Your stepdaughter came forward and gave you an alibi for the night of the hit-and-run."

Korbin was speechless. How had Fallon done that? Had she lied? Why would she? She despised him. Or had she finally forgiven him?

"She said she was parked outside and planned to go in and talk to you about your wife's death, but she ended up deciding not to. But she was parked there for two hours."

"Did she see Damen take my car out of the garage?"

"The report didn't say."

She'd probably showed up right after that.

"She saw you in the house. You had your front blinds open. She was able to say the time you went up to bed. That's when she drove away."

That still left Collette's murder, and he still had the task of taking Damen down once and for all. He'd see him in prison, where he'd never be able to harm anyone else or come after him and Savanna. Plus, if he could expose whatever Damen was planning with Tony, he could discredit Damen's claim of seeing him at the time of Collette's murder. Shift suspicion from himself to Damen. Damen had a motive to hide his association with Tony, and had gone after Korbin in Wolf Creek. If Korbin could find out what they were planning, and he was pretty sure it was illegal, police would check to see if Damen had lied about seeing Korbin at the time of Collette's murder. The email would prove his association with Tony.

"Are police still looking for me?" he asked.

"That, I don't know."

Pounding on his door and the ringing bell gave him ominous déjà vu.

"Did you tell anyone where I am?" he asked Julio.

"Only my brother-in-law."

Who could have been discovered, or could have confessed when confronted with the call he'd made to Korbin. Agent Kidd would not have protected him if it meant he'd have to break the law.

"Time to go. I'll be in touch. Thanks for everything, Julio."

"Good luck, my friend."

Korbin grabbed his jacket and the laptop he'd taken from Damen and went out onto the balcony. He'd thought about how he'd get away if this happened. Hopefully it worked.

Using the fire escape, he reached the second floor and dropped to the ground from there. He'd parked Julio's car there and was in and backing up as police emerged onto the balcony and spotted him.

Korbin raced out of the back parking lot. A police car appeared at the entrance and he had to drive off the curb to avoid a collision. The lights went on and the siren whistled as the policeman started to chase him.

He could not get caught.

Korbin raced the car, one of those new Volvos. He'd never outrun a cop. He drove through the neighborhood, turning as many corners as he could. Another police car joined in the chase and Korbin's confidence faltered. He got out onto the highway and raced for the next exit, which would take him to Golden.

He lost sight of one police car at the exit. The other missed it and was stuck on the highway.

Korbin cut off a car getting onto another highway and weaved in and out of traffic. He took the next turn and another into a neighborhood. Dodging a slow-moving minivan, he turned again and got back onto the highway. He sped as fast as he could to the next exit with no sight of police cars.

Going through the old town of Golden, he maneuvered the back roads until he made it into the foothills. On a two-lane highway, he watched his rearview mirror. No sign of the cop.

He didn't relax yet. Staying on the back roads, he drove to Highway 285 near Morrison and sped up the winding mountain road toward Evergreen.

Realizing where he was headed, Korbin checked himself. He wasn't going to seek refuge. He couldn't even be sure he'd be safe there. He could trust Savanna not to turn him in, but what about her family? Would she be alone? Macon might be there. Going there might be a big risk. But he found he could not stop himself from going there. He was going for Savanna.

Chapter 12

Sitting on a pillowy bench seat in the window of the upper-level turret, Savanna couldn't stay focused on the book. She leaned her head against the glass. There were lots of windows in the Evergreen mansion. This place was good for her to hide out a while, but it wasn't home. It was much more formal than home. The cobblestone circular drive matched the light-colored stone of the home. Trees had been planted just so. And inside, she felt she disturbed perfection every time she sat down or put a drink on a table.

Movement on the drive caught her attention. A familiar white Volvo drew nearer. Her heart registered who it was a fraction of a second before her brain did. Mouth dropping open, she jerked her head off the window and inhaled a much-needed breath.

There was only one way Korbin could have gotten inside the gate.

"Savanna!" her mother yelled. You had to yell in this house.

Savanna stayed where she was. Her mother had let him in.

What was he doing here? At first she was glad, but then she became irritated. Was he that inconsiderate of her feelings? Did he know how she felt? How did she feel?

"Savanna!"

Macon had gone back to his movie set this morning and it was just her and Mom and Dad. Dad was working from home and was with a director in the basement, talking business.

The man in the Volvo was no director. Lawbreaker. Fugitive. He could star in one of Dad's movies.

He parked the car in front of the sweeping stone stairs that led to the entry. The valet stepped up to the car as Korbin got out of the driver's seat. His tall, muscular frame made her ache for him, and also made her fight her attraction to him. A slight breeze ruffled his dark hair.

He spoke to the valet and climbed the stairs, disappearing from her view.

"Savanna Ivy!"

Her mother's impatience propelled her off the bench seat. But she was slow to make her way through the enormous house. As she reached the wide stairs descending to the entry, she heard Korbin talking to her mother.

"My apologies, again, for the unannounced visit," he said. "Thanks for letting me through your security. It's pretty impressive."

"Nonsense. Savanna has told us all about you."

"I hope nothing too disparaging."

How could it have been if her mother let him in?

"Being wanted by the law is disparaging, Mr. Maguire," her mother said, "but we trust our daughter's judgment."

Savanna took each stair in a slow descent. When she saw Korbin, she stopped. He looked up and the simmering heat of his gaze struck her.

After a moment he snapped out of his trance. "Hello, Savanna."

His deep, rich voice fanned her most sensitive nerves. Going rigid in defense, she stepped down the rest of the stairs much more briskly.

She stopped next to her mother, facing Korbin. "What brings you here?"

He cleared his throat. "I'm not sure I can answer that."

"Police?"

Camille gave her daughter a sharp glance.

"No. They found out where I was staying, but..."

The way he looked into her eyes explained enough. He'd ignored her wishes and come anyway. The police hadn't driven him here. He hadn't come expecting to be offered a hiding place. He couldn't stay away.

"Well." Camille clapped her hands together. "It's close to dinnertime. Let's have a barbecue."

"It's the middle of winter," Savanna said.

Camille waved her hand, more of a swat. "You know your dad."

She led the way through the entry and then down another set of stairs to the basement. Korbin took notice of the house, but in an interested way, not an awed or greedy way. He came from money. Savanna found it so refreshing not to have to wonder if it was her money or name that had brought him here.

In the lower-level rec room, Camille asked a butler to

bring everything they'd need for hamburgers. Her dad was sitting at the bar talking on the phone. The director must have left.

"Ah." Jackson Ivy stood and kissed Savanna's cheek. "This must mean the workday is over." Next, he kissed his wife, who glowed with a smile and kissed him back. Jackson turned to Korbin and with all the kissing going on, didn't lean in for one. "We're not traditionally French, but kisses are sometimes our thing."

"I'm not French, either." Korbin shook his hand. He refused to kiss a man. "Maguire. Irish through and through."

Jackson laughed and Korbin realized he'd only been teasing. Damn theatrical types.

"This is Korbin, Dad," Savanna said.

The congenial greeting died out a bit and Jackson withdrew his hand. Not surprising. What father wouldn't be protective of his daughters?

Korbin turned to Savanna. "Did you hear the news?"

Savanna perked up, full attention.

"We don't watch a lot of television here," Camille said.

"My stepdaughter gave me an alibi for the hit-and-run," Korbin said.

"You have a stepdaughter?" Savanna asked. His wife's daughter had lost a mother. Not so shocking by itself but why hadn't Korbin told her? Another secret he hadn't divulged until he had to.

"Fallon Ellgard. She's twenty-three. Niya had her when she was sixteen. We lost touch after her mother died."

Savanna saw how he drifted off into thought. He must have been close to the girl. Was he thinking of a broken family, once a unit? Perhaps the things he didn't speak about were the things that hurt him the most. But they were also the things that would bring about change. This trying time for him was difficult, but maybe it was exactly what he needed. He'd already refused to help Damen.

"She must be so devastated," Camille said. "That's such a young age to lose a mom. She's just starting out on her own."

Korbin nodded, clearly not welcoming the subject. His bad choices had led to her mother being shot. The girl must blame him. Her grief would be hard to comprehend.

"She's a smart girl," Korbin said. "Accepted into Harvard. Pretty. Grown-up for her age. She always was. I think it was losing her dad to cancer when she was eight that did it. She's lost both her parents. I had a good relationship with her, but she was close to her dad. She told me once that she was afraid she'd forget what he looked like." He stopped. Now the girl would fear she'd forget how her mother looked. What he left out of that unexpected disclosure was that he missed her.

Savanna saw that her mom and dad had taken notice along with her.

"Have you talked with her?" Jackson asked.

"She refuses to talk to me."

Confirmation that the girl did blame him. Maybe that's why he never mentioned her. It was one more dark memory from his wife's murder.

"Well, she came forward to give you an alibi," Camille said. "Is it true?"

"It must be. She came to see me, but something stopped her from going to the door. She must have thought about it a long time, though. The police said she was out there for two hours."

Watching him. Maybe that had been enough. A first step toward forgiveness. It also gave a glimpse into the relationship they'd begun to build. His stepdaughter must not want to live without at least some semblance of family. Fallon meant a lot to Korbin.

"How did you ever end up a fugitive?" Camille asked. "You seem like such a nice man."

Korbin looked at her as though he was considering how to answer, or maybe he was figuring it out as he went along. "My parents weren't the most loving people when I grew up. I didn't like their way of life, the formality. I suppose I rebelled and that put me on the wrong path. I barely spoke to them at Niya's funeral."

"Good heavens, why ever not?" Camille asked.

"I disappointed them. They expressed their condolences, but they might as well have been distant acquaintances. I can't imagine what they're thinking right now."

"Probably the worst," Jackson said. "You should talk to them, son."

Korbin met Jackson's gaze but didn't respond. Her father had a way of speaking the truth in not so many words. But he meant no harm, and that came across. If Korbin wasn't offended, he didn't show it. He just seemed tormented over the broken relationship and how to mend it.

Savanna put her hand on his arm. "I'm sure you'll get a chance."

He turned to her, uncertainty shrouding him, but warmth at her gentle concern and care easing away his tension.

"Well." Jackson clapped his hands together once. "I've got some burgers to grill."

"I'll help you." Camille went with him to the table where all the food had been placed.

"Scared them away," Korbin said with a wry grin.

"They're just giving you some space. You're a big man, and not one who looks like he makes confessions like that."

"Try never."

Savanna suspected his mood had everything to do with his stepdaughter. He longed to maintain a relationship with her and she may not let him. There was nothing tying them together anymore, and his criminal past might prevent her from letting him try.

With her parents busy with dinner, Savanna was left with Korbin beginning to regard her much differently. His trouble faded to the background for a moment as seeing each other again came into the forefront of all else. His eyes changed, awareness of her heating them up. Feeling an answering reaction, Savanna tensed.

"Agent Kidd called about Tony," he said, breaking the moment. "He checked out, but he runs a janitorial contracting company that only recently began showing significant profits." He pulled out a flash drive and showed it to her.

"What did you find?" Taking the flash drive, she went to a desk on the far side of the room and awakened the computer.

"I copied the list of all the contactors he employs," Korbin said, following her. "I figured we could go talk to the one in Colorado."

She looked up and back at him when he said "we."

"If you want to go with me."

Irrationally she clamored to gush out a *yes*, thrilled that he wanted to be with her. But wanting to be with her now and wanting to be with her indefinitely were two different things, and she could not forget his baggage, which might be too heavy to take on a new relationship. There was also the danger. Would she really put herself in danger to be with him?

He was an innocent man. Could she just as easily abandon him?

She faced the computer, opening the list. There were about twenty contractors. She read the names of companies and one of them triggered something significant.

"Some of the companies are big," Korbin said.

"That's exactly what I was thinking. Hart is a big bank."

"There are a few banks."

"A water treatment facility." Savanna pointed.

"In LA."

Savanna checked the others. One of the companies in Colorado provided emergency communication systems services. She began to feel a chill crawl down her back from the crown of her head.

"Does this look like what I think it looks like?"

"These could all be terrorist targets."

She looked up at him, this time with no warmth between them. "Why keep records of their employment?"

"To appear legitimate to the hiring company. Even the FBI didn't find anything wrong. Agent Kidd only had a hunch, and he didn't see this list. The companies wouldn't see it, either, only information on the contractor hired."

Facing the computer again, she wondered aloud, "How did Tony link up with these people?"

"He must have known them ahead of time. This has

been planned for a long time. And Damen is helping him."

"How?"

"He wanted me involved. Maybe he needed someone to design a virus."

Forget explosives. This was electronic warfare. Take down vital infrastructure. Banks. Water treatment facilities. Emergency systems. If they succeeded it could be catastrophic.

"They have to be stopped," she said, deciding right then that she was going with Korbin.

"We have no proof."

"Then we have to get it." Where would they begin? "Macon said Damen has a twin brother."

"He does."

"Maybe he knows something."

"It's worth a try." He took out his wallet and found a piece of paper with Agent Kidd's number written down. Then he went to a landline and made the call, putting it on speaker so Savanna could hear.

"Agent Kidd."

"I have something for you," Korbin said.

"Maguire?"

"I need your email."

"Hey, sorry for what happened. I didn't rat you out. It just so happens I have competition for a promotion around here. He found out I'd been talking to my brother-in-law and since he saw the news, he did some digging and learned about the apartment. He must have staked you out or something."

"I got away. Give me your email."

The agent fell quiet for a bit. "What have you got?"

"Maybe something big. Really big. Like a terrorist plot." Korbin explained everything they knew.

"That does sound big. If we can prove it. I'll see what I can do. In the meantime, I've got an update for you on the murder evidence."

Savanna met Korbin's anticipatory look.

"I just found out that a small amount of blood and some other tissue was discovered under one of Collette's fingernails. It looks as though she tried to scratch him and caught him at least partially. Now all we need is a DNA match. Will it be yours?"

"No. It'll be Damen's," Korbin replied.

The next afternoon, Dad was like one of his action heroes.

"I didn't know you had a gun safe here." Savanna took in the ten-by-ten room filled with every imaginable gun and rifle. "Or is this a panic room?"

Jackson handed Korbin an intimidating automatic rifle with a scope mounted to the top and then a couple of pistols, one with a silencer.

"I always said everyone could come to this house and be safe." He examined another pistol and then handed it to her. "This one will be perfect for you."

Standing at the doorway, Camille didn't look pleased. "I still don't see why we can't leave this up to police. Can't the two of them just stay here until it all blows over?"

If the DNA matched Damen's it would only be a matter of time before he was arrested.

Jackson turned to her, Korbin doing the same but not saying anything.

"Korbin is being set up, but the police will still take

him in," Jackson said. "He won't be free to do his own investigating."

"I suppose you have a point," Camille said worriedly as she looked at Korbin. "You aren't going to shoot at police, are you?"

Korbin chuckled. "No. Just run from them."

"Until he can prove his innocence," Savanna said. The guns were for Damen and Tony and anyone else who felt motivated to snuff them out to protect the terrorist plan.

Camille went to Savanna and took her hands. "Are you sure, honey? I don't want you to go. It's so dangerous."

"Not if we're careful," Korbin said. Damen was still in the hospital.

"Honey." Jackson moved close and put his arm around her. "It'll be okay." He rubbed her shoulder. "She has Korbin, and there comes a time when you have to let your kids live their own lives."

"But this is different."

Damen had shot at her at her house, but he'd nearly killed her at Chavis's cabin. Her parents didn't know that and they didn't need to. Although her dad supported her, she could hear the worry in his tone. He had to stop himself from refusing to let her go. Or maybe he knew she'd go anyway, no matter what they said or did. She was old enough to make her own choices.

"I promise I'll bring her back to you," Korbin said. "Both of you."

Savanna glanced at him, asking herself for the millionth time why she was doing this. Why go with him? Ever since he'd gotten stuck on her road she'd been involved in his situation, but this wasn't only about him anymore. If she could help prevent a threat to national security, she was not the type of person who could sit around in a high-security mansion and do nothing. Besides, it wasn't as if they were taking this on by themselves. Korbin's contact at the FBI was helping. Pretty soon, law enforcement would see that Korbin was on their side, and that he was innocent.

Jackson took out a ring of keys and handed them to Korbin. "This is a Class A motor home. You'll stick out but you'll be comfortable."

In other words, it was an expensive motor home.

"Lincoln used one of those when he helped Sabrina, didn't he?"

"He stole a used one," her mother said, disapproving, but not for the substandard quality. Her son had stolen something.

Jackson grinned his affection. "There are two passports in the desk drawer in case you need them," her dad said. "And a driver's license for Korbin."

"When did you get all of that done?" She eyed Korbin.

"This morning," Jackson answered.

He must have some great connections. She decided not to ask further on it. Instead, she moved forward and looped her arm over his shoulder. "Thanks, Dad." She kissed his cheek. "You're the best dad ever."

He gave her arm a squeeze. "You just come home to your mother. I won't be able to live with her if anything happens to any of her kids."

Although he made a joke of it, Savanna wasn't fooled. He was serious.

"I'll be happy when all of my kids settle down and stay out of trouble. The only trouble I want to hear about is labor pains."

"You could make a really interesting biography on us." Savanna went to her mother and gave her the same show of affection. "Don't worry. Korbin's going to clear his name and everything will be all right. You can plan a big party when Damen and Tony are arrested." And anyone else involved in the scheme.

Camille walked with Jackson behind them out of the gun room. She and Korbin were all packed. Camille had gathered enough clothes for them to get by, along with hats and sunglasses and jackets to conceal their looks.

In the circular drive, the motor home was ready for them. Savanna said goodbye to her parents, and Korbin shook Jackson's hand. Her mother wasn't so amenable. It was one thing to want her daughter to find a faithful, honorable man, and quite another to send her off with an armed fugitive.

As they climbed into the RV, Savanna felt on the verge of an adventure and something else. Ever since Agent Kidd had revealed that DNA evidence had been found, the furnace of desire that tempted her so burned hotter. Innocent, Korbin was a much more palatable bachelor. One less thing to stand between them. She'd done this before, though. She'd erred on the side of optimism and didn't look objectively at the situation—or the man. She was forever a believer in good. Everyone had good in them. What she was no good at doing was stopping to question if the person was good *for her*.

In hindsight, the lawyer wasn't. If she had looked closer, she'd have seen it long before she caught him with his ex-wife. Optimism had gotten the best of her. The same had been true with her fiancé. All a person had to do was want something to have it. But in love, both the man and the woman had to want it. She had no radar for what a man wanted. And she realized now that she had to raise her standards for what she wanted. Handsome, successful and compatible were not enough. He had to be handsome, successful, compatible, and honest with both himself and her. He had to be as invested in her as she was in him, and be truthful about how he felt.

Korbin was all of those things. If he didn't pursue her, it wouldn't be because he hadn't been honest. That made falling for him that much more complicated. Dangerous. And irresistible.

Chapter 13

Demarco went back into the hospital room to the chair he'd occupied for hours. Damen was still unconscious. When he'd first seen him the sight had shocked him. One of his eyes was purple and swollen shut. Cuts were all over his face. He looked like a torture victim. Bullied and beaten. It filled him with rage and reminded him of a time in high school.

The quarterback for the school team had it out for Damen after he stole his girlfriend's wallet. He'd stolen the wallet because she'd ridiculed him for asking her out. Back then, Damen had believed anything was possible, that he was capable of doing anything he set his mind to. That he was worthy, even though he was picked on in school.

The girl had laughed and said, "Why would I want to go out with *you*?"

The kids around had all laughed and then the quarterback had appeared, slipping his arm around her waist while everyone snickered and called him names. Damen never knew it, but Demarco had witnessed the whole thing.

The incident had so humiliated Damen, he'd retaliated by stealing the girl's wallet and spending her money on hemorrhoid cream, which he'd put in her locker along with her empty wallet. Everyone had known Damen was the one to put it there.

The quarterback had followed Damen home from school one night, and before Damen reached their place, jumped him and beat him up. Their mom had taken him to the doctor and Damen had refused to press charges. So Demarco had taken matters into his own hands.

He'd followed the quarterback home with two of his biggest friends and they'd beaten him up. Before leaving him, Demarco whispered into the quarterback's ear, "If I see you within ten feet of my brother ever again, I'll kill you."

He'd been alarmed that he'd possessed the darkness to say those words, and had not said them since. But the quarterback had not bothered Damen again.

His brother began to stir on the bed.

Demarco rushed over to the side of the bed. Damen blinked the one eye groggily. He was slowly coming to.

Demarco waited for him to look at him and for him to focus.

"Where am I?" Damen asked in a raspy voice.

"Pagosa Springs hospital. Do you remember why?"

His brother screwed up his brow, and that turned into a wince. "Maguire."

Demarco felt a strong impulse to retaliate against Korbin. His love for his brother compelled him. Or was it a conditioned instinct? He'd protected Damen for so long he couldn't react in any other way. He could almost forget about Collette.

"I told you not to cause trouble with him, Damen."

His brother managed a weak laugh that made him wince. "Demarco. Always looking out for me."

Demarco put his hand on his shoulder briefly. "You're my brother."

His one good eye blinked. "Even after I punch you, you come here for me?"

"I'm trying to help you."

"Haven't you been listening? It's time for you to stop protecting me."

Frustration and sadness pushed tears into his eyes. "I don't want to see you get hurt. I've always hated that, Damen. I only wanted you to be happy."

"I was happy before Korbin did this to me." His cut and bruised mouth curved into a swollen smile.

Demarco laughed. "Stop joking about this. I want my brother back."

"I never left you, Demarco." He lifted his hand and put it on Demarco's. "It's going to be okay."

No, it wasn't. Didn't he see that? How could he think anything would be okay after he killed someone?

"Why did you go after Korbin?" he asked. "He's going to be arrested. Isn't that enough for revenge?" He didn't let on what he knew.

Damen's smile faded.

"Did he discover something about your drug dealing?"

Damen stared at him, his hand sliding off his chest and coming to rest on the bedside.

"You can tell me. I'm your twin brother."

"No, Demarco. Some things I can't tell you. You should just go back to your perfect life with your perfect business and perfect wife. Let me take care of my own affairs. I'm better at it than you think."

Is that how he saw him now? Was he envious? Of him?

"Like murder?"

Damen's expression froze. For a long moment he studied him. "What?"

"I saw you that morning," Demarco said.

Still, his expression didn't change, not that there was much going on there due to a lot of skin damage. "What morning?"

He'd had plenty of time to think on the way here. The detective. His wife. Damen. All of it. As torn as he was over what he saw, he had to at least let his brother in on the fact that he knew. Deciding what to do about it may depend on how his brother reacted.

"The morning after you killed Collette," he said.

Rapid blinks of Damen's eye were all that gave away his surprise. "What?"

"I saw you leave your house with a gun and I saw what you did with it."

For a long time Damen stared up at him from the hospital bed, no doubt deciding how to respond. Deny or tell the truth? "What were you doing there?"

"I've noticed a change in you. You're secretive and you avoid me. I needed to talk to you. I went to your house and you were just leaving. You looked strange and I saw you put a gun in your pants. I followed you."

He pinned him with another long look. "Why didn't you tell me?"

"I didn't have the chance. You left for Wolf Creek."

"Why didn't you tell me when you came to Julio's cabin?"

"I didn't want to believe you did it."

Demarco felt the bond they had still gripping him.

"I didn't. Korbin did."

His lie was a betrayal. "Don't lie to me, Damen. I've been in denial over this. After I saw what you did, I was worried about why you had a gun and why you disposed of it. And then I just didn't want to accept what it must mean. And then I saw the news. You said you saw Korbin Maguire leave Collette's house at the time of the murder."

Damen said nothing.

"You lied," Demarco said, the hurt deeper now. Saying it out loud, confronting him, made it real. His brother's betrayal cut him to the bone. He didn't want to lose him. But he was. And he was furious with him for doing that to him. To them.

"I can explain," Damen said.

"Really?" How had his twin veered into such serious trouble? "You can explain why you're justified in framing another man for your crimes?"

"Demarco—"

"Too bad his stepdaughter came forward and cleared him of the hit-and-run."

"What?"

"Oh." He feigned sympathy. "You didn't know?" He leaned over the bed, bracing his hands on the thin mattress. "She must have arrived just after you stole his car. Yeah. She was parked out front for a couple of hours. Long enough to thwart your plan."

Damen eyed his face. "What's gotten into you?"

"Did you plan to kill Collette after that?" He had

to hear him say it. To confirm it. That it hadn't been planned. That it had been a crime of passion.

"No. Demarco. I saw her meet Korbin. I went to her house after that and we talked. She said she did meet Korbin but she lied about why. I was so angry. After I ran that man over, I had an idea."

"To frame Korbin. Revenge."

"Did you plan to kill Collette?"

Damen shook his head, rolling it slightly on the pillow. "No. After I ran that man over, I went to her house. I needed an alibi . We argued…"

And then he'd killed her. It hadn't been planned. Only the hit-and-run had been planned. Damen had seen what he wanted to see, what his weak ego had seen. "So you decided to kill her?"

"He was going to take her away from me."

And there it was. The truth. An awful truth. "Was he, Damen? Was he going to take her away from you? Or was Collette tired of being treated like a dog? Wasn't it she who was going away from you? It was her choice, not Korbin's. Am I right?"

"Stop it."

"You had it all figured out in your mind, didn't you? Everyone's out to get you. The world against Damen. So Damen fought back."

Damen shook his head. "No."

His anger reached a boiling point. How could Damen have done this? How could he be so stupid? Did he actually think he could get away with it? "You always had it in you. You always fought and bullied your way to respect. When in fact you're just a puny man shaking a big fist."

"Why did you come here if that's how you feel?"

He hadn't felt this way until now. Right now. "I wasn't sure how I felt. But now I am. My own twin brother…a *murderer*. You repulse me."

Damen blanched at first. Finally, something he said penetrated. But it was short-lived. Then grim resolve settled in. "What are you going to do?"

Demarco's opinion of him had mattered for a few seconds and then Damen was back to fighting the world. "You'd rather kill Collette than let her go?" Demarco shook his head in disgust. "What happened to you?" He was so angry on so many levels he could barely see straight. He felt like a fool for enabling his brother for so many years. And yet he felt a horrible, gaping hole opening up in his chest.

As Damen continued to look at him impassively, Demarco's fury and pain mounted. "I asked you a question."

Damen merely blinked. Absolute on his path of destruction. He believed no one could help him. Even Demarco. He had stepped in too many times. When Damen had begun to falter, Demarco should have let him find his own way. How different would things be today if he had let the bullies run their course?

The sound of a knock on the hospital room door tabled Demarco's next attack. One last attempt to talk sense into his brother. He was slipping further and further away and there was nothing he could do to stop it. He'd lost Damen years ago. When? He could not say exactly, only knew he should have distanced himself. Twin or not, Damen was right about one thing. He had to find his own way.

"Ah. He awakens," the doctor said as he entered the room.

Demarco stepped back and watched as the man checked Damen and half listened as he asked several questions. How would this change things between them? Damen had committed murder. What would he do knowing he'd seen him throw the murder weapon away?

He caught Damen's glance and saw the threatened look in his eyes. Demarco met it with indifference and a curse that resonated inside his head. A curse to his brother for causing this tragedy.

What are you going to do? his brother mouthed as the doctor turned his back to write a few notes.

Demarco met his paranoid eye and didn't respond, sickened that he still didn't have an answer to that.

"When can I leave this place?" Damen asked the doctor.

"Let's see how you do today." The doctor wouldn't give an exact time or day of his release and Demarco was glad. The longer Damen was in here the better.

"There's a policeman waiting to have a word with you," the doctor said. "Two of them."

"Here?" Damen seemed surprised that the police were here. And then the confusion cleared. They were here to talk to him about his condition and what had caused it. "Right. Send them in."

Demarco stepped back farther as the doctor left and the first police detective entered. While he introduced himself, the second one entered and gave Demarco a jolt. It was Gunderman. He stayed back and leaned against the wall, glancing at him with a nod of greeting.

The other detective had finished up small talk with Damen and now asked about how he ended up in the hospital. Demarco began to listen.

"How did you know Mr. Maguire would be at Julio Chavis's cabin?" the detective asked.

"They're friends," Damen said. "It was a guess." He struggled to sit up.

Demarco stepped forward to help him, an automatic impulse. His brother looked at him in surprise. He adjusted the pillows behind his back, catching the way Gunderman noticed.

"Why did you try to find him?" the detective asked.

"He killed my girlfriend." Damen slid a glance up to Demarco, silently daring him to intervene.

"So you planned to…what…?"

"Make sure he was arrested." Damen's sarcasm revealed the lie. He'd gone to kill Korbin.

"Why didn't you call police and inform them of this cabin?"

Damen didn't answer right away. "Maybe I needed to talk to him first."

His belligerence shouldn't come as a shock to Demarco. His brother had never been a sharp cheese.

Gunderman moved forward then, standing beside the other detective. Damen looked at him with his one eye.

"I'll take it from here," he said to the other detective. That one nodded and left the room.

"I'm Detective Gunderman from the Denver Police Department." He showed him his badge.

"Are you aware that Mr. Maguire now has an alibi for the hit-and-run?" At Damen's silence, Gunderman said, "That means Mr. Maguire's car was stolen."

Damen stared at the man a few seconds. "Okay…?"

"Did you steal it?"

"Me?"

The cops were onto him. They suspected he may have stolen Korbin's car. But why? What had made them think that was a possibility?

Gunderman was still waiting for a response.

"No," Damen said.

"Where were you that night?"

"You asked me that already. I was working at home until late and then went over to Collette's. After seeing Korbin leave her house, I found her dead."

"Can anyone verify you were at home?"

Damen smirked. "I live alone."

"Mr. Maguire told us he met this woman at the Laughing Grass Pizzeria. The day before her murder. Were you aware of that?"

"No."

Demarco saw how Gunderman remained calm but Demarco sensed he knew Damen was lying. "Here's the problem I have, Mr. Ricchetti. Mr. Maguire's car was found abandoned after a fatal hit-and-run, and then your girlfriend turns up murdered. All in the same night. How does that happen?"

Damen stared at him. He was beginning to realize he might be in trouble. Real trouble.

"I don't know," Damen finally said.

"Mr. Maguire said your girlfriend was afraid you'd hurt her. Her sister and a close friend said the same thing."

"I never would have hurt Collette. I loved her. Korbin is lying."

Demarco found it remarkable that his brother had said "loved" instead of "love." And it wasn't because she was dead. He'd loved her until he thought that she wanted another man and that she was going to leave him.

After a moment watching Damen, Gunderman nodded a few times, noncommittal, disbelieving.

"Are you planning to return to Denver when you're released?" he finally asked.

"Yes."

Once more, he nodded. Then he turned to Demarco. "Can I have a word with you outside?"

Demarco glanced at his brother and then said, "Sure."

He followed the detective into the hallway, where they faced each other.

"Have you given this some thought since we last talked?" Gunderman asked.

He'd thought of nothing else. His life had pretty much come to a screeching halt ever since he'd seen Damen toss that gun.

Gunderman put his hands on his hips with a frustrated sigh. "I'm going to get down to the truth one way or the other."

He wasn't ready to throw his brother to the wolves. Not when he was just inside the hospital room.

"Do you think my brother killed his girlfriend, Detective?" he asked.

"We're looking at every possibility. At this point he's a person of interest."

Demarco was tempted to blurt out what he saw, and mortified that he'd even consider doing so. His own brother. Except his brother wasn't his brother anymore. He wasn't the boy from his childhood. The defenseless brother. He was a criminal.

"I understand the position you're in," Gunderman said. "He's your twin brother. You have an instinct to protect him. But if you're hiding something crucial to this case, you can be prosecuted right along with him."

"Well, I wouldn't want that to happen," he said with a

note of lightness. Inside, he thought of his wife and what prosecution would do to her.

"You have my card," Gunderman said, then gave him a wave in farewell and started down the hall. Demarco watched him go and then intended to go back into the hospital room, but nausea took him to the bathroom before he could go in and face his brother again.

Splashing cold water on his face, he stared at himself in the mirror, eyes round and shadowed with dark circles, his face gaunt.

When Demarco was ready to leave the restroom, he went out into the hall. Standing outside Damen's room, he didn't go inside. His brother was someone else now and it was too late to save him.

Abandoning his own twin brother was the hardest thing he'd ever do. He felt hollow and lost. Wretched. There in the hall, he finally admitted to himself that there was no saving his brother. Damen had turned to crime. Demarco was no criminal, and he refused to be dragged into his crisis. Instead of going back into the room, where he was certain Damen was nervously waiting for him, Demarco started down the hall.

Damen would have to find his own way back to Denver. Now the only question Demarco had was, how much trouble would he be in if he turned in the murder weapon? He'd hidden evidence. Aided Damen in murder. What kind of a price would he pay for that?

Chapter 14

"How well do you know this man?" Savanna looked at Korbin as she walked beside him in snow boots, jeans and classy polka-dot jacket. He was in a black parka with the zipper undone, making him appear even bigger than he was.

"Not well. I've met him a few times."

He rang the doorbell. A few seconds later, an attractive woman answered. Her eyes darted back and forth between them on the other side of the glass outer door and then fixed on Korbin.

"Korbin?" She sounded unsteady. "What are you doing here?"

"We need to talk to Demarco."

"He isn't here. He went to Pagosa Springs to get Damen." She eyed him warily.

"I didn't kill Collette," Korbin said. "Damen set me up."

"Like I said…he isn't here."

"When will he be back? Where is he staying?"

After a brief hesitation and more scrutiny, she said, "I don't know when he'll be back, but he's got an auction tomorrow night. I doubt he'll miss that. It's black-tie. One of his promotional events."

Earlier, Savanna had left Korbin at their RV campsite and went shopping for attire for the evening. Then she prepared in the bathroom of the motor home. When she finished, she gave herself one final appraisal in the mirror. Blue eyes conservatively lined and lips glossed, hair artfully pinned up with a few curls dangling, she had to say she looked good. She hadn't dressed up like this in a long time. Smooth skin above the pretty, glittering beads of the scooped neckline needed no adornment. The diamond earrings were enough. The band of beads ran around her back in a strap and another dipped low above her rear. The A-line chiffon dress wasn't form-fitting, but flattered enough of her figure to be striking. She experienced a second of trepidation before leaving the bedroom. One look at her in this and Korbin would have a challenge set out for him. She didn't mean to entice him.

Walking out into the living area of the high-end RV, Savanna saw him standing near the side door. The slideouts made the RV feel as though they were in a stationary home, luxurious and spacious. He didn't move as he saw her, but his eyes roamed all over her, lingering at her neckline, where a demure portion of cleavage was exposed. The dress inspired innocence, but hinted at seduction. He himself appeared larger than usual in his black satin-lapel tuxedo—shoulders broader, arms thicker. In his rugged face, pale gray eyes glowed with intensity that she had sparked. Dark, thick hair stuck out in all the right places, roguish and beckoning a woman's fingers. And yet he was a classic gentleman with the black bow tie against a trim white shirt.

He met her gaze as she came to a stop before him. "What are you doing to me?"

She smiled without responding, but thinking, *snagging you*.

He put his hand on her back, the bare portion below the strap and above the low hem. She preceded him out the door and she discovered that he'd arranged for a car to pick them up.

"Putting the fake IDs to work, I see," she said.

He opened the back door for her. "It has tinted windows."

Clever man. She sat in the back and he climbed in after her. The driver said nothing, the glass window shut between them. All the way there, a living tension hummed. The challenge of breaking through a guarded heart—his—and letting down her own guard. A thread of restraint held her back.

"Whose estate is being sold at this auction?" she asked. A much safer subject.

"The daughter of an animated-film producer sold her multimillion-dollar estate in Wyoming. This auction contains everything she's getting rid of."

"Small world." Her dad probably knew the woman.

"She collects antiques and the exhibit will have some rare art."

"Sounds like a score for Demarco." He didn't seem to live large. His house was modest.

"He doesn't hold events like these very often."

The car stopped in front of the downtown hotel where

the viewing event was held. Tomorrow the auction would last all day. Korbin opened the lobby door for Savanna and put his hand on her lower back again. Indulging himself? They drew many admiring looks, the kind that young, handsome couples often drew.

Reaching the ballroom, a crowd had already assembled. Tables of appetizers and several bars were spread among displays of antiques. Crystal chandeliers gave off low light. Easels showcased pricey paintings and more hung on the walls, some with their own spotlight.

Savanna was taken in. While Korbin searched the throng, she stopped at a display of beaded jewelry that had once belonged to an Indian woman. There was a story about her printed on a plaque. She moved on to some paintings, studying each one. A floral painting caught her eye, an abstract with varying splashes of soft yellow, orange and green. It would stand out in the right room but not overwhelm.

Korbin leaned closer to her ear in the din of voices and classical music. "There's Demarco."

Three men stood near the opposite wall, a five-by-eight painting looming above, the outer edges of spotlights highlighting a bald spot on one and the fine show of gray on another. The one in the middle was the youngest, with thick brown hair and the look of a bulldog, except he had a really long nose. The one to his left was taller and thinner, more of a Great Dane.

"Demarco is the older one," Korbin said.

The near-forty, slightly graying man. He was fit, trim and about the same height as the Great Dane. She immediately picked up that the two he spoke with didn't belong here. She couldn't say why. Demarco looked every bit his part as host and tomorrow's auctioneer of this collection of rare pieces. The other two wore no ties and held themselves like construction workers. Legs apart. Paws around the top of champagne glasses.

Friends of Damen's?

Demarco leaned in, speaking almost harshly, and then shooting furtive looks as though occasionally remembering where he was. An elderly couple passed and Demarco put on his auctioneer face to greet them. The two men he'd been talking to moved away, going to stand at a tall cocktail table and observe the crowd.

The elderly couple moved on and Demarco turned to some new guests.

"Let's go say hello."

Savanna meandered through the crowd and waited for Demarco to notice them. His smile vanished.

"Excuse me," he said to the pair of women he'd been talking to.

The women glanced toward her and Korbin, and then took their flutes of champagne and went to a nearby statue.

"You're awfully bold coming here," Demarco said. "Hotel security might recognize you."

"Your wife said you'd be here tonight," Korbin said. "I hope you don't mind our impromptu visit."

"It's a public event."

"How's Damen?" Korbin asked.

With a smirk, Demarco said, "He was released from the hospital this morning. Not very happy with you, I'd imagine."

"He's got no reason to be."

Savanna looked around. If he'd been released, he was probably back in Denver by now.

"You must be Savanna Ivy." Demarco offered his

hand. She put hers in it and he bent to give her a top kiss. "I've heard all about you, especially lately."

"Not uncommon, I'm afraid."

"You don't look like you've been kidnapped." He gave her a complimentary once-over, not at all insulting, and then sent a mischievous glance to Korbin. There was a playful side to this one, even though a lot of danger surrounded the reason she and Korbin were there. "Well taken care of. Like a rare gem."

"I do clean up well."

"Savanna lives alone on several hundred remote acres near Wolf Creek Pass," Korbin said.

"I only meant for now. Taken care of, that is." He smiled. "How ever did you make it past the front door? I saw the news about you and Macon."

"I didn't know you followed the rich and famous," Korbin said.

Savanna was sure he wasn't well acquainted enough with Demarco to be that familiar with his tastes. This seemed more of a filler conversation, one Demarco probably hoped would keep them off something he was trying to avoid.

"I don't. Only this one, since you seem to be the one who brought her under the spotlight."

"I'm quite safe with Korbin." Except when she was naked with him.

Demarco looked over to where the Great Dane and bulldog were standing now. Another man had joined them.

Damen.

Weathering a shock wave, Savanna looked to see if he'd come armed and just as quickly realized he wouldn't have gotten into this event if he was. There were guards at the entrance and everyone had to go through a metal detector.

"Looks like Damen made it after all," Demarco said, charm almost diffusing his sarcasm.

The twins were having some differences, it would appear. She didn't ask what Damen was doing here. It wasn't significant that he'd show up for his brother's big auction event.

Korbin continued to watch Damen, not startled to see him out of the hospital and moving around. He showed no sign of fear. Rather, he observed. He watched the interaction among the three men at the cocktail table, gathering information.

"All I ask is that you take it outside if it gets ugly, okay, Korbin? I've seen your handiwork."

Meaning, Damen in the hospital.

"I don't like being told what to do," he said. Damen had thought he could coerce him into doing whatever work he brought his way.

"A lesson my brother is learning too late, it would seem."

"Who's that he's is talking with?" Korbin asked.

"Oh, that's Tony," Demarco said with a note of disgust.

While Savanna had to cover her alarm, Korbin didn't miss a beat. "I've heard of him."

"Adam Liski is the man with him. Your replacement, I'd imagine. Said he was into computers. Although he didn't come out and say it, I got that it was hacking."

"Oh?" Savanna queried.

"Damen found him a few months ago."

"Then he's hardly a replacement," Korbin said.

"Damen didn't ask me to work on Tony's project until a few weeks ago."

"Really? Then he must not be impressed with his progress or he wouldn't have tried to get you. He always thought so highly of you and your work."

Korbin was a good hacker. What a résumé. Savanna slid her gaze his way. He caught the look and said, "I only take the good jobs."

"Damen said this new project will be worth millions."

A plot to take down critical infrastructure? Who was paying Damen? Tony? Who was paying him?

"Why are they here, anyway?" Savanna asked. "Tony, I mean."

"He wanted to know where Damen is, and then why I didn't bring him back to Denver."

"Why didn't you?"

Demarco turned to him with a shielded look, clearly regretting having let that slip. "Doc said he'd be released soon. There was no need. And as you can see, he's getting around fine on his own."

"Is there a reason why you left him in Pagosa Springs? You went there, didn't you? Wasn't it to bring him home?"

"Who said I left him?"

"Didn't you?"

Demarco let out a long breath. "He had his own vehicle. I only left after I knew he was going to be all right."

Savanna saw how Korbin searched Demarco's face. He was fishing for something Demarco wasn't saying. While Demarco's explanation seemed true, there also seemed to be something missing. He was too frustrated, too nervous. He might be tired of his brother skating the line of the law.

"How much has he told you about his business with Tony?" Korbin asked.

"Didn't come here for the cocktails and art, did you?" Demarco quipped.

"What do you know about it?" Korbin wasn't letting him avoid his questions.

"Not a thing. Damen had taken to leaving me out of his messes. He doesn't like it when I lecture him."

"He listens to lectures?"

"He used to listen to mine." Demarco waved off an offer from a waiter for a glass of champagne.

Korbin declined as well.

Savanna took one of the glasses, sipping as she kept her eye on the cocktail table where Damen talked to the other two men.

"Have you noticed anything unusual about him?" Korbin asked. "Anything he's done? Said?"

Demarco's gaze shifted from Savanna back to Korbin. He was unpracticed at concealing lies. He didn't have his brother's devious nature.

"Nothing out of the ordinary," he said at last.

Savanna exchanged a glance with Korbin.

"Except for when he left town to go after you," Demarco said.

"You thought that was unusual?" Savanna asked.

"Well, yeah. Why would he do that?" He made a smirking face, grunting along with it, all a show.

"Why do you think?" Korbin asked.

"Why do *you*?" Demarco countered.

Korbin studied Demarco for a few seconds. "You are aware that police suspect him in both the hit-and-run and Collette's murder, aren't you?"

"Yes."

"They're waiting on some DNA testing."

Demarco's pretense fell away and grim concern took its place.

Korbin took Savanna's hand. "If you know something, take my advice and tell the police now. It's only a matter of time before there's enough evidence to make an arrest."

Demarco's eyes blinked once, a betrayal of how dead-on Korbin was. His mouth pressed into a hard line, opened and then closed again. He wasn't going to talk.

"Let's go."

"But…" She held up her glass.

He took it and put it on the nearest table.

"Why are we leaving? Maybe we can get him to talk."

"It's not him I'm worried about."

Savanna looked back and saw that Damen had spotted them. His unharmed eye glared from across the room, watching their leisurely departure. He didn't dare confront them. Not here. And not Korbin. Not alone. But he wasn't alone. He had Tony.

Out in the back of their car, Korbin used his phone to look up Adam Liski. He hadn't blocked his address and phone number. Telling the driver to take them there, he turned to Savanna, still admiring the way she looked in her dress.

It had been a nice party. If Damen and Tony hadn't shown, he would have let them stay longer.

He grinned, pulling down the middle armrest. She moved out of the way and saw that behind the armrest, which also served as cup holders, there was a refrigerator box. Above that, two glasses fit into a compact holder.

He opened the box to reveal a bottle of iced champagne inside.

She gaped at him. "You planned this?"

"They asked and I said yes."

He went about opening the bottle, expertly doing so without causing the cork to shoot all over the car. Savanna took out the glasses, holding them as he poured.

Feeling playful, she leaned close when he lifted the armrest out of the way and clinked his glass. "To clearing your name."

His eyes stayed with hers as he sipped.

"You look beautiful."

She smiled and then ran her finger down from his black bow tie to his chest. "So do you."

"That dress is a test of my restraint."

"Then it's a good thing we're about to break into Adam's home."

He chuckled. Then his smile eased into a warm, melting moment.

He clinked her glass next. "To you deciding not to plow your road."

Somehow they'd leaned even closer, he with his head just above hers, eyes locked.

Then she jerked back. Stared at him, lips parted, appalled—at herself. Leaning fully against the seat, she sipped some champagne and restored her defenses. Korbin seemed to be doing the same.

Twenty minutes later, the car came to a stop. The brief enchantment that the auction preview had offered was gone. She was still in her party dress, but the fun was over.

"Wait here for us," Korbin told the driver.

Savanna walked with him up the street of the south

Denver neighborhood. Adam lived in an apartment building. Entering the lobby, no one was around at this hour, after ten. They had the elevator to themselves and passed only one person in the hall on the way to the door. Korbin pulled out something from his jacket pocket and began working on the lock.

"You break into buildings, too?"

"Only when I have to."

The door unlocked and he entered first. It was a small comfort to know Adam was at the cocktail party. She didn't like thinking what would happen if he came home early.

Korbin found a laptop on a desk in the living room. The apartment wasn't large, but it was nice and clean. He booted up and began typing several attempts at a password. He rummaged through the desk, looking in drawers, finding files and reading through those before going back to the password attempts.

Savanna wandered around the apartment. Adam had a so-so view of the Denver Tech Center, slashed by a busy highway. Unless he had maid service, he was somewhat of a neat freak. The bathroom was spotless, impressive for a man. The apartment had two master bedrooms, one of which had nothing in the closet. The other looked occupied, with the day's clothes thrown onto a chair. The closet light was on. She went in there and saw a safe with the door partially ajar. Not wanting to touch anything, she went out to the living room where Korbin was growing increasingly frustrated. He'd never guess a fellow hacker's password.

"There's something in the bedroom," she said.

He looked up at her. "What is it?"

"Come here." She went back to the room and showed him the safe.

He knelt and dug through there, coming out with a leather notebook. It was a contact book, but she saw that it also had a list of passwords. He found the one he needed and went back to the computer. As soon as he was on, his fingers tapped rapidly. Several windows came up, most of them showing code Savanna didn't pretend to understand.

After scrolling through several lines, he finally slowed, interpreting the code with a deepening brow.

"This code is complicated but I think I can slow them down," he said, typing away.

"What is it?"

"It will enable them to steal the identities of all employees at each organization where Tony placed contractors."

"That's it?" That seemed off to Savanna. Why go to all the trouble to employ people when all they had to do was use a virus or something? "It can't just be that. Those places are too important to our economy and our way of life."

"I agree." He paused, reading the code he'd inserted into a portion of Adam's. Then he began typing again. "Adam is probably only one piece of this. Tony must have other contacts, other computer hackers working this."

Savanna thought a moment. "One who will design a virus for the emergency systems company. One who will either contaminate or destroy the water treatment plants. That type of thing?"

"Exactly."

She rubbed her arms against the chill that prickled her skin.

He closed the programs he'd opened and then the computer. Standing, he started for the door. "Let's get out of here."

She walked with him down the hall. "What did you do to the code?"

"Planted a virus. It'll take him a while to find it. If he ever does."

"Your first good deed as a law-abiding citizen."

He half smiled at that, and she suspected he wasn't sure if he should take that as a compliment.

"You could do that for a living, you know." Or for something to do. He didn't have to work, like her.

"Hack for the good guys?" Now his smile was genuine. "I suppose I could."

"Have you thought about what you're going to do when this is all over?"

They reached the car and got in. He hadn't answered yet, and she saw that the question had gotten him thinking about something heavy.

"What *are* you going to do?" she asked.

"I should go see my parents."

"What's stopping you?" He'd hinted at their being disappointed, and she could see why, but they were his parents.

"I don't know if they want me to. Not anymore."

"It's never too late, Korbin. They'd want to know you've changed your ways. They'd probably celebrate with you, and welcome their son back."

He laughed cynically. "You don't know my parents."

"They're wealthy and have affluent friends, and you probably embarrass them every time the subject of you and the trouble you're in comes up."

"I have always been in trouble. In school, after school. Now…"

"But you won't be after this." She angled her head as she studied him. "Will you?"

He grunted. "No. Not unless somebody frames me again."

"Then there you go. Things are different now. You should call them. They'd probably like to know you didn't kill anyone. You shouldn't let them keep thinking that you've done these horrible crimes. Can you imagine what that must be doing to them?"

His reluctance over talking to his parents changed to concern. "I hadn't thought of it that way."

Had he thought they'd know he was framed? Even after being estranged for however many years?

"You should call them. Tonight."

Korbin paced the RV living room. Savanna sat with her feet up on the coffee table, having changed into a long T-shirt and shorts. Her hair was still up in that sexy do, but she'd washed all the makeup off. He was still in his trousers, but had stripped down to the white T-shirt and was barefoot. He'd noticed Savanna checking out his chest a few times, but he was too torn over whether she was right about contacting his parents or not.

"Would you like me to leave you alone?" she asked.

He stopped walking. "No." Actually, having her near would make it better, easier. He couldn't explain why. He wouldn't be embarrassed talking in front of her. She was more of an anchor.

"Call them," she urged.

When he just stood there staring at her, she patted the sofa next to her.

He went there and sat. He leaned forward and looked down at his phone.

Savanna reached over and took his phone. Seeing he'd made it to their contact information, she pressed the call button and handed it back to him.

"Hey," he said too late.

"They're your parents, not the IRS."

He put the already-ringing phone to his ear, marveling at her tough-love methods.

"Hello?" His mother sounded shaken. She must recognize the number. Of course, why wouldn't she?

He felt like a dolt. "Mom."

"Korbin." He heard her breathing faster and then she called for his dad. "Are you all right?"

"Yes, I'm okay. I—"

"Where are you?"

"I'm safe. Still in Colorado."

"Oh, Korbin. Why haven't you called us sooner?"

This was not what he expected. "I'm just wanted to call and tell you that—"

"We've been going out of our minds with worry. The news…" She let out a breathy grunt. "It's been pure torture. What's going on, Korbin?"

"None of it is true."

"What? What's not true?"

"I didn't kill anyone. Damen did something that I'm trying to make right. I'm close, but until I have proof, the police will be looking for me."

"Oh, Korbin." There was that disappointment he'd heard before. She told his dad who was on the phone.

"Your dad's going to pick up another line. Didn't we warn you about that boy? Damen was never good for you."

"I know, Mom. At least, now I do."

He heard his dad pick up the line.

"What about Fallon? Did she really see you the night of the hit-and-run? When we heard that…" Another breathy grunt. "We just couldn't believe you'd do it, even by accident. You got yourself in trouble, but not that kind. We just…"

"Yes, Mom, she did see me that night. She hasn't spoken to me since the funeral. But she must have changed her mind, or was close to it."

"So, she didn't go in? We couldn't tell from the news. They didn't say. Have you spoken with her?"

"No, not yet. She didn't come to the door that night, only saw me in the house." She hadn't been quite ready. "I'll try to get in touch with her. With the media…"

"How did this all start? How did you get yourself in this situation?" This question came from his dad. He wasn't as forgiving as his mother.

"I wanted out," he said. "After Niya died…after I grieved for a while, I realized this isn't what I was meant to do. I told Damen 'no more.' He didn't like that." He explained the entire story about Collette. "I don't think he would have killed her if he hadn't known she was leaving and I was helping her."

"He'd have just set you up for the hit-and-run," his mother said.

"Yes."

There was a long silence.

"What will you do after you prove Damen killed her?"

If he could prove it. That was something that wasn't being said. "I'm not sure yet."

"What about this woman we keep hearing about?" his mother asked. "Jackson Ivy's daughter?"

"She's helping me."

"How is she helping you? Macon Ivy told reporters this morning that you got stuck on her road and that's how you ended up together."

His parents had been getting all their information from the media. "She just is."

"You may have gone off with a bunch of thugs, Korbin, but I still know you. There's something there between you. Macon claimed you were innocent and that his sister was in good hands."

"Mother…"

"Honey," his dad said.

"I'm just happy he called."

"Don't forget the choices he's made. And he may still pay for them with prison time," his dad said. "Whether innocent of the crime you're charged with or not, you probably deserve some time behind bars."

"Maybe I do. But not for murder."

"It doesn't matter. I've had it with all you've put me and your mother through. Your mother especially. Did you have it so bad growing up? No, you didn't. Most kids would give a limb to have the life you did as a kid. And look what kind of thanks we get."

"I'm sorry, Dad." There was nothing else to say. He leaned forward, elbows on his knees.

"You've been nothing but trouble since you were fourteen."

"I'd like a chance to change that."

"It's a little late, don't you think? You can't even decide definitively what you're going to do with the rest of your life. You're almost forty. Crying out loud. If you don't know by now, you never will."

"Honey." Now it was his mother who used the endearment.

"You've had plenty of opportunity to change before now. Why should we believe you mean it this time?"

"Because this time I mean it."

"It takes being accused of murder to realize that? Two people have died."

Korbin lifted his free hand and rubbed his forehead. "Three."

Don't forget his wife. She was the one who'd changed him.

"Well, great. Congratulations. My smart son. It takes your wife dying to realize crime isn't worth it."

"Honey, stop." His mother began to cry.

Korbin felt like crying with her. His dad was right. He should have known sooner. Maybe he had, but he hadn't paid attention. He'd gotten so entrenched in the life that he'd missed all the signs. Adolescent rebellion had grown into habit. Routine. And then there had been nothing routine about his wife's shooting.

"I'll call you when it's over," he said. "I'm sorry, Mother." Listening to her weeping was absolute torture. "I never meant to hurt you."

With that, he hung up. It had taken his wife's dying to realize crime wasn't worth it. But if there was ever a way to make something positive in her death, it was turning his life around. To do that, he had to stay out of prison.

Chapter 15

Shutting his car door, Demarco backed out of the parking space in front of his house. Driving out of the lot, he headed for work. Turning on the stereo, the satellite radio was tuned in to a news channel and they were talking about Korbin and Savanna. It was believed that they had returned to Denver. Someone had spotted them in a Class A motor home and police were now searching for them in that. They were turning into a real Bonnie-and-Clyde story. Savanna was with Korbin willingly and there was speculation that Korbin may be innocent.

Movement in the backseat brought his eyes to the rearview mirror.

Damen sat up. "Hello, brother."

What was he doing hiding in the backseat? When he pushed the barrel of a gun to Demarco's ribs, he had his answer.

"You shouldn't have left me in Pagosa Springs," Damen said. "We still had a lot to talk about."

Demarco was scared out of his mind, but he didn't show it. In the past he could reason with Damen to keep him in line. Now he had no idea how to approach him, how to convince him what a mistake he was making. Killing him would only result in another murder charge. He thought of Cora, of their life. When Damen had sneered that he had a perfect wife and a perfect life, he had been right. Demarco felt lucky to have what he had. He was happy. He wished Damen could have found that for himself.

"Now you're going to shoot your own twin brother?" Demarco asked.

"Only if you don't do what I tell you."

"Oh yeah? What's that? Isn't keeping your secret enough?" He didn't care how angry he sounded. He was sick of this.

"Well, see, now there's where I've got a problem. You know I used Korbin's gun to kill Collette. If you go to the cops with what you know, I'll be arrested. And I just can't let that happen."

Demarco hadn't known it was Korbin's gun, but now he did. "If I was going to go to the cops, don't you think I would have by now?" He should have. Right from the beginning. That very morning. He shouldn't have thought about it. He should have just done it and thought about it later. Gone through the grief after the fact.

"You're having an attack of conscience. I know you. I can tell. You had one in Pagosa Springs. That's why you left. You're starting to turn away from me."

"You're turning into a crazy man."

"Then give this crazy man your cell phone."

Demarco pulled it from his shirt pocket and handed it over.

"Good. Now drive to the next exit. We're going to my house."

Demarco drove there, going slow and hoping for a lucky break. None came and Damen didn't change his mind. It amazed him that his own twin could shut off any sentiments he had. By the time he pulled into Damen's garage, he was convinced his brother was quite capable of killing him.

Cora. Cora. I'm so sorry, my love.

When the garage door closed, Damen told him to get out.

Demarco debated whether he should try to fight his brother now. Growing up, Damen had been the tougher one. Demarco was more academic and had no taste for violence.

He went into the house and saw another man there. Damen's mysterious friend, Tony.

"We have more trouble," that one said.

"What are you two up to?" Demarco asked.

"He's the one who's going to make me a lot of money. If you'd have kept your nose out of my affairs, you'd have reaped some benefits of that."

"Hurry up with him, we need to get going," Tony said.

"Where to?"

"Adam had a break-in at his house."

That stopped Damen short. "Who would do that?"

"Has to be Maguire and that Ivy woman. They're getting too close, Damen. It's time to take care of them once and for all."

Damen swore a few times. Giving Demarco a shove, he said, "In the basement."

Demarco went to the stairway door, which was open, and went down the stairs. Tony followed.

"Was anything missing?" Damen asked.

"No, but Adam said he thinks someone was on his computer. We have to assume they know."

Damen spat out more curses.

In the basement, Demarco saw that Damen had been busy remodeling. He'd constructed a square room out of plywood and put in an iron-bar door with a padlock on it. There was a twin bed inside, and the room had been built off the bathroom.

How considerate of his twin.

Demarco turned to face Damen. "What do they know?"

"In the room." He pointed with his gun.

"Damen, there's no need to lock me up."

"It's either that or Tony here is going to kill you."

Tony folded his arms. "That's what we should have done already."

"See?" Damen said. "I'm saving your life by doing this."

If Demarco was locked in this room, his chances of escape were dismal. Hitting Damen's wrist, he shoved him into Tony and made a run for it. He charged up the stairs. On the last step, someone grabbed his ankle and he fell onto the kitchen floor. Rolling to his side, he saw that it was Tony. Demarco kicked his face with his other foot. That sent him backward and loosened his hold.

Demarco got to his feet and ran through the house. Tony was on his heels.

At the front door, Demarco had the handle in his hand when Tony grabbed him and threw him away. Sprawled on the living room floor, Demarco saw Tony pull out a gun.

All he could do was watch, waiting for a bullet.

"Wait!" Damen shouted. "Don't shoot him."

"He's too much of a risk."

Damen stepped in front of Demarco, who sagged in relief.

"Look, I know he's your twin brother, but you're in this too deep, Damen. We have to get rid of him. You can wait out in the car. I'll do it."

"No. He goes in the room downstairs." Damen faced Demarco. "Come on."

Demarco stood and Damen gestured for him to go to the basement. With Tony still aiming the gun, about to kill him anyway, Demarco went ahead of Damen.

In the basement, he entered the room and Damen closed the door and locked it.

"You can't keep me in here forever," Demarco said, watching Damen play with the key and realize what he was saying. Eventually he'd have to let Tony kill him.

"Damen, this is wrong. Get rid of that guy and let me help you. I'll get you a good lawyer for the hit-and-run and Collette's murder. It's not too late. You can still have a good life."

"Shut up. Don't talk. I'm going to make a lot of money."

"Not if you're in prison. Korbin said the police have DNA evidence. Is it yours? Tony doesn't care what happens to you. He will walk away from this. It will only be you who is arrested."

Damen grabbed the bars with one hand. "I said shut up! That isn't true!"

"It is true. You'll be arrested."

"Only if I'm caught."

Demarco had to try another tactic. "What about me, Damen? What about you and me?"

"You always had it good. Everything is always so easy for you. Your wife. Your career. It all fell right into place. You don't know what it's like to have to struggle for everything."

"You could have had the same."

"No, I couldn't. You were the smart one. Well, you weren't so smart when you followed me, were you?"

"A life of crime isn't a life, Damen. You're going to get yourself killed or sent to prison."

"You're as bad as Korbin. Mr. Too Good is what the both of you are. A couple of Mr. Too Goods."

"Let's go, Damen."

Demarco had to reach through to his brother. Somehow. "What are you going to do after you make your money?"

"Take a vacation."

"What about me?"

"What about you? Are you going to rat me out?"

This time when he answered, he'd be lying. "Of course not. You're my brother."

"Well, then I suppose when I can trust you, I'll let you go."

Behind him, Tony snorted. "Like that'll ever happen."

Damen turned to him. He didn't like being laughed at. When they were kids, a boy had bullied him in the playground. Damen had started swinging on a swing and the boy had begun teasing him. There was a girl in the swing next to him. It was all very stupid. The bully had said Damen was a girl because he liked to swing with girls. He didn't play sports like other boys. The boy laughed at him. Damen had stopped swinging, got up and went over and punched the boy. Got him so good he sailed onto his backside and bled out of his nose. He'd been the first of many.

"What do you know about it?" Damen asked, that familiar bite in his tone.

Demarco should have paid more attention to the signs.

"Your brother will say anything to get out of there. Are you that dumb?"

Just like the bully, Damen charged. He punched Tony and sent him to the floor.

"Hey! What'd you do that for?"

"Don't talk to me like that."

"Like what? You're going to get us both caught." Tony pointed to Demarco. "He knows too much."

"He can get me arrested for murder. I don't see what you're so worried about. You can deny you even know me."

Tony stood up, wiping his nose. "Whatever. Come on. Let's go, damn it."

Damen looked back at Demarco. "I'm sorry."

"Damen, don't do this. Think about it. Think about what this will do to your future."

"My future is already a goner if you tell the cops what you saw."

"They won't need me to convict you."

Damen started for the stairs.

"What are you going to do? Kill Korbin and Savanna? Kill me? Kill everybody? You won't get away with it!"

At the base of the stairs, Damen hung the key on a nail and followed Tony to the main level.

"Damen!"

His brother kept going up the stairs.

"Damen!" he yelled louder. When the door closed, he screamed, "Damen!"

But Damen didn't come back.

He had to do something. He had to warn Korbin. Searching around the small room, he noticed a mini refrigerator with a TV on top. He rattled the iron door, checked the hinges to see if he could undo them. Next, he kicked the wall. It was all solid. His brother had built a tree house when they were young teenagers. He was good with wood. Demarco remembered when they'd invited some friends over and one of the boys started arguing with Damen about which actor played in a popular fantasy movie.

Everybody knows that, the boy had sneered.

And in the next instant, Damen had pushed him out of the tree house. The boy had broken his leg and their parents had a tough time talking the boy's parents out of a lawsuit. It was lucky that insurance had covered all the medical bills.

More signs.

He rarely showed remorse. He didn't like animals and animals didn't like him.

As an adult, he'd seemed to have outgrown his childhood faults...for a while. His relationship with Collette had once appeared normal. But now, Demarco had come to find out, she'd been afraid of him. Damen hadn't changed. He was still irrational and solved his problems with violence. And he had just become one of Damen's problems.

Chapter 16

"We're here to see Pavlo Borsuk." Savanna stood beside Korbin at the security desk of NextGen Emergency Communications Systems, or NGECS. State-of-the-art automated doors requiring an access card were on both sides of the island desk. Metal detectors scanned anyone entering the outer doors, and two guards stood post. A lot of good all that would do if someone were already inside.

"What's the nature of your visit?"

"Personal."

"Sign in, please."

Korbin signed his false name and Savanna did the same. The guard called an extension and announced their arrival. He repeated their names. "They said it's personal." He looked up at Korbin and Savanna. Then he hung up. "He'll be right here."

No one seemed to recognize them.

A few minutes later, a tall, thick man with a bushy crop of brown hair and brown eyes appeared through the security doors, followed by another man not as tall and thinner with blond hair. They both wore overalls that must be the required uniform. Pavlo looked to the guard for guidance, and that one pointed to them. The man behind him was looking at Korbin.

Pavlo approached, hiding what had to be his surprise or confusion. "I am Pavlo."

His rich Eastern European accent was muted as though he'd spent a fair amount of time in the United States, learning to blend in. His partner hung back. He must have come along so they could resume whatever janitorial work had been interrupted.

"Mr. Borsuk, we're tracking down all of the contractors employed by United Janitorial Services. We've noticed some inconsistencies and we were hoping you could clear some things up," Korbin said.

"What things? Who are you?"

"We're acquaintances of Tony's. How long have you been employed here?" Korbin noticed how his coworker stood straighter, pushing off the security desk where he leaned, and watching and listening much more intently.

"Five years. You are friends of Tony's?"

"Is that when you became a US citizen?"

The coworker glanced at Pavlo.

"Why do you need to know such things? If you are doing survey, you call Tony." Pavlo started to turn to go. "Let's go, Nate."

"Aside from stealing employee identities, what are you planning?" Korbin asked.

Pavlo stopped cold, then turned to him. "Excuse me?"

"We know all about your operation. You immigrate

to this country, establish citizenship and then get jobs at these kinds of corporations. You lie dormant for years, until it's time to execute your plan. What else is there?"

"I do not know what you are talking about."

Korbin glanced at Nate, who seemed interested to the point of anxiety. "If you give us information, the FBI might be persuaded to go easy on you." Easier, perhaps, than they did the others involved. It may not be wise to suggest the FBI was onto them, and yet that very thing might scare this man into talking.

Pavlo looked closer at him and Savanna. "You are that couple in news. Jorge, call the police. This is the man wanted for that murder."

The guard stared at Korbin, but recognition didn't come.

"They're planning a terrorist attack," Korbin told him, also including Nate in on it. "There are several more like him at other corporations. Foreigners who apply for citizenship and then get jobs like this so they can infiltrate sensitive American companies." To Pavlo he asked, "What job got you a work visa? Janitorial? Did Tony handle all of that for you through his bogus company? Explains why he showed no profit at first. He brought you over here on visas and you all worked lesser jobs until you were able to land this one."

"Call the police, Jorge."

Jorge, a rule-follower, picked up the phone. "Mr. Howard, there are some people up here that you should come and talk to."

He hadn't called police. He'd called his boss.

"Wait here," the guard said.

A mocking smile touched the Ukrainian's mouth. He

waited with them until Mr. Howard appeared, a big African-American man in a suit.

"What seems to be the problem?"

"This is our head of security," Pavlo said. "These two are—"

"Tony Bartoszewicz runs an operation through a front company called United Janitorial Services," Korbin said. "Mr. Borsuk works for him. You hired him under contract. We've traced several United Janitorial Services employees to corporations like this one. What do you think terrorists could do with access to an emergency communications company?"

"That is going too far. Terrorist?" Pavlo sneered as though insulted.

"Some of the other companies are water treatment plants and the biggest banks in the country," Savanna said.

"They are lying. Do you not recognize them? This is the man wanted for that woman's murder."

The head of security hadn't said anything, but he listened. Before he could say more, the front doors opened and in rushed a dozen policemen.

Grabbing Savanna's hand, Korbin shoved the head of security and then punched Pavlo in the nose. It was enough to get him out of the way. Running for the secure doors, he reached Nate. Acting on instinct, he reached for his badge and yanked, breaking the thin lanyard. With Savanna behind him, he opened the secure doors and together they ran down a long hallway, fluorescent lights a runway with closed doors lining each side. Thundering footsteps came up behind them. A woman in a pencil skirt toppled out of the way. A man spilled coffee on the floor. Another stopped short at an intersecting hall.

Korbin chose an exit sign and headed there. He caught a sign made on printer paper that told everyone this was Shipping. Korbin pulled Savanna with him through two swinging double doors. Cool air flowed through an open overhead door. He jumped off the loading dock and turned to catch Savanna, guiding her by her waist until she had her footing. Over her head, he saw security guards and police burst through the shipping room doors.

He ran for the parking lot. Seeing a car find a space, he ran faster. The driver got out and saw them running, saw the throng of pursuers and started to get back into his vehicle. Korbin grabbed the keys dangling from the man's hand and a fistful of his jacket. Tossing him aside, he climbed in after Savanna as she crawled over to the passenger side. He stuck the key in place and revved the engine.

One of the policemen slapped his hand on the trunk as they sped away.

Savanna checked behind them for signs of police and saw none. "We need to ditch this car."

"Let's take the train."

They parked, and walked and ran to the nearby station. Savanna sat next to him, still reeling from their near brush with the law. She was getting good at this. And it was kind of thrilling. Even more thrilling was the man beside her. His thigh was pressed to hers. His quick thinking back there had her marveling. The way he took that man's badge and held her hand. His determination to avoid arrest so that he could clear his name was full of stealth. She believed wholeheartedly that he'd succeed.

She glanced over at him and he caught her. Neither looked away.

At their stop, they got off and walked the rest of the way to their RV campground. In the full light of day, she kept her vigilance on high alert for police or Tony or Damen. Or anyone the two of them might send.

She wasn't sure if it was the excitement of their escape or his capability in doing so that had stirred this titillating reaction in her. Walking up the lane in the campground, a car approached behind them. She turned with him, him taking hold of her hand. Her heart thumped faster from flight-or-fight and him.

At their RV, she stopped to look around with him.

"Looks like we're safe," he said.

"For now." She looked at him. They both seemed content to stand here and do just that. "What made you think to grab the man's badge?"

"He works with Pavlo. And he looked like he knew something."

"You want to go talk to him?"

"Yeah. Tonight."

What were they going to do until then? She glanced around. They should probably go inside.

When she looked back at him, he was watching her in a way that convinced her he wondered the same.

A bicycler buzzed by, shooting into view in front of the RV. Savanna jumped.

The bicycler didn't pose any harm, but the car approaching down the lane did.

"That's Damen," Korbin said, incredulous.

How had he found them? Tony was driving. A gun came out of the passenger window.

Korbin shoved Savanna and she ran for the front of the RV as a gunshot tore into the wood of the picnic table. The car screeched to a stop at their site. Korbin had the keys out and the passenger door unlocked as running footsteps grew closer.

She scrambled into the big RV just as Damen ran around the front of it. Savanna screamed as Tony appeared at the driver's door and tried the handle. It didn't open.

Korbin kicked Damen. The gun flew out of his hand and Damen jumped up and onto Korbin, and they fought on the front passenger seat. Savanna ran through the RV and went to the backroom where she kept a pistol in the bedside drawer. Rushing back to the living room, she found Korbin wrestling with Damen just behind the cab, half in the kitchen. Tony was about to climb in on the passenger side.

Savanna fired the pistol, making him duck and fall out the door.

Korbin kicked Damen and got to his feet, running to Savanna and taking the gun. He swung it around as Damen stood with a knife in his hand.

"Get out," Korbin demanded.

"When you're dead," Damen hissed.

Tony climbed up on the step of the door and aimed his pistol inside the RV. Savanna moved behind the wall next to the side door. Korbin kept Damen between him and Tony.

Remembering Korbin had another gun in the kitchen drawer, she leaned around the wall and reached for the top handle. Korbin was sparring with Damen.

"You aren't going to kill me," Damen taunted, jabbing the knife.

Korbin jumped back to avoid being sliced.

Tony fired the gun, a bullet hitting the wall under the cabinet. Savanna ducked back.

"You're not so tough when I'm not tied," Damen said.

Korbin kicked him, sending him sailing backward onto his back. Savanna leaned forward, watching Tony taking aim at Korbin. She opened the drawer and retrieved the gun as Korbin fired his weapon at Tony, making him crouch behind the passenger seat.

Savanna readied the pistol and aimed for Tony's head while Korbin faced off with Damen again. He was back on his feet with the knife, an evil, confident gleam in his eyes.

"I should have taken care of you when I took care of those gang members who came after me."

If the reminder that those gang members had cost him his wife bothered Korbin, he didn't show it.

"You were such a pansy after that." Damen continued to taunt him. "I always thought she made you too soft. She was the reason you started drifting away."

"From crime?"

"You didn't have a problem with it before you met her."

"Maybe I finally grew up."

"You think you're so much better than everyone else."

Korbin didn't respond.

"I was glad when she got shot. I thought I'd get my friend back."

While Korbin's anger brewed into a dangerous storm that Damen recklessly stirred, Savanna saw Tony disappear from the passenger door. She searched for him through the windows. She saw him in the living room slide-out window. He shot at Korbin but the glass protected him.

Damen lunged with the knife again, catching Korbin on the arm, but Korbin slammed the gun alongside Damen's head. Damen recovered quickly, ramming into Korbin, sending him stumbling backward. Knife raised, Damen tried to stab him in the chest. Korbin gripped the knife handle over Damen's hand and the two fought for their own purpose. Damen to stab Korbin, Korbin to stop him. Damen blocked Korbin from swinging the gun again.

Moving closer, Savanna aimed her pistol. "Stop or I'll shoot."

Damen looked at the gun she held straight at his head. Then, slamming Korbin's arm to the floor, he loosened Korbin's grip on the gun. He snatched the pistol and began to move the barrel toward her. Seeing that Damen was about to shoot her, Korbin used both hands and turned the knife on Damen, sinking it into his chest. Savanna dived for the cover of the table as Damen fired.

Lying on her side, she watched Damen grip the handle of the embedded knife and slump to the floor, eyes on Korbin, wide with disbelief.

Panting for air, Savanna opened the side door and pointed her gun outside, looking for Tony. She spotted him behind the RV, peeking out to see her and then drawing out of the line of fire when he did.

Korbin dragged Damen's body to the door. She got out of the way as he pushed it outside. Savanna looked away from the grotesque sight.

Korbin guided her into the RV. "Time to go. The gunfire is going to bring the cops."

Numb, she stepped toward the front.

"I need you to drive. Can you?"

He'd just killed his friend...who was no longer his friend, but still. He'd killed someone and he was so methodical.

"Savanna?"

Realizing she stood in the cab staring at him, she nodded. He guided her to the seat. She gripped the wheel while Korbin jammed the keys into the ignition and started the engine.

Korbin crouched to see through one of the windows. As soon as the engine started, Tony began firing. Bullets hit the side of the RV.

The danger propelled her back into an adrenaline rush of action.

Looking out the driver's window, she stared for a stunned second at the ding in the glass. The windows were all bulletproof. Panting a few breaths, she yanked the gear into Reverse and gave it gas. She hit Tony's car and kept backing up while Korbin hung on and went to the kitchen to retrieve his gun.

She backed the RV out of the space and hit the side of Tony's car in the process. Out in the lane, she drove forward toward the exit. They'd never outrun him in this. She looked back and saw that Korbin was way ahead of her. He opened the window in the back, a bathroom. Breaking out the screen, he aimed and started firing. Savanna drove as fast as she could out of the RV park. Korbin hung on as she swerved around a turn and then veered to avoid a truck hauling a trailer that had stopped at the stop sign at the exit of the campground. She cut off traffic getting onto the highway. In the side mirror, Savanna watched the long line of vehicles behind a slow-moving Subaru hold Tony at the stop sign. He'd parked beside the truck in an attempt to get out onto the highway as Savanna had. The driver of the truck saw the gun in Tony's hand and ducked and shouted for his wife and kids to do the same. Savanna saw his lips moving and then the detail faded as the RV picked up speed and she raced down the highway.

Korbin stayed at the window. Savanna took an exit and veered onto I-70 west. She drove ten miles per hour over the speed limit, as much as she dared to avoid attracting too much attention. Close to the foothills, she took an exit and drove down several streets until another campground came into sight.

Maybe it wasn't wise to stay in one. Tony would check them all to find them. She passed it and got back out onto the highway, driving into the foothills. Korbin came to sit next to her in front, watching the rearview mirror and twisting to look through the windows.

"Turn here." Korbin pointed to a road ahead.

She slowed and turned the corner. Her hands still shook from all the violence she'd witnessed and survived.

"Are you okay?" Korbin asked.

She nodded unsteadily.

"I'm sorry."

Why was he sorry? She glanced at him. "It isn't your fault." He had such a guilty conscience. Who wouldn't after what he'd been through?

The two-lane road was deserted this time of year. She drove carefully over the patchy ice. "You know this place?"

"There's a dirt road up here and a few places to camp."

Driving in silence a moment, she spotted the road and slowed. The big tires of the RV crunched over gravel and ice. It wasn't an official campsite, just a forest service road.

"Will we get in trouble?" she asked.

His head turned and she felt him look at her.

With a glance she realized by his raised brow what

she'd just asked. She started laughing. A grin sprang up on his face and a few chuckles broke free. The tension from what happened earlier began to lighten.

She found a pull-off that led into the trees. She turned and drove into the shade, out of sight of the road. They'd be well protected here. Finding a flat area, she parked, shut off the engine and then sighed.

"I'll call Dad and have a car sent here."

He still wore a slight smile, but humor had warmed to the hint of sexual awareness.

Savanna stood from the driver's chair and went back to start opening up the RV slide-outs, which they'd retracted when they'd gone to see Pavlo. Finished, she turned from the last living room slide-out to find Korbin standing there.

"Mmph." She bumped into him.

Korbin steadied her with his hand on her waist. The contact sent her closer to forgetting why she should wait to do what she yearned to. What he also yearned to do. After surviving what they had, it was a relief to feel something good.

He drew her toward him and she stepped into his arms.

Breathless, she pressed herself against him, wrapping her arms around his neck while he crushed his mouth to hers. Nothing else mattered but him. He kissed her, but it wasn't enough. Not nearly enough. She dug her fingers through his hair and wordlessly asked for more. He groaned and sank his tongue deep.

Yes.

She kissed him without reservation, moved against him, wished she could bask forever in the power of this feeling she had for him.

Korbin lifted her off her feet. She wound her legs around him, planting kisses all over his face.

"Savanna," he rasped.

"Yes."

"Are you sure?"

"Oh, God." She wished he wouldn't ask her that.

Korbin started walking with her. Her fingers worked frantically to unbutton his short-sleeved shirt. Down the narrow hall to the master bedroom, he laid her on the bed and finished what she started. She removed her top.

As he dropped his shirt to the floor, she admired smooth skin over rippling muscles. He bent down and she ran her fingers into his hair at the base of his neck. Sexy, she thought, running her hands over him, exulting in the heat that radiated off his body.

He undid her bra and gently cupped her breasts. Air cooled her skin over the layer of sweat on her own body. He planted sweet kisses around each of her nipples, then sucked them while his hands worked to unbutton her jeans, pushing them down. He left that task half-done and untied her boots. She kicked them off. He did the same with his and jerked out of his pants, heated eyes watching her remove her jeans and underwear the rest of the way.

Naked and reaching for him, she melted at the sound of his gruff anticipation. He moved between her parted legs and found her. Bracing his hands on each side of her, he pushed inside. He didn't stop. He kept moving. Savanna arched her neck and he sucked the skin there. She sank her fingers into his hair again and splayed her other hand over his back, running it down his sweat-covered skin to his butt, where she squeezed.

He drove into her harder, his face just above hers, eyes intent on her, breathing rough and guttural. She came apart looking up at him. Drowning sensation built to a crescendo. She dragged her eyes closed and groaned with the intensity of her release.

He sank his tongue inside her mouth and rode her gently through her orgasm before he took his own with a few quick, deep, hard thrusts.

Then he collapsed on top of her. She felt his heart pounding as fast as hers, heard his ragged breaths slow with hers.

She kissed his cheek, then found his mouth.

"Are you okay?" he asked.

"Why wouldn't I be?" Why had he asked?

Rolling off her, he pulled her to his side and folded his arm under his head. Savanna drew a pattern on his chest.

"I take it you are," he said, grinning.

Her hand flattened on his chest, not knowing what to say. Didn't want to think much about it. Instead, she slid a leg over him and pushed herself up to straddle his hips. Her fingers kneaded his hard chest. She moved against him.

"Uh." He gripped her hips and moved with her. "You're…mmm…going to have to give me a little more… ah…time, sweetheart."

She laughed, more of a drugged sound, and leaned down to kiss him. "I don't need more time."

His deep chuckle heated her more. "You're right." He rolled them as one, then positioned her underneath him.

Savanna dug the back of her head into the pillow as he pushed her knees apart and kissed his way from her breasts to her abdomen. She sank her fingers into his beautiful hair as he found the place where she needed him most. He took his time about it, sending shivers spreading with each light touch.

She came with a soft sound she couldn't repress and Korbin smiled as he kissed her stomach, then dragged his tongue up to one tight nipple, then the other. Taking her head between his strong hands, he looked down at her for a while, eyes soft and sending her intimate messages.

He kissed her lips, and her heart swelled with tender emotion. His tongue reached for hers and when she caressed him with equal feeling, he pressed harder. His breath grew ragged. She lay pliant while he probed for her, watching his eyes grow fevered and intense. He moved slowly, dragging back and forth until he ignited her again. Then he propped himself up by his hands to arrow into her harder. She lifted her knees.

The whirlwind peaked and settled. Korbin fell on top of her and she welcomed his hot, sweaty weight. He kissed her neck just below her ear and moved off her. Pulling her with him, he held her close.

Savanna rested her cheek on his chest, listening to his heart slow to a normal rate. She kissed his skin.

They basked in the aftermath for a while and then the world returned.

They hadn't eaten yet today. "Let's eat in bed." She meant to keep this enchantment going. Because later, reality would return, and she might not like it.

She got up, naked, even though they were somewhere remote, there was something exciting about walking naked into the kitchen with the window coverings open. She was safe and cozy in here, protected by a man she didn't want to love.

Finding a plate, she put strawberries and cheese on it and grabbed two bottles of water before going back to the bedroom. She rested the plate near Korbin's hips and he relieved her of the bottles while she crawled onto the mattress. Sitting on folded legs, she lifted a strawberry. It was fresh and plump.

"Mmm."

Popping the berry into her mouth, she studied him lying there all sexy on the bed, unabashed and propped on one elbow, muscles flexing, bunching.

"Let's share everything," she said, holding up a second strawberry.

He took her hand and bit the strawberry, then kissed her fingertips with a velvety touch.

Her breath quickened and she marveled at his appetite. Not for food, either. Letting him keep her hand, she reached for a piece of cheese. She brought it to his lips and he took a bite, leaving half for her. She put it into her mouth and chewed with him, falling into the look in his eyes, those wolfish eyes that hungered for her.

Next came another strawberry. This time he sucked her finger after taking it.

"Oh."

He gave a lopsided grin. "My turn."

Taking a berry from the plate, he poised it before her.

"You like fruit," she teased.

"Juicy," he said with a dark whisper. "Like you."

He pressed it to her lips and she took a bite. He ate the other half and brushed his thumb over her bottom lip, no longer smiling.

"Come here," he coaxed.

She sat on her hip, her legs off to the side, and leaned toward him. He put a strawberry between his teeth and she smiled as she took a bite of her half. Her heart scampered warmly as they chewed with their lips touching. He kissed her.

Their breathing resonated in the room.

"Savanna," he rasped, and pulled her head back to his.

She lay down and he moved over her, continuing to kiss her. That's all he did. Kiss her. And then, he lay with her, holding her against him. Savanna could feel him drifting again. Away from her.

Chapter 17

The car had been a good idea. Behind tinted windows, they wouldn't be recognized. Korbin searched the neighborhood as he climbed out of the back, making sure all was clear for Savanna. It was a quiet Saturday morning. She stood with him, eyes a little sheepish but also full of remembered heat as she passed him and headed up the cracked and narrow walk that sliced the front yard in half. Two huge maple trees needed a good trim but kept them in shadows as they stepped up to the covered porch of the 1960s home.

Ringing the doorbell, he looked around again and faced forward when the door opened and Nate appeared. He scanned the neighborhood and let them inside.

A pregnant woman sat reclined on the couch, and two kids about eight and twelve sat on the love seat. The slipcover over it was coming untucked. Bulky furniture crowded the small living room. A coffee table was full of magazines and glasses. The entertainment center was old and too big for the room, and the TV was loud and played a vampire movie.

"Dude, you shouldn't be here," Nate said. "Babe, could you get us some beers?"

Korbin held up his hand. "No." He shook his head at the pregnant woman, who looked glad not to have to get up. "We don't need anything. We won't be here long."

"You got my badge?"

"That isn't why we're here."

Nate's brow went down.

"What has Pavlo said to you about why he's working at your company?"

"Hey, man, the cops already questioned me. I told them all I know." When Korbin and Savanna waited for him to go on, he did. "Pavlo bragged about some crap about how easy it was to get a green card. At first I thought he was joking like he was some kind of jihad warrior. But then I started thinking. He's from the Ukraine, you know? And he's always making fun of me as an American. One night after work, we stopped for some beers and he started talking again. Only this time he said he had friends who were going to change the world. When I asked him how, he patted me on the back and said, 'Don't worry, you won't know what hit you.' It was weird, man. He doesn't drink so he was sober when he said it. Like I'd be dead after whatever thing he was talking about that would change the world."

"He's part of a group who are planning to steal the identities of people who work for companies like the one that employs you."

"That's going to change the world?"

"Not by itself, but what if the computer virus that steals identities does something more than that?"

"What if the virus is a disguise?" Savanna asked at the same time he thought of it.

Nate laughed. "A guy like Pavlo is going to plant a virus that will take down NextGen Emergency Communications Systems?" He laughed again. "He's a freaking janitor."

"He isn't the mastermind behind the virus," Korbin said. "They have others working on it here and must have more in the Ukraine."

There was never going to be an identity theft. Only a virus that would destroy the systems running key organizations.

Korbin's cell phone rang. Checking the caller ID, he didn't recognize the number. He answered.

"If you wish to see your stepdaughter alive, you will do as I say." It was Tony.

Korbin froze with the implications of the call. He hadn't anticipated this, that Tony—or anyone—would go after Fallon. Their estrangement should have been enough. But Tony didn't know they were estranged. And it had been all over the news when she'd given him an alibi.

"Bring Savanna with you." He gave an address. "You have one hour."

Savanna was as ashen as Korbin when she learned what Tony had done.

"I want you to go back to Evergreen."

"No." They'd been arguing about this in the back of the sedan all the way back to the RV. "I'm going with you."

"That's two of you I have to take care of, Savanna."

"You said Tony wanted me to be there, too."

"He did."

"What will he do if I don't show up?"

"Not kill you."

"I'm going and that's final."

The sedan drove onto the dirt road and pulled to a stop at the RV. She and Korbin got out.

"You could get killed."

While that did frighten her, she could not and would not let him go alone. "We're in this together, Korbin. We'll get out of it together."

He faced her before climbing up into the driver's seat. Rather than start an argument, she saw that she'd made some headway. They were in this together. They were together in another way, too.

"All right, but you stay in the RV until it's over."

She didn't agree to that. If he needed her, she'd be there for him.

Tony must have figured out where they'd gone. An RV this size was hard to hide. The meeting place was close. Korbin drove down another dirt road, this one private. As they approached a clearing, a ranch house with boarded-up windows came into view. The outbuildings weren't boarded up, and outside the barn, two armed men stood.

Another appeared in the open door with Fallon in a chokehold, a gun to her head. Her long, curly blond hair was wild and messy. She wore faded jeans and a sweater and no jacket. Savanna saw the tightening of Korbin's face. This was the reason she'd insisted on going with him. Women had fallen victim to violence everywhere he went. He had to stop it. And she was going to help him. Because if she'd ever have a chance with him, he had to be able to put all of this behind him.

She waited in the RV, watching him walk toward the barn. As she predicted, Tony appeared, pointing his finger into Korbin's face. He sent a man to the RV. Savanna got out as he approached and walked toward Korbin, who looked furious that she'd done it.

Three men with guns forced them inside the barn. Fallon whimpered and eyed Savanna. Having been alone when she was abducted and not having a clue as to why, she was frightened to hysteria. She cried as the man shoved her to Savanna, who caught her.

"It's going to be all right," she said low into the woman's ear.

Dust and dirt and cobwebs were thick from lack of care, and milk urns and pump equipment were just as they were left when the ranch had been abandoned. Drains in the concrete floor surrounded stalls on the other side, troughs underneath to catch blood of cattle when the barn had once been used as a slaughterhouse. Disgusting. The creepiness of this place enveloped Savanna.

Tony strode with his hands clasped behind his back, studying his prey, which at the moment was Korbin. Two of the goons with guns covered Korbin, and only one covered Savanna and Fallon.

"You've caused me a great deal of trouble, Mr. Maguire."

"You should give up now," Korbin said.

Tony snorted. "This coming from a man wanted for murder."

"The police are going to find out about you. Nate

knows all about your plans. We just left his house. He's going to tell police, if he hasn't already."

"Nate doesn't know anything."

"The identity theft you're planning is a ruse. Isn't that something? What about the virus you're going to try to infect all those companies with? Nothing?"

It was dangerous for Korbin to push a man like Tony. Right now. When the guns were all trained on them. Savanna looked for a way out. If she could overpower the man before her and Fallon...

"Killing us won't solve your problem," Korbin said.

"Perhaps not, but it will give me great satisfaction. I will gladly claim responsibility for your deaths. And I will go to mine with a smile."

Fallon began crying again. She believed their situation was hopeless. While it did appear that way, Savanna refused to give up. She watched Korbin look over at Fallon. A quiet rage simmered inside of him.

"You." Tony indicated Fallon. "Back up into that stall."

Fallon clutched Savanna's side. "No!"

Savanna pushed her to Korbin. "I'll go." She backed up into the stall, looking down at the drains, seeing the trough underneath through a layer of grime.

Tony walked over to a ledge beside one of the stalls and lifted a rusty knife. Savanna had seen enough documentaries to know what that was for. He'd slice her neck and let her bleed out.

"No." Korbin started toward her, Fallon clinging to him. But the two men moved forward with their guns, aiming not at him but at Fallon.

Tony strode toward her, the rusty instrument hanging from his hand and a sick smile curving his mouth. The armed man watched, not paying close attention.

Savanna looked at Korbin, trying to assure him she wouldn't go down without a fight. He saw her and checked the two guns on him.

Tony lifted the knife. Savanna grabbed his wrist and pushed him into the man with the gun. Korbin shoved Fallon so that she sprawled to the ground. Savanna went down and pulled her toward her while Korbin fought two armed men.

She watched in horror as one of them was about to shoot him. But he wrestled a gun from one man and shot that one.

As he was about to shoot the third to the stunned disbelief of Tony, a group of men in black rushed into the barn yelling, "FBI. Drop your weapons!"

And it was over just like that.

Tony and two of the armed men were cuffed and hauled off, and the shot man was taken away on a stretcher. One of the agents talked to Korbin while two more stood guard over Savanna and Fallon.

"I'm Savanna Ivy." She stuck out her hand to Fallon, who was still scared and pale.

"I know. I heard all about you."

Of course she had. "I've heard a little about you."

Fallon turned to her. "You have?"

"Yes. Korbin told me. He feels awful about your mother. It's changed him."

Fallon looked reluctant to believe it. "Is today any indication?"

"Yes. He's fighting for his life back, the one he should have had with you and Niya."

"He told you her name?"

"He told me a lot about her."

"But...I thought the two of you were..."

Savanna smiled, a fake one, really, because secretly that hurt. "We were, but…" She shook her head. "He isn't ready for that yet."

"When I heard, I…" Tears sprang easily to the girl's eyes, still sensitive from her ordeal. "My mother. Shot. I couldn't fathom it. And because Korbin…"

"It isn't Korbin's fault that Damen got involved in this. He wants to have a life with you in it, and not just because you're Niya's daughter. He loves you."

"You're awfully understanding for someone who's romantically involved with him."

Savanna shrugged. "I've been through this before." The second choice, the expendable one. The one who wasn't quite enough.

Fallon observed her a while. "If Korbin loves you, he'll stick around."

"Yeah, I know the drill."

"No, I mean it. He loved my mother and he stood by her no matter what. He never cheated on her and he treated her like a queen. I see that now. It took me a while, but I saw it."

Savanna smiled through the ache in her heart. "Yeah, I know that about him."

"May we have a word with the two of you?" an agent came over to them and asked.

Savanna saw that Korbin was being handcuffed.

"What are you doing?"

The agent glanced back. "We don't have a choice. Your boyfriend is a hero, but he's still a suspect in a murder. We have to take him in."

Chapter 18

Demarco kicked the plywood again, trying to loosen the nails. But the boards were nailed good to the beams and weren't budging. He paced his tiny space. Where the hell was Damen?

Hearing someone at the front door, he started yelling.

"Help! I'm in the basement! Help!" He kept screaming, "Help!"

A few moments later, he heard glass shattering. Whoever was there had heard him. He sagged against the cool metal of the bars for a second.

"Demarco?"

"Cora?" Cora had found him.

"Demarco!" He heard her feet thudding above and then reaching the basement door. She rushed down. Seeing him, she breathed and said, "Oh," as she reached the barred door, gripping it with her hands.

"Oh, Demarco."

"How did you find me?" he asked.

"I guessed he might have taken you to his house. I was hoping and praying."

"You're a good guesser. The key." He pointed. "It's hanging by the stairs."

"Oh." She wasn't accustomed to so much excitement, violent excitement. He vowed to keep her from ever going through anything like this for as long as he lived.

Her fingers shook as she maneuvered the key in the lock. When it snapped open and the door swung free, he felt a rush of gladness.

Taking her into his arms, he hugged her and kissed her all over her face. "I love you."

Her hands bracketed his face. "I love you, too." She had begun to cry. "Oh, Demo. I have terrible news."

She still held his face. He braced himself for what was coming, already knowing.

"Damen is dead."

He shut his eyes. Would prison have been better? He'd have probably gotten life.

"Police found him in an RV park. They believe he tried to kill Korbin again and Korbin ended up killing him."

Damen had failed as Demarco thought he would. While he'd hoped Damen would survive his bad decisions, it was still difficult to realize he'd never see his brother again. Damen was gone.

"They asked if we'd go to the coroner's office to…" She fought back tears. "Identify the body."

He nodded. Taking her hands, he held them between their bodies and looked into her eyes. "There's something else I need to do."

Even though he felt stings of anger that Korbin had killed his brother, his course was set. And even though he feared what Gunderman would do to him once he turned in the weapon used in Collette's murder, he had to do the right thing. From now on, he would do the right thing and not think twice about it.

"What is it?"

"Let's get out of here." Keeping one of her hands, he led her up the stairs.

In the car, she asked, "What is it you have to do?"

"I'll show you. Let's go home."

For the rest of the ride there, memories of Damen shook him. He and Damen when they were five, blowing out candles together and then playing with the new army toys they'd gotten. Damen laughing. Camping out with their friends. Shooting off illegal fireworks. The innocence. Damen had been good then. Before his first girlfriend. Before animals growled at him whenever he got too close. Before he'd done his first crime.

And then Demarco had met Cora. He'd fallen so in love. Damen had never found that. At times, he'd watched Demarco and Cora with a glint of resentment. Demarco caught it sometimes. He hadn't wanted to believe his brother hated him for finding love. If there ever had been a woman Damen had loved, it was the one he'd asked to marry him. Demarco hadn't seen him look at her the way a man did when he loved her. But he'd claimed he had. And then the woman had found another man. The wedding was called off.

That had been the turning point for Damen. He began spending time with felons. His group of friends expanded. He'd connected with Korbin, probably the only good man out of the whole bunch. And then a new breed of criminals. Korbin had been smart enough to walk away. Now this.

Cora pulled into their garage and he preceded her into the house. He went to the guest bedroom closet that they used as storage. He reached up and took down a shoe box.

Cora stood in the room, watching. He took the box to the bed and set it there. Then he opened the lid. Inside, the gun Damen had used to kill Collette was inside a gallon-sized plastic bag. He felt Cora's hand squeeze his forearm and only then realized she'd put her hand there.

"Demo...why didn't you tell me?"

"I didn't want to frighten you. And I wasn't sure what to do with it."

"I-is this...?"

"Yes."

"But...how...?"

"I saw him." Replacing the lid on the shoebox, he took her hand. "Come with me. I need to show you something else."

"There's more?"

Damen had taken his cell phone and had destroyed it so no one could track him. But Demarco had recorded a video of Damen on his own phone, and copied it to his laptop. At his laptop, he opened the file and let Cora sit down to watch. She did, with both hands flattened on the desk. He could see her profile and it grew increasingly horrified. When the video ended with Damen turning from the river, she put her hand to her mouth. He could feel her thoughts. How could Demarco have ever doubted his brother had killed Collette?

"That was Korbin's gun," Demarco said. "He must have given it to Collette because she was afraid of Damen, and Korbin was going to help her get away.

Damen thought they were having an affair, but she must have been planning to escape him. That's why he killed her. In a jealous rage."

"You knew?"

"Cora...I..."

"All this time, you knew he did it and you said nothing. You didn't even tell me."

He could see that last part bothered her most. "I'm sorry. I had a hard time accepting that Damen could do such a thing. But now, looking back, I recorded this because somewhere inside of me I knew I'd had enough. I could no longer protect him. It just took me a while to accept it, to mourn the loss of Damen. Because I knew I was going to lose him."

"Oh, Demo." Cora was both sympathetic and reproachful. "If police have this—" she held up the phone "—it proves Korbin couldn't have killed her."

Demarco nodded. He'd gone over this a hundred times already. "Even if I claim to have seen Damen leave his house, Korbin still could have killed her. But he didn't have time to get rid of the gun. He was being arrested for a different crime—the hit-and-run. Korbin was being held for questioning at the time this recording was taken."

"Why dispose of the gun if it was Korbin's?" she asked.

"He killed Collette in the heat of the moment. He probably wasn't wearing gloves then. Only when he stole the car."

Cora stood. "You have to give this to police."

There was nothing stopping him now. "That's the one more thing I have to do." Evil and corruption would be gone from their lives from here on out.

"You should have given it to the police as soon as you saw him and made this video."

"Yes. That would have been the right thing to do. After this, I'm going to devote my life to you and me and doing just that. The right thing."

Chapter 19

Korbin saw Demarco waiting in front of the police station as he walked with Savanna through the doors. Demarco had known all along that he was innocent. Korbin should be furious. What if he had never come forward? The DNA evidence may have been enough to prove he didn't kill Collette. That was the only reason he wasn't furious, that and the dilemma Demarco had found himself in. Damen had caused a lot of people unwanted drama.

Reporters swarmed him and Savanna, thrusting microphones at them and hurling questions, most of which he didn't catch. Savanna, or her parents, had sent some security guards, who formed a barrier for them.

"The FBI has made arrests of several janitors across the country," a reporter said. "What were they planning?"

"What kind of attack did you thwart?" one of the reporters shouted.

"How does it feel to be a national hero?"

Korbin grinned at that reporter. Him? A hero? Cameras went off and he faced forward again.

"Hey, Savanna, how did you two meet?"

Demarco waited by the sedan that would take them away from here. Korbin stopped before him. Detective Gunderman had told him that he turned over Korbin's gun and the video of Damen. No charges had been placed against Demarco for withholding the evidence in exchange for his cooperation and testimony.

"I wanted to apologize in person," Demarco said.

What should a man say to another apologizing for nearly ripping his life apart? He could think of nothing, so he said nothing.

"I don't expect you to forgive me. But I do have a surprise for you." He opened the back door and Korbin saw Fallon sitting inside. She looked tentative and moved deeper into the vehicle as more cameras clicked and video cameras rolled.

Korbin looked at Demarco, who shrugged. "I watched the news. I figured the least I could do is get things started in the right direction for you and your stepdaughter." He handed him a card, an invitation. "And invite you to my next antiques auction review. You had to leave early from the last one." He looked at Savanna. "It would be a shame to waste such a beautiful dress."

Korbin shook Demarco's hand. Some day he'd forgive him. When all of this was a distant memory. All except... he looked over at Savanna. Would she also be a memory?

"Thanks," he said to Demarco.

Demarco gave him a slight bow. "I hope to see you soon."

Getting into the car, he looked at Fallon with her long,

curly blond hair and striking blue eyes. Savanna got into the front and the car began to move. Behind them, Korbin saw Demarco talking to reporters. When the sedan turned a corner, he disappeared from sight. He turned to Fallon. She looked at him in that tentative way, still not sure how she felt about him.

"I was going to go home, but I ran into Demarco on my way out of the station," she said.

"I'm glad you didn't."

She opened her mouth to say something and then shut it. Then she tried again. "Why is it so important that I be in your life?"

Had she really asked that question? "You've been like a daughter to me since you were fifteen."

"I hated you when I was fifteen."

"Yeah, but that didn't last. Every stepkid hates the one who isn't their real parent. It's a stage. As soon as you saw what a great guy I was, you came around."

She smiled. "You can be a real charmer. No wonder my mother fell for you so fast."

He chuckled and then noticed Savanna's head turning as though she wanted badly to look at them. This couldn't be an easy exchange for her to hear. But it was important that he make Fallon understand how he felt about her, that she meant as much to him as any kid of his own would.

"We were a family," he said. "And even though your mother isn't here anymore, you're still part of my family. You're the only daughter I'll ever have."

Fallon lowered her head, and he felt her uncertainty.

Korbin reached for her hand, taking it from where it was curled into her other hand to hold it in his. "If I could change what happened, I would."

Fallon lifted her head, all the pain of her loss shining in her eyes. "She trusted you."

He stayed silent, letting her say what she needed to say.

"She knew what you were into, but she wasn't afraid because she had you." Tears sprang to her eyes, each one a dagger into his heart. "How could you have let her die like that?"

Korbin grasped her hand and kissed the back of it, then put it back down and covered it with his as he struggled with the familiar guilt. "I've asked myself that same question many times. I should have known she was in danger. I should have protected her. But I didn't. I didn't know what Damen was getting us into. He never told me. But I promise you, if I had known, your mother would have been nowhere near that place. I would have gotten us away from here. From Damen. You have to believe that."

"You didn't know?"

"No."

Fallon wiped her eyes, her tears stopping. "I don't know how to feel about you."

"You don't have to feel anything."

"I'm afraid that…every time I see you, I'm going to be reminded of how my mother was gunned down like a gangster."

"It might be that way for a while. But I'd like a chance to build a new relationship with you. To eventually change that perception. I may have done my share of crimes, but I never meant to hurt anyone. I loved your mother. There isn't anything I wouldn't do to have her back. If only…" He could see her walking beside him, smiling, the breeze in her hair, loving him. "She was just walking too close to Damen." She'd been walking too close. The gunman had missed and hit her.

"Why did she have to fall in love with you?"

That was a painful thing to ask. But all of her awful thoughts had to be aired.

"If it would mean she'd still be alive, then I wish she never had." Unfortunately, no one got a second take in this life. The film was made, a real horror.

"I miss her so much."

Korbin said nothing. There was nothing he could say. He had loved Niya with all his heart, but she was gone.

"Tell you what," he said. "In about a month or so, let's get together for lunch. We'll talk some more. Take it slow and go from there. If you decide you don't want me in your life, if it's too hard for you, then I'll understand. But I'll always be here for you, no matter what."

A tiny smile poked the corners of her mouth and she nodded. "Okay."

The car stopped and he realized it was to drop Fallon off.

She leaned over and hugged him. "Thank you."

For saving her? For understanding? It didn't matter.

"I'll call you," he said.

And she was gone. Korbin watched her go inside her apartment building, feeling his life begin to take a turn in the right direction for a change. There was, however, one more thing he had to do.

When they reached a busy street where he was sure to catch a taxi, he said, "Stop the car."

Savanna swung her head back to look at him.

The driver pulled over and Korbin got out. He opened the passenger door and extended his hand. Savanna took it and got out, bewildered and leery. As he looked at her beautiful face, her striking blue eyes, all of the chaos he'd experienced in the last year came to a head.

He had so many mixed-up emotions running through him right now he didn't know which one to address first. It wasn't a very manly feeling. He needed to be straight. True. Grounded. Sure. And he was none of those things. He was a criminal who'd gotten his wife killed. He was aimless. Drifting. Somehow he had to find his anchor, and while he was pretty sure she stood before him right now, he had to get out of these stormy waters so that he could see land.

"Savanna…"

Resignation lurked in her eyes. She lifted her finger to shush him.

He took her finger and lowered it. "No. Hear me out."

"Why? So you can tell me you're leaving? No, thanks." She turned to get back into the car.

Korbin took hold of her arm and swung her back around, meaning to bring her against him. With her lips forming an O, she flattened her hands on his chest as he adjusted her comfortably into his arms.

"A lot has happened over the last few days." Murders. Shoot-outs. Chases. Falling in love…

"You have a life where I don't fit," she said. "I get it." She started to push his chest to get away.

He held her firm. She wasn't going anywhere. "With Fallon?"

"Yes. If I'd seen that coming, I'd…" She didn't finish, but her rapid breathing revealed how hurt she felt. She was fighting tears.

Tenderness rose up in him and he wished he could spare her that.

"What?" he asked gently. "What would you have done? Stop what happened? There was no stopping that."

Her brows scrunched together. There was no stopping them.

"As I was saying…" He waited for her breathing to calm and for her to look into his eyes, really look. When she began to melt into him, something he loved to see, he said, "A lot has happened in the last few days."

"Yes. One of which is that I fell in love with you. I'm an idiot. Why do I fall for the wrong guys all the time? The ones who never stick around?"

He raised his brow in silent admonishment. "Will you listen to me for two minutes?"

She patted his chest, anxious and fretful.

Korbin lowered his head and kissed her. She tensed at first, but as he moved over her mouth and finally got her to relax and enjoy it, he eased away, finding and locking her gaze again.

"I don't know where I'm at in my grieving process," he said, softening that with another kiss. "I don't know what I'm going to do with my future." He kissed her again. "I'm confused. And the reason I'm so confused is I think I've fallen in love with you."

Savanna's eyes stared up at him unblinking, her mouth wide again. "I don't understand. Are you leaving me?"

"For now, yes."

She started pushing again.

"When I come for you, there will be nothing between us, Savanna. Are you listening?" He kissed her again, a few short pecks that turned into one long and slow one. "You deserve all of me. Not pieces at a time. I thought I was making progress grieving for Niya, but I wasn't. Not until I met you. I'm making progress now. But I need to know without a doubt that I'm over her, and most importantly, that I don't blame myself for her death. That has to be all the way behind me before I can come to you as a whole man, one who will belong to you and only you."

For the second time today, he watched tears well in a woman's eyes.

"I'm going to go stay with my parents for a while." She sniffled. "I'm going to see you again?"

"Yes, Savanna. I just don't know when. Can you wait for me?"

She took longer than he liked to answer. "Yes."

"Are you sure? You don't seem sure."

"I'm sure. I love you."

I love you, too almost came out of his mouth unbidden, but he stopped it. Telling her that now, with his past such a jumble in his head and heart, wouldn't be fair or honest.

"I think I love you, too," he said. "I want to be able to come back here and tell you that for real."

"Oh, Korbin." She flung her arms around him and kissed him with all she had.

He kissed her for several more minutes. If he kissed her any longer, he wouldn't be going anywhere but the nearest hotel.

Easing back, he took her face between his hands and kissed her once more before stepping back.

She was breathing fast and tears still shone in her eyes as he turned and walked up the street to flag down a taxi.

Savanna sat in the turret window, book on her lap, staring out at the falling snow. It had been a week since Korbin left her standing on the sidewalk, watching him get into a taxi and disappear from her life. Such a flutter of torn emotions had churned through her that she could barely get back into the sedan. As the days rolled by, her heartache only intensified. But it was different from the other times. This was bittersweet. She felt such strong love for him she could hardly contain it. Like now, staring out the window, yearning for a love that had promised to come back but hadn't yet. Yearning so much that it hurt.

Her entire family was in Evergreen right now. She'd locked the door to this library. It adjoined the room where she was sleeping. She'd locked that door, too. She had to be alone with this lonely love consuming her.

Pounding on the door interrupted her quasi-peace.

"Savanna? Open up." It was Macon.

"Leave me alone."

"Let me in." He pounded again. "Mom's about to send everybody up here to break down the door."

She'd do it, too. With a hard sigh, she left her perch and unlocked the door. Macon leaned with his forearm on the door frame, looking disheveled and rakish.

Savanna moved out of the way so he could enter. When he did, she closed and locked the door.

"How long are you going to stay up here?"

"I don't know. I was thinking about going home." For once, being alone hadn't appealed to her, which was why she'd come here. And also the press. They were relentless. But now the sanctuary of her home was calling to her.

"You aren't going anywhere unless you can convince Mom you're okay." Macon sat down on a wing-backed chair and put his feet up on an ottoman.

Savanna sat in the other chair beside him.

"So, he's not coming back, huh?"

"He said he was."

"Did he?"

Thinking back to what Korbin had said, she wasn't so sure. "Yes, but…"

"You don't trust him."

No. Yes. She realized she did trust him. He'd meant what he'd said. He'd be back. Some day. She might suffer from a broken heart for the third time in her life, but she wouldn't fault him. He would be the most honest and faithful man to have broken her heart.

"Well, then stop watching for him."

"I'm not watching for him."

"You sit in that window pretending to read a book when all you do is stare at the road."

"How…"

"I see you sometimes."

"Spying on me?"

"You're my sister. I hate to see you hurting. Makes me want to go find him and beat him up for you."

She smiled. "Stop it."

"*Modern Citizen Magazine* wants to do a feature on the two of you."

She gaped at him. *Citizen* was the most venerable entertainment magazine out there. "What?"

"Yeah. You saved the country." He grinned. "And there's the other matter of a budding romance everybody is dying to hear about."

Savanna rolled her eyes. "How do you know they want to do a feature?"

"Their chief editor called Dad. Asked him to talk to you. Apparently they've tried to get a hold of both you and Korbin, but neither of you is answering your phone."

"I'll come downstairs, just, please, stop talking about that."

He chuckled. "At least you don't have someone claiming you left them in Aspen."

Macon's ex-girlfriend had gone public with their breakup. She said that when he'd gone to help Savanna, he abandoned her in a hotel without a word.

"She was an airhead anyway. You can do better."

"No actresses, I've decided."

She stood up. "Come on. Help me show Mom I'm okay so I can go home."

Korbin had just dropped Fallon off at the airport. She'd spent the weekend at his parents' house. She had no living grandparents and had never met his mom and dad. They'd all gotten along great. Fallon had no family other than him. She seemed to be warming to the idea of having one with them. And as always, his next thought was of Savanna. Family. It was a new life. He still couldn't make the transition. It all felt so surreal. His life was close to settling. When would he go for her? Now? It felt right…and then not. He still shied away from it.

Dropping his rental car keys into the doorman's palm, he nodded his thanks and went to find his mother. She was in one of the living rooms, the less formal one. She smiled when she saw him. He'd made progress earning his parents' forgiveness. His dad was much calmer now. Not completely trusting, but on the way there.

His mother patted the cushion beside her. "I want to talk to you about something."

"Where's Dad?" He went there and sat.

She turned off the television. "Out in the garage working on his motorcycle. Getting ready for spring."

His dad owned a Harley. It was the one thing he didn't hire someone to take care of.

"Dad said the chief editor of *Modern Citizen Magazine* called him."

"They've left me messages."

"Aren't you going to call them back?"

"Do you think I should?"

"It would be a joint interview. You and that woman, Savanna Ivy."

Excitement and reticence flopped in his stomach.

"What happened with the two of you?" his mom asked.

How could he explain that to his mom?

"Why aren't you with her right now?"

"I'm here."

"Yes, and we appreciate that, but we'll always be here, honey. If you wait too long, you're going to lose her."

He stared at his mother. She was so insightful when it came to him. He'd forgotten that.

"Why did you leave her behind? Why not bring her with you here?"

"I had to set things right with you and Dad. And Fallon."

His mom angled her head, all-knowing. "Honey, it's okay to let her go."

He sat back against the chair.

"Even Fallon agrees." When he shot a look at her, she said, "We talked just before she left. She asked why you weren't with Savanna. She said she was a nice woman, and brave."

"She's okay with it?"

"She said you should go get her."

Fallon was okay with him moving on?

"It's been a year, Korbin. That's enough time to show your respect and love. Fallon doesn't doubt your love for her mother. And she doesn't expect you to live alone the rest of your life."

While that helped, he still couldn't take that leap.

"Let her go, Korbin." When he just looked at her, she said, "Just do it. Just go back to Colorado and tell Savanna that you love her. I can see that you do. You had the same look with Niya. It's okay if you love again. A lot of people don't get another chance at it. Don't let it pass you by because you feel guilty. What is that saying? *Feel the guilt and do it anyway.*"

"It's not just that. What am I going to do with my future?" He was no longer a criminal. What would he do with his time? He needed direction.

"Do you love her?" his mom asked.

And the answer came into his eyes.

"Then go get her. Make a future with her. You both can figure it out together."

It was the most sensible thing anyone had ever said to him. All at once everything became clear. Savanna. Him. Fallon. Family.

Chapter 20

Savanna's mother came with her to Wolf Creek and they were baking cookies when someone rang the doorbell. Savanna wiped her hands and went to the door. It was Hurley.

"Hi, Hurley."

He extended an envelope. "This is for you."

She eyed his grin as she took it. "What's this?"

It was thick, as though there was a card inside.

"An invitation." His grin was suspicious.

There was a card inside, blank except for something handwritten.

Meet me at Silver Plume. Be there before the storm.
Korbin

Sparks of excitement and shock inundated her. She looked up at Hurley.

"He asked me to take you there."

"He did?" Behind him in the driveway, a snowmobile was running. She was so surprised and thrilled she was bursting inside. She threw a hug around Hurley and then jumped up and down. "I have to pack! Give me a second." She kissed Hurley's cheek and ran inside.

"Mom!"

"Who is it?"

"Korbin! He came back!" She went still. "Oh my God, I have to get ready."

"What? Why?"

She kissed her mom's cheek. "Hurley's taking me to him."

"Now? Savanna, what's gotten into you?"

"Korbin is meeting me at one of Hurley's yurts." Her mother could never guess the significance of that yurt. Savanna covered her mouth with her hand. He was here. He'd come back for her.

Savanna trotted up the stairs with waving hands. In her room, she packed sexy lingerie and a few other articles of clothing into a backpack and then raced downstairs. In the closet off the front entry, she quickly dressed in winter clothes and then put the pack on her back.

Her mother smiled, leaning against the wall where Korbin had once stood with a gun.

"My daughter in love," her mother said. "You tell that boy if he doesn't treat you right he'll have me to answer to."

Savanna walked over in her snow boots and kissed her mom on her cheek. "Sorry to leave you like this."

"It's good. I can go home now. I always hated thinking of you all by yourself in this house." She lifted her head to look around. "It's so isolated. Don't you ever worry about wild animals?"

"No, Mother. I love it here."

"Is this where you and Korbin will live?"

"Yes. At least I hope so."

"What about your motivational speaking?" her mother asked.

"I don't need it anymore." Suddenly she realized that was true. Speaking positively helped her feel interesting, but she didn't need that anymore. She was interesting without any convincing. Korbin made her feel that way. She fit him. They belonged together.

"Do you have your phone with you?" Camille asked.

"There's no service where I'm going." And she didn't want any when she got there.

Her mother kissed her cheek this time. "I love you. Call me when you get back home. And tell me when the wedding is."

Savanna could just smile big. A wedding! With Korbin. Her heart did an ecstatic flop.

She left the house and ran to Hurley, who'd climbed onto the snowmobile. It was a clear day, but the forecast had called for snow later that night. As Hurley drove the snowmobile away, she blew a kiss to her mom, who watched from the open front door.

It was a lot faster on a snowmobile. Hurley stopped beside another snowmobile parked in front of Silver Plume. Savanna got off and waved goodbye to him.

Her heart was racing wildly, as though she'd skied there. Taking a deep breath, she opened the yurt door.

Korbin was in a long-sleeved T-shirt, jeans and no shoes. His light gray eyes were fixed on her. He seemed anxious, but passion simmered underneath that.

She closed the door. It was warm in the yurt and the only light came from the wood-burning stove and candles. There was a huge vase full of red roses on the table, which was set for dinner. Whatever he was cooking smelled lovely.

"Hi," she said.

He started toward her. When he reached her, he slid a hand to the nape of her neck and kissed her.

"Everything okay?" she asked.

"More than okay."

"You seem…tense."

"I was. And then you walked through the door and everything made sense again."

She smiled. "Got it all figured out, have you?"

"It took a little convincing, but yes."

"What kind of convincing?"

"My mom. Fallon. They made me see that I have to move on."

She looped her arms around him. "I can't tell you how happy I am to hear that."

"And I came to the realization that my life would be lacking without you."

She sighed with exaggeration. "Finally. A man for me."

"A rich one."

"A faithful one."

"Always. I will never betray your trust, Savanna."

Korbin was a man who did what he said and said what he meant. And he was all hers. For the first time in her life, she believed that.

* * * * *

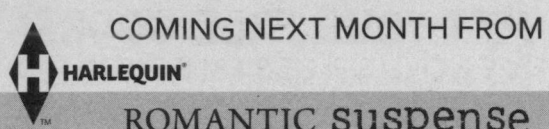

COMING NEXT MONTH FROM

HARLEQUIN®

ROMANTIC suspense

Available February 3, 2015

#1835 CARRYING HIS SECRET
Marie Ferrarella's 250th book
The Adair Affairs • by Marie Ferrarella
Elizabeth Shelton has always had a crush on Whit Adair, her boss's son. But now, having just discovered she's pregnant with Whit's child after a one-night stand, she soon becomes the next target of her boss's murderer...

#1836 OPERATION POWER PLAY
Cutter's Code • by Justine Davis
Widow Sloan Burke falls hard for Detective Brett Dunbar, who rescues her when she's in trouble—but is she prepared to love another man who puts his life on the line daily? The next life in jeopardy could be hers.

#1837 SILKEN THREATS
Dangerous in Dallas • by Addison Fox
Wedding dress designer Cassidy Tate turns to security expert Tucker Buchanan when a botched burglary uncovers a decades-old secret in the floor of her elite boutique. Danger and passion can't help but collide in this once-in-a-lifetime story.

#1838 TAKEN BY THE CON
by C.J. Miller
FBI agent Lucia Harrington teams up with a former con man to catch his criminal ex-father-in-law. To bring down her man, she won't break the rules, but Cash Stone sees things differently. In love and crime, there are no boundaries.

REQUEST YOUR FREE BOOKS!
2 FREE NOVELS PLUS 2 FREE GIFTS!

ROMANTIC suspense

Sparked by danger, fueled by passion

YES! Please send me 2 FREE Harlequin® Romantic Suspense novels and my 2 FREE gifts (gifts are worth about $10). After receiving them, if I don't wish to receive any more books, I can return the shipping statement marked "cancel." If I don't cancel, I will receive 4 brand-new novels every month and be billed just $4.74 per book in the U.S. or $5.24 per book in Canada. That's a savings of at least 14% off the cover price! It's quite a bargain! Shipping and handling is just 50¢ per book in the U.S. and 75¢ per book in Canada.* I understand that accepting the 2 free books and gifts places me under no obligation to buy anything. I can always return a shipment and cancel at any time. Even if I never buy another book, the two free books and gifts are mine to keep forever.

240/340 HDN F45N

Name	(PLEASE PRINT)	
Address		Apt. #
City	State/Prov.	Zip/Postal Code

Signature (if under 18, a parent or guardian must sign)

Mail to the **Harlequin®** Reader Service:
IN U.S.A.: P.O. Box 1867, Buffalo, NY 14240-1867
IN CANADA: P.O. Box 609, Fort Erie, Ontario L2A 5X3

Want to try two free books from another line?
Call 1-800-873-8635 or visit www.ReaderService.com.

* Terms and prices subject to change without notice. Prices do not include applicable taxes. Sales tax applicable in N.Y. Canadian residents will be charged applicable taxes. Offer not valid in Quebec. This offer is limited to one order per household. Not valid for current subscribers to Harlequin Romantic Suspense books. All orders subject to credit approval. Credit or debit balances in a customer's account(s) may be offset by any other outstanding balance owed by or to the customer. Please allow 4 to 6 weeks for delivery. Offer available while quantities last.

Your Privacy—The Harlequin® Reader Service is committed to protecting your privacy. Our Privacy Policy is available online at www.ReaderService.com or upon request from the Harlequin Reader Service.

We make a portion of our mailing list available to reputable third parties that offer products we believe may interest you. If you prefer that we not exchange your name with third parties, or if you wish to clarify or modify your communication preferences, please visit us at www.ReaderService.com/consumerschoice or write to us at Harlequin Reader Service Preference Service, P.O. Box 9062, Buffalo, NY 14269. Include your complete name and address.

Elizabeth just found out she's pregnant after a one-night stand with her boss's son. And she's the sole witness to her boss's murder. The only one who can protect her is the last man she wants in her life...

Read on for a sneak peek at Marie Ferrarella's 250th Harlequin installment,

CARRYING HIS SECRET

After getting out of his car, Elizabeth crossed to her own, taking careful, small steps as if she was afraid that tilting even a fraction of an inch in any direction would send her sprawling to the ground.

Discovering her boss's body the way she had had thrown her equilibrium into complete turmoil, and she found herself both nauseous and dizzy.

Or maybe that was due to the tiny human being she was carrying within her.

In either case, she couldn't allow herself to display any signs of weakness—especially around Whit.

At the last moment, just before she got into her car, Elizabeth turned and looked in Whit's direction. "If you need to talk—about anything at all," she emphasized, "call me. You have my number."

"I won't need to talk," Whit told her flatly.

He wouldn't call, Elizabeth thought, sliding in behind the steering wheel of her vehicle. She closed the door and tugged her seat belt out of its resting place. The man could be unbelievably stubborn, but there was absolutely nothing she could do about that except to express her heartfelt sorrow and regret. That and be there if Whit discovered that he did need someone to turn to.

Would Whit take over the corporation? Would he just pick up the mantle and act as if it was all only business as usual?

His manner just now indicated that most likely he would, but the man wasn't a robot or an android. He was going to have to make time to grieve over his loss. If he didn't, eventually it would catch up to him and cause a breakdown.

Whit was too good at his job to allow that to happen. But she was still uneasy. After all, he was a man, not a machine.

She had to find a way to make sure that didn't happen. For his sake, as well as for the memory of Reginald Adair… and the life of her child.

Don't miss Marie Ferrarella's 250th Harlequin installment, CARRYING HIS SECRET!

Available February 2015, wherever Harlequin® Romantic Suspense books and ebooks are sold.